KW 7-1-19

Did you read this book - Leave your mark

cb									

Victorville City Library
15011 Circle Dr.
Victorville, CA 92395
760-245-4222

RALPH COMPTON:
RAWHIDE FLAT

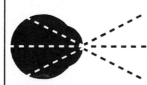

This Large Print Book carries the
Seal of Approval of N.A.V.H.

RALPH COMPTON: RAWHIDE FLAT

JOSEPH A. WEST

THORNDIKE PRESS

A part of Gale, Cengage Learning

GALE
CENGAGE Learning™

Detroit • New York • San Francisco • New Haven, Conn • Waterville, Maine • London

GALE
CENGAGE Learning

LIBRARY OF CONGRESS CATALOGING-IN-PUBLICATION DATA

West, Joseph A.
  [Rawhide flat]
  Ralph Compton Rawhide flat : a Ralph Compton novel / by Joseph A. West.
    p. cm. — (Thorndike Press large print Western)
  Previously published under title: Rawhide flat, 2009.
  ISBN-13: 978-1-4104-2159-3 (hardcover : alk. paper)
  ISBN-10: 1-4104-2159-7 (hardcover : alk. paper)
  1. Marshals—Fiction. 2. Bank robberies—Fiction. 3. Brigands and robbers—Fiction. 4. Large type books. I. Compton, Ralph. II. Title.
PS3573.E8224R38 2009
813'.54—dc22   2009031819

Published in 2009 by arrangement with NAL Signet, a member of Penguin Group (USA) Inc.

Printed in the United States of America
1 2 3 4 5 6 7 13 12 11 10 09

THE IMMORTAL COWBOY

This is respectfully dedicated to the "American Cowboy." His was the saga sparked by the turmoil that followed the Civil War, and the passing of more than a century has by no means diminished the flame.

True, the old days and the old ways are but treasured memories, and the old trails have grown dim with the ravages of time, but the spirit of the cowboy lives on.

In my travels — to Texas, Oklahoma, Kansas, Nebraska, Colorado, Wyoming, New Mexico, and Arizona — I always find something that reminds me of the Old West. While I am walking these plains and mountains for the first time, there is this feeling that a part of me is eternal, that I have known these old trails before. I believe it is the undying spirit of the frontier calling, allowing me, through the mind's eye, to step back into time. What is the appeal of the Old West of the American frontier?

It has been epitomized by some as the dark and bloody period in American history. Its heroes — Crockett, Bowie, Hickok, Earp — have been reviled and criticized. Yet the Old West lives on, larger than life.

It has become a symbol of freedom, when there was always another mountain to climb and another river to cross; when a dispute between two men was settled not with expensive lawyers, but with fists, knives, or guns. Barbaric? Maybe. But some things never change. When the cowboy rode into the pages of American history, he left behind a legacy that lives within the hearts of us all.

— *Ralph Compton*

CHAPTER 1

Sometime during the roaring, hurtling night, two nuns perched like black crows on the seats opposite Deputy United States Marshal Augustus Crane. The women watched him intently, their bright black eyes glittering.

Warned by an instinct as ancient as man himself, Crane woke.

His uneasy glance moved to the nuns, but he sensed no threat. He smiled, touched his hat, then looked out the window, where sparks from the locomotive's stack danced past like fireflies. Beyond lay pitch darkness, and the only sensations of speed were the rattling of the coach, the *clack-clack* of steel wheels on iron rails and the shifting orange light from swaying oil lamps.

One of the nuns made a small sound and Crane again turned to them.

Both held rosaries, ebony beads separated by tarnished silver chains. The beads clicked through their fingers and the nuns' mouths moved, whispered prayers hissing through their lips with the sound of slender snakes.

The women's skin was as yellow as old parchment, drawn tight to their bones. Shallow wrinkles threaded around their eyes and foreheads, and starched white wimples framed their faces like war helmets. Their black habits were frayed and showed signs of constant darning.

They could have been thirty years old, Crane guessed, or a hundred. He decided, if he got close enough to them, they would smell of dust, holy relics of the ancient dead and the smoke of wax candles.

Sitting just inside the door, the back of the marshal's wooden seat was jammed against the wall. The rest of the carriage, bathed in the trembling half-light, stretched away from him.

There were only two other passengers. A puncher, dressed in a sweat-stained hat and faded range clothes, dozed off, drunk, his chin on his chest. The other man, also asleep, wore gray broadcloth — a drummer, Crane figured, or a businessman of some kind, of which there were many around, all of them getting rich off Comstock silver and the backbreaking labor of miners.

Surprised, Crane heard one of the nuns

talking to him. Her voice was melodious and cultured, the educated tone of a gentlewoman.

"You are planning to disembark at Rawhide Flat, Marshal?" She noted Crane's surprise and added, "The star on your chest is quite obvious."

"It's the end of the line."

"For many people, I'm afraid." The nun tried a smile, did not succeed, and said, "I am Sister Marie Celeste. My companion is Sister Theresa Campion."

"Pleased to make your acquaintance, Sister."

Crane looked at the other nun. Her head was tilted back, her gaze lifted to the roof of the carriage as she tolled her beads. Blue-veined lids closed over her eyes, beautiful lashes fanning black and lacy over her cheekbones. Her lips moved ceaselessly.

"There is trouble in Rawhide Flat," Sister Marie Celeste said. "That is why you are here?"

Crane nodded. "Yes. I have an arrest to make."

"The black man?"

"Yes. Him."

"I am told he will hang."

"A judge will decide."

"But he will hang nevertheless," the nun

said. "Judges find it easy to hang a black man. Not many people care."

"If he's guilty, he will hang. Yes."

"Oh, he's guilty. Not much doubt about that."

"I don't know anything about him. I've never met the man or spoken to the arresting officer."

"Sheriff Paul Masterson arrested him." The nun's eyes went to the rectangle of black ink that was the window, and without turning she said, "Sheriff Masterson is a very hard man." She looked at Crane again. "I think you are too" — she again tried to smile and this time succeeded, conveying surprising warmth — "what the cowboys call a hard case."

"Goes with the star, Sister," Crane said. He was amused. "When you hire on for the job, the first question they ask is, 'Are you a hard case?' "

"They ask aspiring nuns that very same question, Marshal."

Crane laughed. "Yeah, I guess they do."

The young cowboy stirred, drawing the marshal's attention. Blinking like an owl, the cowboy looked around him, dry tongue smacking inside an arid mouth. His gaze met Crane's and held it for a couple of heartbeats. Then the puncher glanced away.

10

He stared out the blank window, not wanting to ever look into Crane's eyes again.

The nun was talking. "Sister Theresa Campion is praying for you, Marshal."

Crane was startled. "Praying for me?"

"Yes, for your welfare."

The other nun was now staring straight ahead, seeing nothing, ticking beads tumbling through her fingers. Her face held a strange radiance, as though it were lit from within by a magic lantern.

"Sister Theresa Campion saw you in a terrible dream. That's why she says the rosary for you."

Crane had been trying to stifle a yawn. Now Sister Marie Celeste's words did it for him. "Is she sure it was me?"

"A tall man with white eyes, hair as black as jet, a star within a circle pinned to his shirt, a blue revolver with a bone handle at his waist . . . Who else could he be but you?"

Crane was not by nature a superstitious man, but he felt a shiver slide along his spine. "What did she see?"

"Fire . . . and death."

"Whose death?"

"Among others, her own." Sister Marie Celeste's eyes burned like coals. "You will kill her amid fire."

A silence echoed between Crane and the

nun, and the marshal studied his options on how to fill it. In the end he settled for humor. He smiled.

"Sister, I may be a hard case, as you say, but I make it a policy never to shoot nuns. I don't shoot priests either. I also don't kill babies, kittens or puppies."

"We saw you at the train station, Marshal. Sister Theresa Campion said, 'That is the man in my dream.' She was so sure."

"I thought nuns had only good dreams, about heaven and Jesus."

"Not always. Sometimes we dream of hell."

Sister Theresa Campion's eyes opened. She turned to Crane and smiled at him. Her teeth were small and irregular, but very white. "I don't know if putting faith in dreams is a mortal sin. But perhaps it was not a dream after all, but a vision."

"I won't shoot you, Sister." Crane grinned. "I plan to pick up my prisoner and return to Virginia City on this train. I'll be in Rawhide Flat an hour, no longer."

The nun shook her head, the starched wimple rasping slightly against her dry cheek. "That is not for you to say, Marshal. The Lord's will will be done. If he has ordained a violent death for me at your hand, so be it."

Caught unawares, Crane sat higher in his seat and desperately tried to angle the conversation away from dreams and doom. "Do you ladies reside in Rawhide Flat?"

Sister Marie Celeste answered, "We have a house there, the Convent of St. Michael the Archangel. Ours is a teaching order, and we hold classes for the children of the silver miners — reading, writing and ciphering mostly, but also some arts and crafts."

"All that must keep you busy."

"Not really. Most of the mining children attend schools in Virginia City or Carson City. Rawhide Flat is a cattle town and a fair distance from most of the Comstock mines."

"Cattlemen have kids."

"Yes, they do, and we teach a few of those as well."

Crane was not normally a talking man, and he tried again to dip into the word well but found it dry. The nuns were watching him expectantly, as though hanging on his every utterance.

The conductor, however, saved the marshal from the need to speak. The man swayed through the carriage, a large brass railroad watch in his hand. "Rawhide Flat in fifteen minutes, folks," he said. "End of the line."

The conductor vanished into the next coach. The Virginia and Truckee train was made up of two carriages and a single boxcar that carried only Crane's horse and the cowboy's mustang.

The marshal glanced out the window, where the departing night was now giving way to a gray dawn. To the west, the ten-thousand-foot peaks of the Carson Range still wore the darkness like a cloak and were not yet visible.

Crane sighed and stretched his long legs, carefully avoiding the skirts of the nuns' habits with his spurs. He searched, finding enough words to tell a small lie. He said, "It's been a real pleasure talking with you ladies." His eyes moved to Sister Theresa Campion and he grinned. "No more bad dreams, huh?"

The nun gave him a smile of incredible sweetness and Crane rethought her age. She might be only about eighteen.

"Trust me, we will meet again, Marshal," she said.

"That I doubt. The kind of places I frequent are not for nuns."

"Nonetheless, Marshal, I know we will meet."

Crane gave up the struggle. He'd heard how stubborn nuns could be and this one

14

must be typical of the breed.

He rose to his feet, touched his hat to the sisters, then turned and opened the door to the small platform at the end of the carriage. He stepped outside, closed the door behind him and gulped a few breaths of fresh, cool air.

He was more troubled by the nuns' talk than he cared to admit.

But as he built a smoke he began to rationalize it.

Strip away the black habits and you'd find that the sisters were just women, and females were inclined to all sorts of strange notions and fancies.

Crane thumbed a match into flame, sheltered it with cupped hands and lit his cigarette. As blue smoke twisted around his head he leaned against the door of the coach, feeling the vibrations of the wheels under his feet.

He smiled. He was in town to pick up a prisoner, not shoot nuns. The entire conversation had been ridiculous, the quaint fantasy of women who had been shut up in cloisters for too long.

The train was slowing and the brightening landscape of hills, brush and hardwood trees no longer hurtled past at breakneck speed. Crane could make out a few houses

15

in the distance and white-faced cattle drinking at the creeks. It was a tranquil scene, one that convinced a man he could get his business done quickly and be on his way.

Then why did he feel on edge?

Crane flicked away the butt of his cigarette. It was the nuns. There was no other reason. He'd taken men into custody before, dozens of times, all of them hard cases of one kind or another. Apart from his having to shoot a couple, most of his arrests had gone smoothly.

The marshal nodded to himself. Yes, it was the nuns. It had to be those two black, ill-omened crows cawing of death and fire. They would have put any man on edge.

CHAPTER 2

A jade sky ribboned with bands of red and deep violet arched over Marshal Crane's head as he led his saddled buckskin down the ramp from the boxcar and onto the flat.

The air smelled of morning and the dung of the empty cattle pens that surrounded the railroad station and elbowed close to the track.

Hissing like a dragon, the locomotive vented steam, and the fireman was inspecting the wheels, a hammer in one hand, an oilcan with a slender spout in the other.

The young cowboy from the train was already in the saddle. He gave Crane a last lingering look from boots to hat, swung his yellow mustang to the west and cantered away.

Smiling, the marshal nodded to himself and in the manner of men who ride lonely trails, he voiced his thoughts aloud. "Good for you, kid. It pays a man to be aware. If you live long enough, you'll make your mark."

Crane's pale gray eyes moved to the station platform. There was no sign of the broadcloth suit, the nuns or other passengers. An errant gust of wind lifted a scrap of paper and drove it against the ticket office window. For a few moments the paper fluttered like a trapped moth, then, bored, the wind let it drop to the platform again.

Crane led his horse past the station, crossed a stretch of sandy ground tangled with stands of prickly pear and brush, and stopped when he saw Rawhide Flat's single street stretching away from him, a thin morning mist still clinging to the rooftops.

The town was a typical collection of false-fronted saloons and hotels, stores, a livery stable and a dance hall. Crane couldn't see it, but the clang of a hammer on red iron told him there was also a blacksmith's forge.

Opposite where he stood, according to the painted sign nailed over the door, was the Convent of Michael the Archangel. Accustomed to the adobe, Spanish-style missions of Arizona and Texas, the marshal was surprised.

The convent looked like an ordinary schoolhouse, a bell with a dangling pull rope hanging to the right of the door. Moreover it was very run-down. The timber boards were warped, jerking out rusty nails, and if it had ever been painted, no sign remained.

Wind and cold had weathered the walls to a silvery color and the mission looked like a prairie ghost fading away in the dawn light.

Crane built a smoke and looked the place over more carefully.

Presumably the nuns' quarters were at the back and there would also be a chapel. He lit his cigarette and saw that the frame building was longer than most, and crooked, rusted tin chimneys poked through the peaked tar-paper roof at several places.

He didn't know if the nuns had taken a vow of poverty, but if they had, they were wearing it on their sleeves. It was as though they were happy to be punished for crimes they didn't commit.

Odd, the marshal thought — a ramshackle schoolhouse in a cow town that was no doubt making money hand over fist from the Comstock. Did Rawhide Flat harbor a grudge against the sisters or was it just indifference?

Angrily Crane shook his head. Damn it, what did he care about a bunch of nuns? Their talk had gotten to him. They'd crawled inside his head and planted a seed of anxiety in his brain that had grown into a

19

hanging tree and now he was dangling from a noose of self-doubt.

He was not going to kill a nun, not today, not tomorrow, not any time. The entire notion was crazy. He pushed it from his mind, angry at himself, angrier at the sisters.

Crane tore his eyes away from the convent and back to the street. No one was stirring this early in the morning. The only living thing he saw was a coyote that watched him briefly, then slunk into an alley.

The marshal had the horseman's distaste for walking when he could ride, but he led the buckskin into the middle of the street to get a feel for the town.

Puffs of yellow dust kicked up from the horse's hooves as Crane stepped slowly along the middle of the street. The saloons were still shuttered and dark. Strange that, because bartenders liked to make an early start to prepare for the morning's business. The stores were also closed, their signs creaking in the wind, windows staring blankly at the brightening morning.

The blacksmith had ceased his hammering and the town was hushed. But it was an uneasy quiet, edged like a knife. It was as though Rawhide Flat were watching him, holding its breath as it waited for something to happen. Even the gusting wind sniffed at

Crane suspiciously, wondering what he was doing, why he was there.

Ahead, the marshal saw a squat frame building about fifty yards beyond the town limits, its heavy pine door and single barred window facing into the street.

The cabin had a brooding, unfriendly look, made worse by the pack of rooting hogs that grunted and slobbered a few yards in front of the door.

It had to be the sheriff's office and Crane quickened his pace, only to immediately slow when a stench hit him like a fist. The marshal had smelled dead men before, men long dead, and now he got a whiff of it again.

Scenting blood, the buckskin jerked up its head, bit jangling, eyes showing white arcs of fear. Crane soothed the horse, then looked closer at the hogs, five huge black animals that must have escaped from a slaughter pen somewhere.

Their snouts were stained scarlet, jaws dripping strings of saliva, and the thing on the ground they pushed and pulled was the body of a man. To Crane's left a second body lay sprawled, but the hogs hadn't yet started on it.

Walking closer, the marshal kept the buckskin on a tight lead.

The body ahead of him was too torn up to be even recognizable as human, but the one to the left had been a puncher, judging by the spurs on his heels and the wide-brimmed hat that lay a few feet from his head. A Winchester, half buried in dust, had dropped beside him.

Crane swung wide of the hogs and their feast and stepped beside the dead cowboy. He hooked the toe of his boot under the man and rolled him over on his back. The face was blue, swollen, the purple tongue protruding. The puncher's brown eyes were open, but, in the anonymity of death, held no expression. He'd been hit in the center of the tobacco bag that hung over the pocket of his shirt. The man had been dead when he hit the ground.

Good shooting.

The marshal's bleak eyes flicked to the other man. Hog snouts were deep in his belly and his body was writhing and arching in convulsive movement as though he were being eaten alive. How he had died . . . well, now there was no way of telling.

His cold eyes lifting to the sheriff's office, Crane studied the place closely but saw no sign of life, though a line of smoke, straight as a string, rose from the iron chimney, carrying with it the smell of coffee.

He led his nervous horse to the other side of the jail and looped the reins around a water pump, out of sight of the gorging hogs. He walked back to the door. The reaction from inside was immediate. The door opened a crack and the double barrels of a scattergun poked between the gap.

"Mister," a rough, tired voice said, "think carefully about what you're going to say in the next five seconds. If I don't like the sound of it, I'll cut you down to britches high."

There's a time for doing and a time for talking. Crane recognized this as a time for talking. Fast.

"Deputy United States Marshal Augustus Crane," he said quickly. "I'm here to take the prisoner Judah Walsh into federal custody."

"Step closer. Let me take a better look at ye."

Crane did as he was told.

"Thought you was a bearded man."

"I was. Kept getting in the way of the bacon an' beans, so I shaved it off."

"My name's Paul Masterson. Mean anything to you?"

"Yeah, I've heard about you. None of it good."

The man called Masterson laughed and

23

opened the door wider. "Come on inside. I've got coffee on the bile."

"I could use some."

Crane stepped into the office, a narrow space furnished with a roll-up writing desk, a table and a couple of chairs. A potbellied stove stood in one corner with a smoking coffeepot. Next to the stove, a jumble of yellowed wanted dodgers and town ordinances was nailed to the wall.

Beside those, draped in black crepe, hung a Civil War portrait of General George Armstrong Custer.

"A great man," Masterson said, seeing Crane's interest.

The marshal nodded and smiled. "Not anymore."

"I scouted for him once, back in 'seventy-four, during his first expedition to the Black Hills country. He was a fine gentleman, if somewhat headstrong in the pursuit of Indians."

Masterson handed Crane a cup of coffee. It was scalding hot and he quickly put the tin cup on the table. "Tell me about the dead men, Sheriff," he said.

He laid slight but significant emphasis on the word "Sheriff," establishing the pecking order of the lawman's narrow world.

The marshal's cold eyes were fixed on

Masterson, but the man seemed unconcerned. "Three nights ago a bunch of the boys, punchers and ranchers mostly, got likkered up and tried to take my prisoner. They didn't get him."

"You killed those two outside?"

"Those two, and maybe one other."

"All your talking was done when you started shooting, or did you even try?"

"Marshal, beware of strong drink. It can make you shoot at sheriffs — and miss. The only talk those cowboys wanted to hear was gun talk. The ranchers were not in a conversational frame of mind either."

"Why didn't you let them remove their hurting dead?"

"Oh, they tried, later. But I dusted the ground around them with a few shots and they scampered." Masterson's smile was razor thin. "See, how it was, after old man Wilson's hogs escaped and got to work on the bodies, I figured those boys would see what was happening and think twice before they tried to rush the jail again." The sheriff's glance went to the window. "So far they haven't."

"Some might say that you gave them too harsh a lesson in civic responsibility. The dead men look like punchers, near as I can tell."

25

Masterson nodded. "Joe Anderson and Bill Paulson. Both of them worked for the Rafter-T up Sullivan Canyon way. I didn't know them very well, but as far as I recollect they were steady hands, but always on the prod. A tad too high-strung for their own good I always thought."

"And Judah Walsh was a puncher?"

"Horse wrangler, but that's not the reason the ranchers around here want him out of jail. Not by a country mile."

Crane tried his coffee. It had cooled some, was strong and bitter, and he drank deep. He was aware of a growing tension between himself and Masterson over the deaths of the cowboys and maybe one other.

Both he and the sheriff were named men, and now they'd met like two tigers in a narrow cage. Crane sought some way to maneuver without pushing Masterson too hard.

Masterson gave it to him.

"I heard you were running with the Clements brothers and that feuding bunch down to Gonzales County, Texas," he said. "Then I heard you'd killed the two Shadley boys in the Gem saloon in El Paso, and then I heard it wasn't them but their pappy you kilt. I never did get the right of it."

Crane recognized Masterson's talk as a friendly overture of sorts and he decided to play out the string.

"The Shadley boys braced me in the Gem, saying something about Mannie Clements knifing one of their cousins," Crane said. "We had words. Then they went for their guns. A day later Saul Shadley came at me with the six-gun, upset over the deaths of his boys. Well, I guess ol' Saul wasn't familiar with the rule that says a man with a pistol shouldn't go up against a man with a sawed-off shotgun."

"You killed him?"

"Yes. But he was notified."

Crane crossed the floor and poured himself more coffee.

"All that was a spell back," he said. "After the Shadley killings I was with the Rangers for a couple of years, did more chasing after Comanches than anything else. Then through Governor Hubbard I was offered this appointment in Nevada."

"And now you're here in Rawhide Flat."

"Uh-huh, now I'm here." Crane built a smoke, lit it, then said, "And you're here. How did that come about? Last I heard you'd been shot trying to rob the Katy cannonball."

"You heard right. Damn rube passenger shot me in the ass with a .32." Masterson's eyes lifted to Crane. "Know what our haul was in that train robbery? A crate of bananas and thirty-five dollars. I was so vexed I went back into the carriage to find that rube and kick his teeth down his throat, blaming him for my troubles, like. But the next thing I know, he's taking pots at me with another Smith and Wesson. I gunned him right there in his seat."

"So a pumpkin-roller shot you in the ass, you spent the thirty-five dollars and ate the bananas, then what?"

"Then I got out of the railroading business. I took this job, figuring all I'd have to do is sit back in a rocking chair, drink beer and maybe buffalo a few drunken punchers on Friday nights."

"But it blew up in your face."

"Real fast. A week ago the Cattleman's Bank and Trust got robbed of fifty thousand dollars, most of it in paper money, but also some gold and silver coin. Then everything went to hell in a handbasket." Masterson shook his head, like a man pondering the fall of great empires. "Damn right it did."

Crane dropped his cigarette to the dirt floor, shredded it dead with the sole of his boot and said, "Take a deep breath, Sheriff. Then tell me about it."

CHAPTER 3

"Marshal," Paul Masterson said, "a lot of folks are getting rich off the Comstock, people who've never set a foot underground, merchants and cattlemen mostly.

"The ranchers around Rawhide Flat supply beef to the miners and bank their profits right here in town. The local businessmen, store owners and saloon keepers do the same."

"So the fifty thousand was theirs," Crane said.

"Yeah, and in one day they saw their savings vanish. The profit margin for beef is thin, and now most of the ranchers are facing ruin.

"They're riled up and they're mean and getting meaner." Masterson nodded in the direction of the street. "You see one result of it out there. Once I counted among my friends the men who rushed the jail, tried to kill me and free my prisoner. No longer."

Crane poured more coffee. Then, his big Texas spurs chiming, he crossed the floor and sat on the edge of the desk. "Tell me about the robbery. Where were you?"

"The day of the robbery, a widow woman who lives a few miles outside of town sent her daughter for me. The kid said her ma had trapped the wolverine that had been killing her chickens and asked if I could please come and shoot it for her.

"I rode out there and it wasn't a wolverine she'd trapped. That didn't surprise me none. You seldom see those critters east of the Sierra Nevada. She'd caught a kit fox, so I shot it, told her to skin it out and sell the pelt next time she was in town.

"When I rode back to Rawhide Flat, the bank had been robbed and two people were dead."

"Judah Walsh killed them both?"

"Nobody knows who killed the bank manager, but Walsh admitted to shooting the female teller. Her name was Martha Spooner, an old maid who lived behind the bank with her cats. As far as I can tell, she gave Walsh sass and he put a bullet into her brisket."

"You went after the robbers?"

"Sure. My posse killed three of them on the east bank of Lake Tahoe about ten miles to the west of town. Just about all the lumber around there has been cut to shore up the Comstock mines, so they'd no place to hide. We caught Walsh alive."

"And the money?"

"The robbers had stashed it somewhere and only Walsh knows where it is. We searched for a couple of days but didn't find a nickel."

Crane glanced out the barred window into the blue morning. Yellow dust hazed the air and from somewhere drifted the smoke tang of frying bacon.

"The ranchers want to beat the information out of Walsh," he said. "That's why they rushed the jail, huh?"

"Hell no. Judah knows he's facing the rope for murder and bank robbery. Against a stacked deck like that, the only chip he's got left to play is to tell the ranchers where the money is hidden. In return, he wants a fast horse, a hundred dollars and free passage out of the state.

"The ranchers and just about everybody in town want to give it to him. I can't blame them. If I were facing financial ruin I'd be inclined to agree."

"So they tried to rush the jail and take him?"

"That sums it up."

"You tried beating it out of Walsh?"

"Waste of time, Marshal. Walsh isn't about to talk and put his head in a noose."

"Pity you can't just shoot him."

"Yeah, isn't it though."

Crane looked around the office. "You got whiskey here?"

"Bottom-left drawer of the desk. Starting early, Marshal?"

"It's for Walsh."

"Loosen his tongue with booze, huh?"

"Something like that."

"It won't work."

"It's worth a try. Now open his cell and leave me alone with him. Sheriff, let's do this nice and easy, like we were visiting kinfolk."

CHAPTER 4

The door of the sheriff's office opened into a short hallway and then into a room mostly taken up by a pair of narrow cells. Masterson unlocked Walsh's cell, then closed the office door behind the marshal.

Crane stepped to the bars and for a few moments studied the man lying on his back in the cot. "How you keeping, Judah?" he asked finally.

The man's eyes fluttered open. He turned, saw Crane and sprang to his feet. He almost ran to the iron bars. "The ranchers send you?"

"Not yet," Crane said. "I've come to talk" — he held up the whiskey bottle — "and bring you breakfast."

Horse wranglers don't run to size, and Walsh was no exception. He was a couple of inches less than medium height, thin, wearing a ragged plaid shirt and baggy, stained pants that had once belonged to a much bigger man, and were tucked into scuffed, mule-eared boots. His skin was very black, his curly hair tight to his scalp.

But it was his eyes that captured Crane's attention. They were almost bright gold in color, and flecked with green. In a woman's face they would have been beautiful, but in a killer like Walsh they were strangely incongruous, like emeralds in a cesspit.

The man rasped the back of his hand across his mouth. "I could use a drink. It's been a while."

Crane smiled, his hand on the cell door. "Mind if I come in, Judah?"

"It's a free country."

"Only for some of us, unfortunately."

Crane handed the bottle to Walsh and watched the man lift it to his lips and drink deeply. He reached into his shirt pocket and produced the makings. "Smoke?"

Walsh took the tobacco and papers without comment and sat on the edge of his cot. His eyes lifted to the tall lawman. "What's a United States marshal doing in Rawhide Flat?"

"I'm here to take you to Virginia City for trial, Judah."

"No you ain't. Them ranchers want to know where the money is hid and they ain't about to let me go."

Crane thumbed a match into flame and lit the black man's cigarette. "Tell me, and I'll tell them, Judah. The fact that you told me where the money is hid to stop more senseless killing would sit well with the jury at your trial. You could say you've found Jesus and did it out of the goodness of a pure heart. Judah, there wouldn't be a dry eye in the courtroom, mine included."

Walsh took another drink from the bottle, then dragged on his cigarette. He spoke through a cloud of blue smoke.

"I ain't telling you where the money is hid. Them other people that was in the bank know I shot the teller lady. A black man who kills a white woman is going to swing in Nevada, no matter what. The only chance this nigger has of dodging the rope is to make a deal with the ranchers."

Crane made a show of thinking deeply, his hand kneading his chin. "Alas, what you say is true, Judah. The color of a man's skin does count for something in this state." The marshal brightened. "Tell you what, Judah. Show me where the money is hidden and I'll put you on a good horse and give you an hour's start before I come after you."

He took a step closer to Walsh and spread his arms wide. "I can't say fairer than

35

that, can I?"

"You go to hell," the man said. "I ain't showing you or nobody else less'n he's nursing cows."

"And that's your final word on the subject, Judah?"

"I'm done talking. Now get out of here. Leave the bottle."

Smiling, Crane kicked out viciously. The toe of his boot slammed into the bottom of Walsh's cheekbone. As the man's head snapped back, the marshal followed up with his spur, the rowel tearing open the tight skin of Walsh's cheek to the bone.

Walsh screamed, crashed to the floor and his back came up hard against the wall.

"Still done talking, Judah?" Crane asked. His voice was soft, almost kind, as though he were addressing an errant child.

The black man moaned in reply. His hand held his mangled cheek and blood seeped through his fingers.

The door to the office opened and Masterson stepped beside Crane. He glanced at Walsh without reaction and asked, "Did he talk?"

The marshal shook his head. "Not yet. But he will, or I'll cut him to ribbons."

His eyes hazed with shock and pain, Walsh spit blood and yelled, "Damn you, I'm telling you nothing and you can't beat it out of me, not now, not ever."

Crane took his watch from his pants pocket and glanced at the time. "Judah, our train leaves in less than two hours," he said. "By then I'll know where the money is hidden."

"Just don't kill him, Marshal," Masterson said. "Dead, he's no use to anybody."

Crane smiled. "I won't kill you, will I, Judah? You'll just wish you were dead."

He bent, picked up the whiskey bottle, stepped to the door, then turned. "See you soon, Judah."

The man looked at him fearfully, as though he were a torturer who had just entered the scarlet chamber with sadistic eyes and a glowing poker in his hand.

Crane laid the bottle on the table and crossed to the gun rack. He took down a Winchester .44-40 and asked Masterson, "Is it loaded?"

The sheriff nodded. "I keep it loaded. Recently at least."

Racking a round into the chamber, Crane opened the door and stepped outside. He looked at the feeding hogs for a moment, then brought the rifle to his shoulder and cut loose. His fire was rapid and accurate, and the hogs squealed and dropped one by one.

A black pig with splotches of white on its back and chest tried to make a run for it. Crane fired and the speeding hog tumbled like a bouncing rubber ball and lay still.

The marshal rested the rifle barrel on his shoulder and his cold eyes swept the street. A few men, attracted by the noise of the shooting, stood on the boardwalks, looking at him.

"You men," Crane called out, "pick up your dead, what's left of them."

The townspeople glanced at one another uncertainly; then one of them broke and ran, disappearing into a store close to the station.

Crane waited. He was aware of Masterson stepping beside him. The sheriff carried two Remingtons butt forward in holsters hung from a single wide belt with a U.S. Cavalry buckle. It was an unusual rig, but from all Crane had heard, Masterson could clear his guns and shoot with incredible speed.

The sheriff was a man to have at your side or a man to fear at your back. Crane hoped he'd never have to find out which.

"You think this is wise?" Masterson asked mildly.

Crane nodded. "Uh-huh. I think you've

already made your point. Besides, unless they're frying in a pan, I don't like hogs."

A few slow minutes ticked past. The sun was rising and the morning was growing hot. Fat black flies buzzed lazily around the bodies of the dead man and the hogs, making a small sound in the quiet. The air smelled of blood, dust and drifting powder smoke.

A commotion at the end of the street attracted Crane's attention. The man who'd run away was standing on the boardwalk gesticulating toward the door of the store, seemingly urging someone to hurry.

Moments later a tall, skinny man in a black tailcoat stepped through the doorway, attempting to fasten a celluloid collar to his shirt as he walked. A second man appeared, dressed like the first, but this one was short and stocky, a black beard hanging to the waistband of his pants.

"Simeon Pearl, the undertaker," Masterson said. "The man with the beard is his assistant, Jacob Shirley." The sheriff turned to Crane and smiled. "Shirley is a frustrated man. He isn't married and the whores will have nothing to do with him. They say he stinks of corpses and makes them think of death and Judgment Day."

"Hard life being an undertaker, I would

think," Crane said. He was talking to Masterson, but his eyes were on the approaching men.

"As bad as being a lawman?"

The marshal shrugged. "Ain't nothing as bad as that."

Simeon Pearl studded his collar in place and checked both bodies. He lingered for a long time over the man partially devoured by the hogs. The stench of death hung in the air like a black fog.

Crane thought that the undertaker's quickly jerking head, hunched shoulders and glittering black eyes gave him the look of Mr. Poe's raven.

Pearl raised his eyes to the marshal. "Oh dear, this will be most difficult," he said. He turned to his assistant. "Do you not agree, Mr. Shirley?"

The other man nodded. "Most difficult indeed, Mr. Pearl. A challenge for our skills, wouldn't you say?"

The wind flapped the tattered tails of Pearl's coat and he looked as though at any minute he would take off, fly to the roof of the jail and croak, "Nevermore. . . ."

"Once again your clarity of thought has ascertained the problem most directly, Mr. Shirley," he said. His voice sounded like rusty nails being drawn out of a pine board.

"Yes, a challenge. And very much so, I fear."

"You don't need to make him pretty," Crane said. "Just plant him, and the other one. Then tell the owner of the hogs to haul them away."

"And who, sir," Pearl asked, "are you? I observe a badge of office on your breast, but from here I can't determine what it says."

"It says I'm Deputy United States Marshal Augustus Crane. Now move that mess off the street."

"Let me say that the metropolis of Rawhide Flat is honored by your presence, Marshal," Pearl said. His eyes angled to Masterson. "We sorely need some decent law and order around here."

Crane could almost see Pearl's brain flit from one subject to another. The undertaker's eyes grew crafty. "Marshal, let me get to the crux of the present . . . um . . . problem, no beating around the bush. As my colleague, Mr. Shirley, would say — clearly stating the case — who will square accounts for the interment of the deceased?"

Masterson spoke. "Both those men were Rafter-T riders. Give your bill to Ben Hollister. He got them killed."

Pearl grimaced. "Mr. Hollister is a hard man, grown harder by the recent unpleas-

antness. He may not honor his obligations."
Pearl turned to Shirley. "Is that not the case,
Mr. Shirley?"

"Indeed it is, Mr. Pearl."

Suddenly Crane was sick of it . . . sick of
the two chattering magpies hopping around
the bodies . . . sick of this town . . . sick of
Judah Walsh . . . sick of everything.

He knew what was happening to him. It
had happened many times before. The dark
angel that followed him everywhere, in good
times and bad, had again enveloped him in
its wings, raking talons across his past until
it bled, blighting his future.

Crane reached into his pocket, found a
ten-dollar gold eagle and threw it at Pearl's
feet. "Bury them, damn you."

The undertaker dived on the coin like a
bird on a worm. Pearl straightened and said,
"A rubber tarpaulin, I think, Mr. Shirley.
And a good stout cart, preferably drawn by
a beast of burden. And I think . . ."

Crane turned away, not wanting to hear
any more. He stepped into the office and
Masterson followed him. The sheriff's eyes
were troubled.

Crane sat at the table and looked at Masterson. "For what it's worth, I believe you were
justified in shooting the cowboys. It's a

lawman's sworn duty to protect his prisoner."

The marshal's delivery had been flat, emotionless. And Masterson, with his honed gunfighter instincts, picked up on it. "The Sideboard restaurant is open. You should get yourself some breakfast. Make you feel better."

"I'll feel better when I get out of this damned town. I need a drink, that's what I need."

"Then have one. Saloons are open as well."

"I'd get drunk and kill somebody. I don't want that."

Masterson filled a cup from the coffeepot and laid it in front of Crane. "Spreading your rage thin, aren't you?" he said. "All of a sudden."

"What do you mean?"

"Used to know a man like you down Cimarron way in the New Mexico Territory. Feller by the name of Clay Allison. Heard of him?"

Crane nodded. Then he said, "I know of him, and he wasn't like me."

As if he hadn't been listening, the sheriff said, "Clay was all right most of the time, but every now and then something he called the 'black thing' would come over him.

That's when he'd spread his rage around and do most of his killing."

It was Crane's inclination to tell the sheriff to shut his mouth and get the prisoner ready for the train. But when he looked into Masterson's hard blue eyes, he thought he detected genuine concern, or at least interest.

"I'm followed by a dark angel," he said. "It sneaks up on me, brings back my past but shows me no future except shadows moving in a fog. When it takes hold of me, I want to curl up in a ball and melt into the earth and sleep forever without dreams."

"You feel like that now?"

"Yeah, I do."

The sheriff said, "I've killed ten men. They don't keep me up o' nights."

"Masterson, where's your angel? I don't see it."

"If it comes to a fight, is that what you'll do, curl up on me?"

"I'm a professional killer, Sheriff, just like you are. Killing is all I know. It's what I'm good at. I won't curl up on you." Crane tried his coffee, then carefully set it on the table. "It won't come to a fight. Get Walsh ready. The train leaves in thirty minutes and I'm taking him with me."

Masterson was suddenly alert and his eyes

locked with Crane's. "I don't think that's going to happen. Listen . . ."

CHAPTER 5

Crane heard it, the *clank-clank* of a steam engine pulling out of the station, its bell tolling a dirge for the death of his plans.

The marshal jumped to his feet and ran out the office door. In the distance, the locomotive was chugging plumes of black smoke into the air.

Crane swore loud and long as he ran around the back of the jail for his horse. He swung into the saddle and hit the street at a flat run.

Somehow he had to stop the train.

But Crane suddenly ran out of street. Ahead of him a line of about twenty riders blocked his path, strung out in a skirmish line from one boardwalk to the other. All of the men had rifles, butt plates resting on their thighs. They were punchers, well-mounted men in wide-brimmed hats who would know how to use the Winchesters they carried.

46

Crane came to a sudden realization that he was losing this. The hard-bitten riders ahead of him wanted Judah Walsh and he couldn't buck odds of twenty-to-one. He drew rein, defeat weighing on him like raw iron.

He watched the riders walk their horses toward him. He could give up Walsh, let the ranchers recover their money. When he returned to Virginia City without his prisoner, no one would raise an eyebrow. Such things happened all the time along the Comstock, guilty men escaped, outlaws vanished into the mountains and not too many people cared. Everybody was too busy getting rich.

The angel was at Crane's shoulder, its whisper thin as a razor in his ear. "Let it go. . . . Just let it go. . . ."

The riders stopped about ten yards from the marshal, close enough that he recognized the young puncher from the train. Two men detached themselves from the rest. They drew rein and sat their horses, studying him.

One of the riders was a tall, blond man, huge in the shoulders and chest, an expression of arrogance, ruthlessness and cruelty on a handsome face that reminded Crane of one of the more depraved Roman emperors.

The other man the marshal knew. Joe Garcia was a two-bit gunman out of Fort Worth, Texas. Garcia was half Irish, half Mexican and all son of a bitch, and he seemed to have been born with an inflated idea of his own importance. He was said to have killed a dozen men. How many had their wounds in the front, Crane didn't know, but he guessed very few.

The emperor was talking, his tall black horse up on its toes, prancing, eager to go. "My name is Ben Hollister. I own the Rafter-T, north of town."

Crane said nothing, and he saw a flash of irritation in Hollister's eyes. This man walked a wide path and he was not accustomed to being ignored by those he considered underlings.

Hollister opened his mouth to speak again, but Paul Masterson's voice stopped him.

"On your left, Marshal. Shotgun."

Crane nodded, most of his attention on Garcia. The little gunman was treacherous and sometimes pulled a derringer he kept hidden in his boot.

"Since you're here, you best listen to this, Masterson," Hollister said. "It's now" — he took a watch from his vest and glanced at the time — "eleven thirty. You have until this time tomorrow morning to hand over Judah Walsh." His cold eyes moved to Crane. "And don't count on the train. It won't be coming back until this business is settled."

"And if we don't give you Walsh?" Masterson said.

"Then we'll tear your jail down and take him."

"It's been tried, Hollister."

"Next time will be different. I'll be there."

"And me," Garcia said, grinning.

Crane was being pushed, and he didn't like it. His depression was replaced by a slow rage in him, an emotion just as black and equally dangerous.

"Hollister," he said, "my pa always told me, 'When you take the measure of a man, take his whole measure.' The fact that you'd hire a back-shooting tinhorn like Joe Garcia tells me a heap about you."

The little gunman sat his saddle, smiling like a hungry coyote on the trail of a wounded rabbit. "I can take you, Crane. Best you hobble your lip."

The marshal turned his horse so he was directly facing Garcia. His voice sounded like silk being drawn across steel. "Skin the Colt, Joe. Get your work in."

"No!" Hollister turned angrily to the gunman. "Back off, Joe. Kill a United States marshal in Rawhide Flat and the authorities will play hob."

"Kill a marshal now, kill him later." Garcia shrugged. "It don't matter none to me."

Crane said nothing. He'd told the man to reach for the iron and that was the extent of any conversation he wanted with Garcia. His talking was done.

Hollister must have sensed that because he said, "You've both heard my demand. Now act on it."

The big rancher swung his horse away and yelled to his men, "Boys, we'll make the Texas Belle our headquarters." A ragged cheer went up as Hollister led his men to the saloon.

Crane watched him go, a man dressed in black broadcloth, his pants tucked into expensive, handmade boots. The rancher's swagger and confident grin suggested raw power and the willingness to wield it. Because of the bank robbery he could be facing ruin, but he gave no indication of concern. Was that because he knew that Judah Walsh would soon be in his hands?

Whatever the reason, Crane decided that Ben Hollister was no bargain and come tomorrow morning he could be a handful and then some.

It was a thought to trouble a man.

"More riders coming in," Masterson said. He was looking out the window into the half-light of the dying day. The rain that had threatened earlier had not materialized and a few stars hung in a clear lemon and amber sky.

Getting no response from Crane, the sheriff threw another mild sentence in his direction. "All the saloons are busy."

"Hollister won't make a move until morning," Crane said.

"Think we can hold them, Marshal?"

"Call me Augustus, for God's sake."

"Gus?"

"That fits." Crane rose from his chair and stepped beside Masterson. "No, we can't hold them. We'll kill a few, but we will not hold them."

"Hollister won't kill a federal marshal, but he'll have no qualms about gunning a tin-star sheriff."

"When the shooting starts, those boys out there will be aiming at both of us. The death of a marshal is an inconvenience that can be explained away later."

"You have any ideas . . . Gus?"

"I'm working on it."

"That dark angel still troubling you?"

"It's sitting on my shoulder, but right now it's leaving me alone." Crane smiled. "Maybe it's because I'm too scared to be depressed."

Masterson was looking out the window again. "I see hands from just about every cow outfit there is. That big redhead standing outside the Bon-Ton is Long Tom Feeney, foreman of the Flying H, and the little feller with him is Good Time Charlie Bone of the J and L. There's a pair of hellers for you."

"Seems like the wolves are gathering," Crane said.

"Seems like." Masterson stiffened. "Somebody's coming."

Crane pulled his gun and stepped to the door. He glanced at the sheriff. "Any man who comes through the door who ain't acting like he's visiting kissin' kin — I start blasting."

"No, don't. It's Maxie Starr. She works in the Texas Belle."

"Friend of yours?"

"You could say that."

Crane opened the door and the woman stepped quickly inside, the wind bringing a gust of perfume with her.

She crossed the floor quickly and laid a basket on the table. "I brought you some grub, Paul. I know you boys aren't exactly welcome on the street."

Maxie Starr was a dazzling blonde, her blue silk dress cut low, revealing the generous swell of her milky breasts. Her glossy hair was pulled back in a ballerina chignon and a thin black ribbon circled her slender neck. Her eyes were sapphire blue, her cheekbones high and beautifully sculpted, and her mouth was wide and generous. The fine arcs at the corner of her lips suggested she smiled often and easily.

Suddenly finding it hard to breathe, Crane decided she was one of the most beautiful women he'd ever seen.

"You shouldn't have come here, Maxie," Masterson said.

"And let you starve?"

"If Ben Hollister sees you here it could go badly for you."

The woman smiled. "He and the others are still early in their drinking. They haven't yet taken the next step to the amorous stage."

Masterson gestured in Crane's direction. "Deputy United States Marshal Augustus Crane. He likes to be called Gus."

As the marshal touched his hat, Maxie said, "The nuns at the mission were talking to me about you. For some reason I got the impression they fear you. You been hard-talking nuns?"

Crane smiled. "Nothing like that. One of them had a bad dream about me, that's all."

Maxie did not return his smile. Her beautiful eyes suddenly looked as unfriendly as the windows of a haunted mansion. "It must have been a really bad dream," she said, "to scare the sisters like that."

Dismissing Crane, the woman turned to Masterson. "Paul, every rancher and cowboy from miles around is in town, and riffraff from the mines, willing to shoot anybody for whiskey and ten dollars. Hollister is boasting that he'll have two hundred fighting men in Rawhide Flat by midnight."

"Long odds," Masterson said mildly. He looked at Maxie. "I'm beholden to you."

The woman smiled. "I owe you, Paul. Remember?"

"Maxie, you don't owe me a thing."

"I'd say shooting a miner off me who was all set to carve his name on my belly with a Green River knife is a pretty big debt."

"It went with the star."

"Maybe so, but I won't forget it." Maxie glanced at the railroad clock on the wall. "I'd better go. I'll be missed if I stay much longer." She turned to Crane. "It's been nice meeting you, Marshal."

Her stiff features indicated she was not telling the truth. Crane touched his hat again. "My pleasure, ma'am."

Masterson's eyes were smiling, seemingly amused at the reserved formality between the two. Crane figured the sheriff was thinking that Maxie had been right — the nun must have had a powerful, bad dream.

Maxie stepped to the door, then ran back and grabbed Masterson's hands in hers. "Get out of town, Paul, now. Leave Judah Walsh to Hollister. The man means nothing to you."

"He's Gus' prisoner, Maxie. He'll have to make that decision."

Maxie looked at Crane but spoke to Masterson. "Gus is a man who's lost the habit of enjoying life, Paul. Don't put your fate in his hands."

Then she was gone and only the lingering memory of her perfume remained.

CHAPTER 6

Paul Masterson removed the cloth from the basket and looked inside. "See what we got, Gus. Maxie did us proud." He laid food on the table. "Beef sandwiches, half an apple pie and two bottles of Bass ale. Can't beat that, huh?"

"And the condemned ate a hearty meal," Crane said. "I guess I'd better feed Walsh first."

"I'll do it. When you talk to him he ends up getting cut with a spur."

The sheriff took a couple of sandwiches to Walsh and when he returned Crane asked, "How is he?"

"He hears the commotion on the street and figures this time tomorrow he'll be well on his way to California with a hundred dollars in his jeans and a good horse under him."

"He could be right."

Masterson bit into a sandwich and spoke

around a mouthful of bread and meat. "Do you make a habit of terrifying nuns, Gus?"

Crane laid his own sandwich and beer on the table. "Not as a general rule."

He told the sheriff what had happened on the train, then added, "Like I said, the sister had a bad dream. Trust me, I don't go out of my way to shoot nuns."

Masterson grinned. "I'd be worried though. Nuns are in good with God. Maybe he really did give the little sister a glimpse of the future."

"Masterson, don't you start up. Your friend Maxie was bad enough."

"Call me Paul."

"I can't shorten that name. Pity."

Crane crossed the floor in a couple of long-legged strides and looked out the window. "Where's the prisoner's horse, and yours?"

"The livery of course. Mine's is a sorrel with four white socks and a blaze face. Walsh was riding a steel-dust Morgan. Why do you want to know?"

"Because we're getting out of here. We're taking Walsh to Virginia City."

"Gus, why don't you just ride away from here, leave Walsh in his cell?"

"I thought about that, thought about it a lot. But if I did what you say, I'd have to turn in my badge because I'd have failed in my duty. The man's not only a robber — he's a cold-blooded killer and I can't turn my back on that."

The marshal's smile was slight. "I have enough bad memories as it is. I don't want to add another to the list."

"I don't know you that well, but even so, if you ever want to talk about them, those bad memories I mean, all you —"

"I'll keep that in mind, Paul."

Masterson nodded and backed off, giving Crane space. "All right, how do you want to play this?"

"We'll wait another hour until the boys are well and truly likkered. Then I'll head for the barn and bring back the horses."

"I should go. I know the town better than you."

"Thanks, but I think I can find the livery stable. Just have Walsh out here and ready to go when I get back. We may have to leave in an all-fired hurry."

Darkness had crowded into Rawhide Flat and the sky was full of stars. A horned moon was on the rise and out among the silvered hills a pair of hunting coyotes called back and forth. The saloons along the street were ablaze with light, jammed with the roars of men and the laughter of women, the laughs ringing false as cracked bells, a discordant counterpoint.

Competing tinpanny pianos battled for space, their notes getting hopelessly tangled, falling into the street like shattered shards of glass.

Crane removed his badge from his shirt and placed it in his pocket. He angled from the jail to the boardwalk and pulled the brim of his hat low over his eyes. It was difficult for a man who stood four inches over six feet in his boots to try to be inconspicuous, but it was a risk he'd have to take.

Behind the main buildings along the street lay a crowded warren of shacks and cabins. Blundering through those in the dark was a sure way to attract unwelcome attention, especially from dogs.

Crane passed a few stores, then crossed the rectangle of yellow light spilling from the front door of the Bon-Ton saloon. He caught a fleeting glimpse of a throng of men standing belly to the bar, girls in silk dresses of blue, yellow and red moving among them like tropical birds.

He had almost reached the point where the boardwalk was interrupted for an alley, when a rough voice hailed him from the shadows. He stopped as a man emerged from the gloom.

"You got the price of a drink?" the man asked. It was more threat than question. His eyes were in shadow, his face heavily bearded and he wore the plaid shirt, heavy canvas pants and lace-up boots of a miner. Greasy hair fell over his shoulders from under a battered plug hat and a revolver in a cross-draw holster was buckled around his belly.

"Sorry, no," Crane said. He made to move on.

The miner's hand shot out and grabbed Crane's by the bicep of his right arm. The fingers of a hard-rock miner are incredibly thick and strong, and they dug deep, the man's long, dirty fingernails like talons.

It took him about half a second to realize he'd made a bad mistake.

Crane jerked his arm away and down. When his hand came up he was holding his Colt. The marshal crashed the gun against the miner's temple, drawing blood. The man staggered back a step and Crane followed, swinging again. This time the Colt's barrel smashed into the bridge of the miner's nose and he dropped to his knees, then fell on his back, his legs bent under him.

Crane shook his head at the perverse timing of this uncalled-for inconvenience.

The man's face was a mask of blood and he was moaning softly. The marshal grabbed the miner by the collar of his shirt to drag him into the alley, then grew still as a woman stepped toward him along the boardwalk.

Dressed in a severe brown dress, she wore a hat of the same color, its drabness relieved by a decorative bunch of imitation red cherries.

The woman was one of the town's respectable matrons, no doubt the wife of a merchant or businessman. Crane shifted his position to shield the miner's bloody face as the matron walked past him. Her eyes stern, she looked like someone was holding a rotten fish under her nose.

"He's drunk," the marshal slurred, "and so am I. Hey, can I buy you a drink, pretty lady?"

Sniffing, the woman moved on. After she crossed the alley and regained the boardwalk again, she turned and snapped, "Disgraceful!"

"Don't get your corsets in a knot, old gal," Crane said, playing a drunk to the hilt. "Come an' have a drink."

The woman quickened her pace, her boots thudding on the walk until she vanished into the night.

Quickly Crane dragged the miner deep into the alley. He was about to walk away when the man groaned and tried to get to his feet. The marshal pulled his gun again, lifted the man's hat and smashed the barrel across his head. This time the miner lay still, making no sound.

The man would either wake up with the worst headache of his life or not wake up at all. But Crane told himself he'd had no choice. He couldn't risk the miner raising the alarm and a bunch of drunken cowboys, ready for any distraction, raising the hue and cry to find his assailant.

"You should have minded your manners around strangers," Crane said to the man. Good advice, even though he could not hear it.

The marshal turned away and regained the boardwalk. Behind him a drunk staggered from one saloon and into another and a frock-coated gambler stepped to the edge of the walk and lit a thin cigar.

Crane's confrontation with the miner had not been seen, and for that he was thankful.

The mission of St. Michael the Archangel was in darkness. The nuns would be early in bed, but as Crane passed, he thought he heard a woman cry out in her sleep. A shiver ran down the marshal's spine.

Was Sister Theresa Campion dreaming about him again?

The windows of the nuns' quarters were shuttered against the moonlight and around the building purple shadows angled, deep and mysterious. Here the raucous din of the saloons was muted and even the wind was stilled, its breath caught up by the brooding darkness.

The mission itself seemed . . . Crane searched his mind for the right word . . . sinister . . . as though it knew him and was patiently waiting . . . and watching.

But for what?

Shaking his head, Crane dismissed the thought. He was acting like a maiden aunt who hears a rustle in every bush. He was on edge, maybe even scared, but of Ben Hollister and his rough riders, not a tiny, eighteen-year-old nun.

The wind's pent-up breath escaped in a loud sigh as Crane crossed fifty yards of open ground to the livery. Behind him, at the mission, a shutter had torn free and was banging back and forth like the beat of a demented drummer.

Despite the number of riders in town, there were few horses in the barn and no one was around. Crane let his eyes become accustomed to the deeper darkness ahead of him, then stepped into black ink, thick with the musky odors of horses, dung and hay.

A tiny mewing sound to his left stopped him. He looked down and saw a small calico cat emerge from the shadows, then sit, staring up at him. Crane had met cats before and he had learned that they expect great formality from strangers and a display of fine manners and good breeding.

He got down on one knee, keeping his distance. "How are you, little feller?" he asked. "Sorry I can't stay and talk. I'm in a hurry."

The calico's amber eyes studied Crane's face for a few moments. Then it rose and pushed against him, purring softly. Figuring that he'd passed the cat test, the marshal picked up the little animal and held it against his chest. He stroked the calico's soft fur and said, "Let's find the horses, huh?"

Enjoying the gentle touch of the man's strong hands, the cat purred happily in reply.

The blaze-faced sorrel was easy to find in the dark and the steeldust occupied the next stall.

Crane put the cat on the floor and whispered, "So long now, little feller. Go catch a mouse." He rubbed the calico's head, its little pointed ears brushing against the palm of his hand. The cat stood hesitantly for a moment, then, on silent feet, disappeared into the gloom.

Crane saddled the horses and led them to the door of the stable. He studied the street. The saloons were as busy as ever and if anything noisier, and the boardwalks were now crowded with men moving from one place to another in search of new excitement.

Over at the Bon-Ton the boys had pushed the piano and the pianist outside into the street, and a crowd of men and a few women were roaring "Lily Dale" at the top of their lungs.

As the marshal watched, one drunken rooster detached himself from the throng, drew his gun and took several pots at the sheriff's office. This drew a huge cheer from the crowd, but Ben Hollister stepped out of the Texas Belle and ordered the shooting to stop.

Crane shook his head and smiled. More than a few of the boys were going to be in no state to fight anybody come the glaring morning light.

Taking the street to get back to Masterson's office was now out of the question.

Crane swung into the saddle of the sorrel and left the barn at a walk, leading the steel-dust. He headed north into the darkness for half a mile, then swung west. After a few minutes he rode due south, keeping Rawhide Flat to his left, its lights twinkling in the gloom.

The trail ahead of Crane was a river of darkness, relieved here and there by streaks of iron white moonlight that silvered the branches of piñon, juniper and sagebrush.

The wind was gusting from the east and the marshal fancied he could hear the *thud-thud-thud* of the stamp mills in El Dorado Canyon a couple of miles away. The Techatticup, Wall Street and Savage mines were operating twenty-four hours a day and Crane had heard they'd already ripped five million dollars in gold and silver from the canyon hard rock.

Hidden in the darkness to the west stretched miles of hill country cut through by a myriad of creeks. As he'd seen from the train, the cottonwoods along their banks, even this late in spring, had only now begun to leaf out.

The cottonwood knows that winter in northern Nevada ain't over till it's over, and the weight of snow on leaves can splinter their weak branches.

Crane left the lights of Rawhide Flat behind him, then looped north again. He rode up to the rear of the sheriff's office and tied up the horses.

He had not been seen.

Keeping to the shadows, the marshal walked around to the front door and stepped inside. He looked around, at the empty office and at the door to Walsh's cell hanging ajar. A quick search told him all he needed to know.

Paul Masterson and Judah Walsh were gone. So was the sheriff's rifle.

CHAPTER 7

A tangle of worry and anger rode Crane as he sat at the table and tried to plan his next move.

It was no use speculating on what had happened. It was an exercise in pointlessness and in the end all it gave a man was a headache.

The marshal reached into his pocket, found his badge and pinned it to the front of his shirt. It was a big country and he could spend days searching for the missing men and never find them — especially if Ben Hollister had stashed them somewhere.

But sometimes the best solution is to meet a problem head-on and go right to its source. Crane reckoned that this was one of those times.

He drew his Colt, thumbed a round into the empty chamber under the hammer, then crossed the floor and took the Greener from the rack.

He searched the drawers of the rolltop desk and found what he was looking for, a box of twelve-gauge shells. He filled a pocket with the ammunition, then laid the shotgun on the table and built a smoke.

What had to be done had to be done, but he was in no hurry to do it. Walking into a saloon filled with drunken, hostile men, every one armed and willing to kill, was no small thing. The thought was enough to give any man pause, and that's what Crane was doing, thinking and pausing. He smoked the cigarette and then another.

The clock on the office wall said it was fifteen minutes after midnight.

The noise from the street outside had grown considerably, a strident cacophony of clinking bottles and glasses, hoarse, shouting male and female voices, yammering pianos, the whole rollicking racket punctuated by the festive revolver as drunks took pots at the moon and maybe each other.

It was time.

Deputy Marshal Crane took a deep breath and picked up the shotgun. He immediately laid it down, wiped damp palms on his pants, then took up the Greener again.

A wave of black depression swept over him and he had to force himself to open the door and step outside. What he was about to do went with the badge and to his mind there was little of the heroic in his actions.

The West was a male-dominated society where men of all stripes, good and bad, were rewarded for learning the practice of violence and the ways of the Colt. In such a male culture lawmen were regarded as heroes, but so were outlaws. To brace lawbreakers in a saloon was expected of Crane, as was the right of the outlaws to resist.

There would be no heroes in the Texas Belle that night . . . only men doing what the West required of them, and Crane would have it no other way.

The crescent moon had horned aside a few stray clouds and was soaring high in the sky. Stars hung like paper lanterns in a Chinatown alley, spreading their cold light, and the wind sighed steadily from the east, chilled by the cooling desert. It nuzzled Crane suspiciously as he walked.

The forlorn piano still stood in the street, abandoned by pianist and songsters, but the saloons were still in full swing, so noisy that the marshal expected their roofs to lift off at any minute and leave the revelers to celebrate in the moonlight.

For a few moments Crane hesitated at the door of the Texas Belle. He swallowed the lump in his throat, adjusted his grip on the shotgun, then stepped inside.

The thick air of the saloon was hot and heavy with the smell of whiskey, cigar smoke, cheap perfume and man-sweat. Crane felt like he'd just walked into an invisible wall.

It took a while before people noticed the tall, grim man with the badge on his chest and a scattergun in his hands.

Gradually the loud chatter and laughter faltered. Voices slowed and finally died away, like withered leaves falling from a tree. All eyes turned to Crane, the expressions on the faces of the men hostile and challenging, those of the women bold, smiling and calculating.

The marshal's voice cut into the uneasy silence. "Ben Hollister," he said. "Show yourself."

Slow moments ticked past, then the tall, lanky, young cowboy Masterson had named as Long Tom Feeney detached himself from the bar. He stood in front of Crane, his legs spread, thumbs in his gun belt.

"Who the hell do you think you are, Mister?" he said. "Comin' in here like you're the damned bull o' the woods." The cowboy was smiling, but his eyes were wild, shining with whiskey and recklessness. He was on the prod, anxious to kill his man.

Crane was on edge and his patience was wafer thin. "Prove your manhood some other night, boy," he said. "Now step aside or I'll cut you in half right where you stand."

The puncher tensed, looking at Crane, calculating his chances in the expectant silence, but a voice from behind him said, "Let it go, Tom. If you don't, Marshal Crane will kill you for sure." Hollister stepped beside the cowboy. "Won't you, Marshal?"

"Where's Sheriff Masterson and Judah Walsh?" Crane asked, ignoring the man's question.

Hollister looked genuinely puzzled. "What the hell are you talking about?"

"They're missing. I think you know where they are."

Puzzlement gave way to anger on the rancher's face. "You mean you let Walsh escape?"

"I mean, he's gone and so is Masterson."

Crane read Hollister's scarlet face. Reluctantly he realized the man was telling the truth; he'd had nothing to do with the disappearance of the sheriff and his prisoner.

A man pushed beside Hollister. He was tall and impossibly skinny, dressed in a black frock coat, a stained, collarless shirt and a battered stovepipe hat. Under the coat he wore two guns in shoulder holsters and in his right hand he carried a Bible. A braided dog whip dangled from his wrist.

The old man's prominent blue eyes and long gray hair and beard gave him the look of an Old Testament prophet and he spoke like one.

"He's lying to us, Ben," the man said. "He has freed the iniquitous and now he speaks to us with a serpent's tongue."

For all his arrogance and bluster, Hollister had spent a lifetime taking the measure of men. His eyes met Crane's and he summed up the marshal in his own mind.

"He's not lying to us, Reuben." He turned to the man. "I hired you for one job. Now I'm giving you another: find Walsh and bring him here."

"And the sheriff?"

Hollister shrugged. "If he gets in the way, kill him."

Crane's smile was thin. "Paul Masterson won't be easy to kill. If the preacher there goes up against him, he'll find he's got a cougar by the tail."

Without taking his eyes off Crane, the rancher turned his head. "Garcia!"

When the little gunman pushed though

the crowd, Hollister said, "Go with Reuben Stark and his sons and as many others as you need. I want Walsh."

Garcia nodded, sliding Crane a look of pure hate and malice.

Stark turned and yelled, "Abe! Ike! Eli! Jeptha! Get over here!"

The crowd parted and four bearded men emerged. Stark's sons were dressed like their father in shabby frock coats, but they wore battered, wide-brimmed hats and had gun belts buckled around their hips. One of the brothers had a smear of lipstick on his cheek.

"Come with me," Stark said. "We have a man to find and another to kill."

The man with the lipstick smear scowled and said, "But, Pa, it's dark out there. How we gonna find men in the dark?" He leered at his brothers. "Besides, right now I got something better in mind."

The sound of Stark's hand slapping his son's cheek was like a rifle shot. As the man staggered back, the old preacher screamed, "Jeptha, he who unites himself with a whore is one with her in body. Verily I say the two will be one flesh and wallow as one in filth."

Jeptha Stark wiped away a trickle of blood from the corner of his mouth and glared at his father. "One day, old man, I swear I'm going to kill you."

"Get out there in the street with your brothers and find that niggra!" Stark snapped. "Go!"

Garcia pushed past Crane. Stark and his sons followed, trailed by a dozen or so cowboys and an equal number of hangers-on and barflies. "Fifty dollars in gold to the man who finds Walsh!" Hollister yelled at their retreating backs, and the men cheered.

The old arrogance was back in the rancher's eyes. "Why, you're still here, Marshal?"

"This isn't over, Hollister. If you find Walsh I want him surrendered into my custody. I'll take him to Virginia City to stand trial for murder."

"Damn it, man, so he shot a dried-up old spinster with nobody to mourn her but a cat. Every rancher around, including me, is facing ruin and the only man who can save us is Judah Walsh."

"I want him, Hollister. He's a cold-blooded killer."

Anger flared in the rancher's face. "And how many have you killed in cold blood, Crane? The only thing that separates you from Walsh is the star on your chest. You kill with the blessing of the law, and he doesn't, that's all."

The rancher shook his head, then softened his tone. "Why should we argue when the solution to the problem has been staring us right in the face?

"Here's my proposition: We get Walsh to tell us where the money is hid. Then we give him a hundred dollars, put him on a horse and wish him well. Once he's outside the town limits, you go after him and make your arrest."

Hollister spread his hands. "I can't say fairer than that."

Crane admitted that the man made sense and it could very well be a way out of this mess. "And Sheriff Masterson?"

"I have no interest in Masterson. If he's still alive and kicking when this night is over, take him with you and no harm done."

"He killed a couple of your men."

"And badly wounded another. But when I get my money back, I'm willing to let bygones be bygones."

"Why didn't you think of this earlier?"

Hollister smiled. "I'm a hard, uncompromising man, Crane, and sometimes I go bullheaded at a thing. Now that I've taken time to think it through, I'm willing to seek the middle ground."

"And the only loser is Judah Walsh."

"Do you give a damn?"

"No, I guess I don't." Crane hesitated, then said, "All right, we play it your way. Tell me at once if you find Walsh. And, Hollister, I'll take it hard if any harm befalls Paul Masterson."

"He means nothing to you."

"I like him."

"Then I'll tell the boys to go easy on him."

The cowboy who'd challenged Crane when he walked into the saloon stiffened and opened his mouth to speak, but Hollister quickly glared the man into silence.

It had been a small exchange and it probably meant nothing, but for some reason it troubled the marshal deeply.

CHAPTER 8

Crane returned to the sheriff's office and replaced the Greener in the rack. He added wood to the stove and shoved the coffeepot on to heat.

The cell adjoining Walsh's had a cot and he planned to stretch out and get some sleep later, after he took the horses back to the livery stable. Wherever Masterson was, it was unlikely he'd need them now.

He started to roll a cigarette, but the sound of two fast gunshots sent him sprinting for the door.

Outside in the street what looked like one of the Stark boys was standing at the alley where Crane had dragged the drunken miner.

"I got him!" the man shouted. "I got Masterson!"

When Crane arrived at the alley, Jeptha Stark, a smoking Colt in his hand, was telling anyone who'd listen that he saw Masterson creeping toward him and cut loose. "I hit the son of a bitch twice," he yelled, his eyes shining. "Plugged him dead center."

Led by Ben Hollister and Reuben Stark, men had crowded into the alley, one of them holding aloft an oil lamp. After a few moments, Hollister pushed back through the milling mob of gawking onlookers.

"You killed the wrong man, damn you," Hollister snapped. "You plugged a miner."

"I know the man," somebody standing behind the rancher said. "His name is John Horne and he always done more moochin' drinks than he ever done mining."

Old Reuben Stark's face was livid. "Boy," he said to Jeptha, "didn't I always teach you to make sure of your target afore you kill a man?"

"I was dang certain it was him, Pa, comin' at me in the dark."

"You shot a drunk, boy."

"No harm done, Reuben," Hollister said mildly. "It was an honest mistake."

"And it still counts as a kill, don't it Mr. Hollister?" Jeptha said.

The rancher said nothing, but Reuben Stark made it clear that he would not be mollified.

"It ain't a kill, boy," he said. "I'll tell you when you can notch your gun and this ain't one o' them times."

Jeptha sneered. "I'm claiming the kill, old man."

Reuben cursed wildly and screamed, "A foolish son brings grief to his father and bitterness to the one who bore him!" He lashed out with the dog whip that hung from his wrist, cutting his son across the face.

The scarlet scar of a welt blossomed on Jeptha's cheek and he cursed and went for his gun.

Reuben Stark was surprisingly fast. He reached into his coat and a Colt appeared in his hand as though he'd just performed a conjuring trick. As his son cleared leather, the barrel of the old man's gun crashed onto his wrist.

Jeptha shrieked and his revolver fell into the dust from his suddenly limp fingers.

Reuben stepped closer, beating Jeptha with the dog whip, raining powerful, slashing blows on the man's head and shoulders.

Punctuating each word with a cut of the whip, Reuben, with a fury that verged on madness, screamed, "The-son-who-raises-a-hand-to-his-father-is-an-abomination!"

Crane turned to Hollister. "Seems to me we'll have another killing on our hands if you don't call off your dog."

For a moment the rancher didn't respond, his eyes glittering, fascinated by the beating Jeptha was taking. Finally, as though he'd just wakened from sleep, he pointed to a couple of his men, then at the raging Stark, and said, "Get him away from here."

Reuben was hauled, kicking, into the saloon, screaming curses on his son's head.

Hollister shrugged and grinned. "That old man is as mean as a caged cougar and crazy as a loco'd calf."

Jeptha had been beaten into the dust. Now he rose and reached for his gun with his left hand. As he flexed his swollen wrist he lifted his blazing eyes to the Texas Belle where his father was still inside raving, and said, "One day I'm going to kill him, just like he killed his own old man."

"Stark, you and your pa are a credit to the community," Crane said.

He brushed through the crowd, grabbed a lantern from a glassy-eyed cowboy and stepped into the alley. He raised the light until it shone on the dead man's face. As he suspected, it was the miner he'd buffaloed earlier in the evening.

"Mister, you should have stayed in the mines," he said.

Crane led the horses back to the barn, along

a street that was suddenly quiet and subdued. A piano still played in the Texas Belle, but most of the crowd had gone to find a place where they could sleep off their whiskey.

The moon was dropping toward the horizon, haloed in a hazy ring of blue and rust red, and only a few stars glittered in a sky slowly shading from black to deep violet. The wind was rising, kicking up veils of dust, tugging playfully at the brim of the marshal's hat.

When he returned to the sheriff's office the clock on the wall stood at one thirty. Crane poured himself coffee, sat at the table and built a smoke. He hadn't slept since the train, and then only fitfully, and he was very tired. Normally he did not let himself get too exhausted, since it was an open invitation to the dark angel, but since his arrival in Rawhide Flat he'd had no other choice.

Blue cigarette smoke curling around his head, he closed his eyes, letting himself drift. But the opening door brought him instantly to full wakefulness, his hand dropping to his holstered gun.

Maxie Starr looked like she'd been through it. Her lipstick was smudged and a tendril of loose hair fell over her eyes. She had bruises on her arms and shoulders from rough handling by drunken men, a beer stain on the front of her dress.

She spoke up without ceremony. "All right, Marshal, where is he?"

"Who?"

"You know who. Where's Paul?"

"You mean you don't know?"

"I mean I don't know."

"They've been hunting him, that crazy old Reuben Stark and his sons among them. I don't think they'll find him, though."

"Why do you say that?"

"Because Paul is smart. Wherever he and Walsh are holed up, it will be safe."

"I wish I was that confident," Maxie said. "Any coffee in the pot?"

"Help yourself." Crane watched Maxie for a few moments, admiring the lithe grace of her shapely body. She was a lovely woman, but her beauty was just beginning to fade into fine lines and a hardening mouth, the result of a profession that demanded much and gave little in return. He said, "Don't worry, Paul will come to no harm. I told Hollister I didn't want him hurt."

The woman turned and her eyes flared. "Hollister! You told Hollister you didn't want him hurt. Ben Hollister will kill Paul the first chance he gets."

"That's not what he told me."

"I don't care what he told you. Hollister wants Paul Masterson dead."

Maxie sat down opposite Crane, her steaming coffee cup on the table in front of her. She looked directly into the marshal's eyes.

"Do you really think Ben Hollister will forgive and forget after Paul killed two of his hands and a third is back at the Rafter-T coughing up black blood and unlikely to last another day? If he let their deaths go unavenged he could never count on the loyalty of his riders ever again.

"Mister, without that loyalty no rancher can survive for long. Cowboys are a close-knit group and when the word got around that Hollister stood by and did nothing after his men were gunned by a tin-star sheriff, he'd soon discover that he can no longer hire punchers.

"How long do you think he'd last in this country when he can't round up his herd or hire men to drive it to the railhead?"

Crane nodded. "I know about punchers, Maxie. I went up the trail from Texas with John Slaughter when I was fourteen, then three times after that."

"Then you know better than anybody why Hollister can't let Paul live."

Crane took out the makings and offered

them to Maxie. The woman expertly built a cigarette that the marshal lit for her. Then he rolled one of his own.

"Hollister made me a proposition," he said. "He told me that after he catches Walsh and gets the man to lead him to the stolen money, I can have him."

"And Paul?"

"That's when he said he wouldn't be harmed."

"And you believed him?"

"Then? Yes, I guess I did. Now I'm not so sure."

Maxie drew deep on her cigarette. Ash fell on her dress and she immediately brushed it away. "Marshal, Hollister knows that after he kills Paul Masterson he has to kill you. You'd try to arrest him and he'd be waiting for you."

"It's no small thing to kill a United States marshal, even a deputy marshal."

Maxie smiled. Then, as though she were talking to a child, she said, "Gus, about the age you were riding up the trail for the first time, I was working in a saloon in Denver. Men in saloons talk, about gunfighters, lawmen, outlaws and who's the best with a gun and who just killed who. Do the names W. T. Bentz, Frank Griffin, Madison Mitchell and Jacob Owens mean anything to you?"

Crane shook his head. "I can't say they do."

"Every one of them was a deputy United States marshal killed in the line of duty, and those are just a few of the names I remember men talking about. There were many others I don't recollect. But I know this — all of them wore a badge just like yours and it didn't protect them from bullets."

Maxie ground out her cigarette under a high-heeled shoe, then said, "By this time I'm betting that Hollister has it figured. If he kills you and Paul, there won't be a big hue and cry because people vanish in the Comstock all the time, and lawmen are not immune. Besides, everybody is so busy making money they won't care."

Crane creaked back on his chair, waves of tiredness washing over him, as Maxie reached for the makings again. "Any idea where Paul and Walsh might be?"

"They're on foot, so he's right here in Rawhide Flat. Paul has a few friends in town, not many, but a few. He could be with any one of them."

"I need names."

The woman smiled. "Later, after you've had some sleep. You're about dead on your feet."

Maxie rose, the cigarette burning low

between her fingers. She took a last puff and dropped the butt on the floor. "I'll be back this evening."

Crane nodded. "Ol' Paul lit out and threw me to the wolves, didn't he?"

Maxie shook her head. "I guess he figures you're all growed up and can take care of yourself."

The marshal smiled. "Take care of your ownself, Maxie."

"You too, Gus. Yeah, you too."

CHAPTER 9

Crane woke, the lumpy straw mattress on his cot paining him. He swung his feet onto the floor, then sat in the thin beam of watery dawn light blading through the cell window. Despite the knots of pain in his back he felt refreshed, though he figured he had slept only four or five hours.

The marshal rose, stretched, put on his hat and boots, then walked into the office. There was still a dull red glow of life in the stove and he added a few pieces of wood. He thumbed open the lid of the coffeepot and glanced inside. Empty.

Where did Masterson keep his coffee?

A search of the desk revealed a small sack of Arbuckle, and Crane laid it on the table. He remembered that there was an iron water pump out back.

Walking into the fine-spun glow of morning he looked around carefully, but there was little to see. The town seemed deserted, the boys sleeping off their drunks, postponing the raw-whiskey headache that would come aborning with the day. The Pine Nut Mountains were a far purple to the east, the vast sky arching over the peaks streaked with scarlet.

His tanned face bronzed by the fire in the sky, Crane took time to light a cigarette, then stepped to the pump where he rinsed out the pot and filled it. He returned to the jail, threw a handful of coffee into the pot, then set it to boil.

Crane ran a hand over his stubbled chin and remembered that his razor and spare shirt were in his saddlebags back at the livery. He'd get them later. Right now all he wanted was coffee and a quiet hour.

It is said that a watched pot never boils, and that was Crane's experience as he sat at the table and watched for signs of bubbling life from the coffee on the stove. Several times he checked the pot, only to find the brew simmering but not yet on the boil.

A few slow minutes dragged past and Crane got to his feet again. But he never reached the coffee. Running steps sounded in the street outside; then the door burst open. A small, breathless man wearing a white apron and an expression of horror rushed inside.

"Marshal . . . the livery stable," he gasped. "Oh my God, come quick."

Crane reached for his gun belt. "What's happened?" he demanded.

But the man's hand flew to his mouth, his cheeks bulged, his eyes popped and he ran outside. Crane heard him throwing up against the wall of the jail.

The marshal stepped into the street and miserably the retching man pointed a shaking finger in the direction of the barn. "Go . . . go," he said, frantically laboring for breath. "Oh my God . . ."

Crane glanced along the street. Already a dozen people, mostly the town's respectable element, were hurrying toward the livery stable. After one last glance at the suffering man, the marshal followed them.

About thirty people were jammed into the barn and Crane had to push his way through a shield wall of backs before he saw what they were seeing.

The crowd was keeping a respectful distance between them and Maxie Starr. All had a look of fascinated revulsion on their faces, but none were there to mourn. The fate of a nameless saloon whore meant nothing to them except as a delightfully shivering diversion in a day that had promised to be as dull as any other.

The only light in the barn came from the door and the open hayloft, but Maxie's naked body, a slender, white marble column streaked with crimson, gleamed with its own unearthly radiance.

Maxie had been hung by her wrists from a beam, a gag banded tightly over her mouth, her unbound hair falling over her shoulders.

The woman's back and hips had been flayed with a whip until the flesh had been stripped from her bones in ribbons of scarlet. The ribs showed white as did parts of her shoulder blades and spine.

The woman had died hard, screaming soundlessly under an attack so frenzied and full of hate it looked like the work of a madman.

Crane stepped closer to Maxie's body.

A crudely lettered sign, scrawled by a bullet on the back of an old dance hall poster, had been hung around the woman's neck.

THUS DEATH TO
ALL THE WHORES
OF BABYLON

Crane removed the placard, then studied the bandanna that had been tied at the back of the woman's head. The ends showed wrinkled twists that suggested the gag had been released, then retied several times.

After an initial whipping, the gag had been untied, probably to answer her tormentor's questions. By then, Maxie would have been too weak and shocked to cry out for help.

The repeated whipping and questioning had gone on for a long time before death had extended to her its small mercy.

Now the people behind Crane began to chatter excitedly among themselves, the women letting out delighted little squeals of horror. A man in broadcloth, pince-nez glasses perched on the end of an imbiber's nose, stepped beside the marshal.

His eyes were shining, eager. "Who done for her, Marshal, huh? Who do you reckon whupped her?"

A black depression settled on Crane, then quickly turned inward, becoming a blazing rage. He grabbed the man by the lapels of his coat and pushed him away. "Get the hell out of here!"

He turned, his face stiff with fury, darkness narrowing his vision to a tunnel streaked with red. "All of you out, now!"

"Here, that won't do," a gray-haired man protested. "You can't treat us like this."

Other voices joined in loud agreement.

Crane pulled his gun and fired two shots

over the heads of the crowd. "Get out!" he yelled. "In two seconds I'll kill any man or woman who isn't gone from here."

The expression on the lawman's face and the smoking Colt in his hand convinced the mob that he'd summed up his feelings and meant what he said.

A stampede for the door followed and a few moments later Crane stood alone.

He punched the empty shells from his gun and reloaded, his face settling into grim, hard lines.

Right then he wanted to kill Ben Hollister real bad. Even if the man hadn't flogged Maxie to death himself, he had given the order. Hollister figured the woman knew where Paul Masterson was holed up and he'd killed her trying to get information that she did not have.

Looking at Maxie's torn body, Crane made up his mind. Before the sun reached its highest point in the sky, Hollister would be dead. There would be no grant of mercy, no appeal to higher authority. The rancher would die like a yellow dog with Crane's bullet in him.

That, the marshal swore.

Right now, Crane had an unpleasant task ahead of him. He took a small, folding knife from his pocket and was about to cut Maxie's bonds when he was stopped by someone calling his name. A woman's voice.

The marshal swung around and to his surprise saw four nuns standing at the door, one of them with a folded, clean white sheet over her arm.

"We will take care of her," Sister Marie Celeste said. She passed the sheet to one of the other nuns.

"She's nothing to you," Crane said, a brutal rage still raking him with spurs that dug deep and hurt intensely.

"She is one of God's children," the nun said. "She is everything to us." Sister Marie Celeste's cool dark eyes leveled on Crane's. "The body must be washed and prepared for burial and prayers for her immortal soul must be said over her. Can you fulfill that function, Marshal?"

All the pent-up anger drained from Crane. "I'll cut her down," he said.

"No, we will do that."

The nun took the knife from Crane's hand, then nodded to the other sisters. The women silently wrapped the sheet around Maxie's naked body and held her as Sister Marie Celeste cut the ropes.

Carefully, so she would not touch the ground, the nuns lifted Maxie's body between them, then carried her from the barn.

Aware that Sister Marie Celeste was still looking at him with cool appraisal, Crane said, "Thank you, Sister."

His response was inadequate and the marshal knew it, but he did not have the words to say more.

The nun nodded. "You have your duty, Marshal, and I have mine."

She turned and left, the rosary beads hanging from the belt of her habit clicking.

Crane stepped to the door and looked down the street. A few of the respectable towns-people were crossing from one boardwalk to the other, but there was no sign of cowboys or miners.

The sun had only just begun its climb into the sky, but the blue morning was already warm, threaded with gold light.

An overloaded brewer's dray with staked sides creaked and swayed past the stable, its mule team straining into the harness. A cloud of gray, alkali dust followed the wagon's progress and drifted in the breeze like a flock of ghosts.

The marshal had been in haste to kill a man. Now he decided that Hollister could wait until he'd had his coffee. Besides, if it came to a draw and shoot, the coffee would help give him an edge.

Crane left the sheriff's office at eleven o'clock, walking into a day so burning hot that just taking a breath of the thick, dry air felt like eating a spoonful of scalding soup.

The sky was the color of washed-out denim and the still sun held no promise that there was relief from the heat to come. Only the mountains, their lower slopes green as mint in a glass of iced tea, looked cool, but they were aloof and impossibly distant.

The marshal walked purposefully in the direction of the Texas Belle. He had come to kill Ben Hollister, his earlier anger of the morning replaced by a slow fire in his belly and death in his eye.

A rust-colored dog glanced at Crane, looked longer, then slunk away, its tail between its legs. Half a dozen hogs rooted noisily among the restaurant waste tossed in an alley, and somewhere a late-rising rooster crowed with hollow pride that the new day had begun.

There was something in Crane's walk and face that caused people to stop and watch him pass. None showed the admiration due a resolute lawman, only puzzlement and a shadow of fear. The marshal was wearing the gunfighter's mantle and such men were best avoided.

Crane was halfway to the saloon when the sound of a gunshot stopped him in his tracks. Then he started running. . . .

CHAPTER 10

Crane burst through the door of the Texas Belle, then stopped, assessing the situation, his Colt already in his hand. Years of dangerous living by the gun had taught him to sum up a scene in an instant, and he did now, trying to make sense of what he was seeing.

The bartender had been bending over the slumped body of a dead man and he straightened as the marshal entered.

"Bill Moore," he said.

The name meant nothing to Crane.

His eyes flicked to the back door of the saloon. Ben Hollister stood just outside, looking around him, gun in hand.

Crane stepped to the body. The man was sprawled over a table, his face in a plate that held the remains of his breakfast. He had knocked the coffeepot over and brown liquid, stained with his blood, seeped, steaming across the tabletop.

Bill Moore, whoever he was, had been

shot in the back of the skull, his blond hair already matted red. Crane pushed the man back in the chair and his head lolled onto his chest.

The bullet had exited just above his right eyebrow, punching out a hole as big as a silver dollar. His eye was gone, leaving a sightless socket.

Crane turned to the bartender. "How did it come about?"

The man opened his mouth, tried to speak but shut it again. There was a tormented expression in his eyes as he tried to form words that refused to come.

Hollister had stepped inside. He holstered his gun as he walked closer to Crane.

"Whoever he was, he's long gone," Hollister said.

"Tell me about it," Crane said.

"Isn't it obvious?"

"Obvious or no, you tell me, Hollister." The man fought down the urge to drive his fist into the big rancher's face. The time for violence would come soon, but not right then.

Hollister was also on the prod, his angry blue eyes bleary from the kind of rotgut hangover that would have made a lesser man yearn only for death.

The rancher swung the upper part of his

body around and pointed to an open window at the rear of the saloon. "Shot came from over there."

"I open the windows in the morning to get rid of the stink in here," the bartender said. He'd added nothing of interest to the conversation, but had found his voice.

Crane nodded in the direction of the dead man. "The bartender says his name is Bill Moore. Who was he?"

"One of my hands," Hollister said. "Trailed with ol' Charlie Goodnight back in the day, then tried to build his own spread down the Castle Mountains way. After two years of drought and one of locusts, he gave up and came to work for me."

"Who would want to kill him?"

"Nobody. He was all right."

"Then why is he dead?"

"He was mistook for me, I reckon."

Hollister saw the shadow of disbelief in Crane's eyes, and decided to spell it out.

"I'm a drinking man, and sometimes I can't face bacon and eggs first thing in the morning. Moore was here, and he was a chowhound. I told him to sit down and finish my breakfast. He did, and a minute or two later somebody shot him."

Crane glanced around the saloon. Hollister's broadcloth coat was draped over a chair. He wore a white shirt, as did the dead man, and his hair was the same shade of blond. From the back Moore could have easily been mistaken for Hollister, especially by a bushwhacker who only had time for a quick, snap shot.

"You got a lot of enemies, Hollister?"

"Only two: you and Paul Masterson."

Crane nodded. "I can't talk for Masterson, but you're right. I'm your worst enemy."

"You plan on finishing the job Masterson started? The big difference is that I'm facing you, Crane. I won't go down as easy as Bill Moore."

The marshal let that go. He said, "Did you hear about Maxie Starr?"

"Yeah, from maybe ten different people this morning who —" Suddenly a look of horror chased the anger from the big rancher's face. "Hey, wait, back down there, Marshal. You don't think I had anything to do with that? I never left the saloon all night. Ask the bartender here." Hollister turned. "Sam, tell him."

The man called Sam looked at Crane. "He's telling the truth, Marshal. Mr. Hollister was at the bar all night. He never even sat down until I brought him his breakfast this morning, and that's a natural fact."

"You could have given the order, Hollister. Let somebody else do your dirty work."

Now a clean anger was back in the rancher's face. "Crane, I don't make war on women. I liked Maxie. I was good to her and I'd never have done anything to harm her."

"Maybe you thought she knew where Masterson was holed up."

"If Maxie had known that, she would have told me. Like I said, I was good to her. Not many men were."

"Then who flogged her to death? You tell me, Hollister."

"I don't know, Crane. But as sure as God is in his heaven, I aim to find out."

There comes a point when a man's talking is over. Hollister, arrogant and belligerent, had reached it.

"Crane, I've told you the truth." The man stiffened. "I think Masterson blames me for Maxie's death, just like you do and that's why he tried to kill me this morning. Now, if all that don't set well with you, skin that hog leg and let's have at it."

Doubt nagged at Crane. His years as a lawman had taught him to recognize the truth when he heard it.

Hollister seemed genuinely saddened, or at least concerned, by the woman's death and the marshal doubted he was a good enough actor to fake it. It's one thing to kill a guilty man; quite another to gun down one who may be innocent. And Crane felt conflicting emotions tug at him.

If not Hollister, then who had brutally murdered Maxie? Only a crazed man would . . .

A disturbing thought came, unbidden, into the marshal's head: where was Reuben Stark, the man with the dog whip?

He asked Hollister the question.

It took the rancher a while to answer. Hollister had been ready for a gunfight he was not sure he could win and every taut-strung nerve in his body had to loosen, bring him down and clear the tunnel vision that had seen only Crane.

Finally he said, his voice steady, "Last I heard he was riding out with his sons hunting Masterson."

"When did he leave the saloon?"

Hollister shook his head, then looked to the bartender for help.

"Near as I can remember, Stark and his boys left around two, said they were going for their horses and then they'd kill themselves a sheriff."

Crane nodded grimly. That would be about the time Maxie had left his office.

A seed of suspicion grew in his mind. Stark was supposedly working for Hollister, but what if the crazy old man had his own secret agenda? If he could find Masterson, he could kill the sheriff and then have Walsh lead him to the money. The entire fifty thousand would be his.

Had Stark found out that Maxie had a more-than-friends relationship with Masterson and would probably know where he was? Did he kidnap her and then mercilessly flog her with his dog whip in an attempt to get information the unfortunate woman could not give?

Suddenly it all added up, and by the strained look on Hollister's face Crane guessed that the rancher had been doing his own thinking and had reached the same conclusion.

But he came at it from an angle the marshal least expected.

"They say there are a bunch of people, sodbusters for the most part, living in the Pine Nut foothills, who are waiting for an avenging angel of the Lord to arrive and smite the sinful of the Comstock," Hollister said. He smiled faintly. "That takes in a heap of territory and a powerful amount of sin."

"Who's the 'they' that are doing all the

saying?" Crane said, irritated as he tried to make sense of what the rancher was telling him.

"Prospectors, punchers and the like."

"Have they seen the people?"

"No, just heard stories."

"I don't catch your drift, Hollister. How does this link up with Reuben Stark and the murder of Maxie Starr?"

"There's been a story going around for a while, just a rumor, mind, that Stark is their leader."

Crane tried to dab a loop on that statement. "What's in it for him? A crazy old man waiting with a bunch of loco people for an angel to arrive. Not much profit in that."

"Could be that's why he needs the fifty thousand. He's got to feed and clothe his followers, and before winter arrives he'll have to build cabins for them. All that takes money."

As though he was trying to keep Crane off balance, Hollister said, "Recently, there's been a string of robberies and killings west of the mountains. Nothing real big, miners murdered and robbed of their pokes, the Pioneer stage held up and a passenger killed, the murder of a preacher and his son. The killers took the man's horse and buggy and his silver watch."

Hollister smiled. "Could be Stark has decided to give the avenging angel some help."

"Any idea where Stark and his sons could have gone?"

"Like I told you, he's hunting Masterson. It's a big country and he could be any-where."

"Maybe, but I'm going after him."

"I'll come with you. I liked Maxie, liked her a lot."

"Not a chance, Hollister. I don't trust you and I don't ride with a man I'm afraid to turn my back on."

The rancher's face burned. "I've never back-shot a man in my life."

"There's always a first time."

"That's cold, Crane. You're a hard man, a mighty hard, unforgiving man. And you ain't exactly a joy to talk with."

"Goes with the badge," the marshal said. His eyes met Hollister's and locked. "One more thing: I may be gone for two, three days — who knows?" he said. "When I get back I want to hear that Paul Masterson is still alive."

"That's hardly up to me."

"I think it is. Maxie said he's probably holed up right here in town and you've got reason enough to gun him. If Masterson gets shot, his fault, nobody's fault, I'll still come looking for you." Crane's eyes iced. "From this moment, all my talking is done. Keep the sheriff alive or I'll come for you and kill you, Hollister."

But the big rancher would not be pushed. "So be it," he said. "I'll be waiting."

Crane stopped at a general store and sacked up a few trail supplies, a canteen and a small coffeepot. Remembering that there was an old Henry rifle in the rack at the sheriff's office, he also bought a box of .44-40 shells. The marshal retrieved the rifle from the office and Masterson's bedroll he'd found in the spare cell, then headed for the livery.

As he passed the Texas Belle he saw Hollister lounging against a post, smoking a cigar. Joe Garcia stood close to him in that wide-legged, thumbs-in-gun-belt stance he always adopted, calculated to make him look like a dangerous man. Garcia grinned insolently at Crane as he walked by, and Hollister said, "Good luck, Marshal."

The marshal said nothing and walked on, this time unable to gauge the sincerity, or lack of it, in the rancher's tone.

Tightening the cinch on the buckskin's saddle, Crane turned when he heard heavy footfalls behind him.

"Howdy, young feller. You figgerin' on pulling your freight?"

The speaker was a skinny old man with a stubble of gray beard on his chin. He was wearing a battered black hat, baggy pants tucked into heavy, mule-eared boots and a ragged vest that had once been red but had faded to orange.

"I'll be back in a couple of days," Crane said.

"Maybe so, but I reckon you already owe me two dollars fer horse board an' feed. Around these parts, oats don't come cheap, if they come at all."

"You're right, two dollars is mighty expensive," Crane said.

The old man shrugged. "This is the Comstock. Hell, everything is expensive."

After he tied his sack of supplies to the saddle horn and slid the Henry into the rifle boot he'd taken from Masterson's saddle, the marshal led the buckskin out of the stall and stopped near the old-timer.

He reached into his pocket and counted out the two dollars into the oldster's hand. "A feller could go broke around here real quick."

"Ain't that a fact," the old man cackled. "Happens to fellers all the time in Rawhide

Flat." He grinned, showing few teeth and those black. "Name's Mitch Holly, by the way. I own this establishment."

Crane nodded, gave his name, then, clutching at any slender straw, said, "You ever hear tell of a man called Reuben Stark?"

Holly's eyes flickered from the marshal's face to the star on his chest and back again. His face was guarded. "An' who wants to know, you personal, or the law?"

"Both."

The old man clammed up for a few moments.

"Sure I know him. He's a crazy old coot, even crazier nor me. An' he's killed more'n his share, I can tell you that."

"You ever hear that he leads a bunch of loco people out in the hills?"

"Heard that."

"Is it true?"

"I'd say it is, on account of how one time he sure enough asked me to jine up. Tol' me to sell the stable, give him my money and wait for the day of vengeance."

Crane smiled. "I see you didn't."

"Mister, I said I was a crazy old coot, but I ain't stupid."

Crane tried another tack. "You heard about the woman who was murdered here last night?"

"I did, heard it this morning." He shook his head. "Terrible thing. See, I was visiting a widder woman of my acquaintance out by Sullivan Canyon an' didn't get back until an hour ago." Holly's face changed. "Here, you don't think —"

"No, I don't think."

"Then you suspicion ol' Reuben?"

"Maybe."

"He's capable, an' he carries that dog whip o' his everywhere."

"Mitch, do you know Sheriff Masterson?"

"Who doesn't? He's a mean one. Kilt a couple of cowboys —"

"Yeah, I know. Any idea where he might be?"

"Long gone, I hope."

"How about Judah Walsh?"

"Marshal, everybody wants to know where he is. Stole the town's money, then hid it somewheres."

"He's with the sheriff."

"Know that too. By now Sheriff Masterson has the money and I don't think we'll get it back. Them two boys is long gone, I reckon."

Crane led the buckskin outside and swung into the saddle. Holly stepped beside him.

"You going after Stark?"

"Could be."

"Then watch out for the Archangel Michael."

The marshal was startled. "What did you say?"

"The avenging angel that's goin' to clean up the Comstock an' kill all the whores. Stark tol' me his name, says he's Michael the Archangel and that he's got a sword made o' fire."

CHAPTER 11

After Crane left the stable he rode past the mission. A nun was ringing the school bell and students, a few girls but mostly sullen, towheaded boys, were walking into class, their reluctance marked by slow, shuffling gaits. A youngster took a last look at the sky before going inside, like a man on the gallows about to be hanged.

The marshal kneed the buckskin into a trot, his mind working.

Was it only coincidence that the mission was named for Stark's avenging angel? The man was pure evil and surely the sisters, used to rassling with the devil, recognized it and would shun him.

Evil is in itself impotent; it only exists and doesn't build, grow, create or produce, the very antithesis to the nun's role.

But Stark had robed himself in the raiment of a righteous man, quoting the Bible, determined to strike down the sinner. Had the nuns, appalled by the greed, licentiousness and easy sin of the Comstock, ignored their scruples and joined the man in an unholy, crusading alliance?

And worse, did they have a hand in Maxie Starr's murder?

Crane tried to put that thought out of his mind, telling himself he was fantasizing, building houses on a bridge he hadn't even crossed yet.

Still, the possibility ate at him painfully, like a virulent, spreading cancer.

Crane was staking all on a roll of the dice. He knew Stark and his sons could be anywhere, but he was betting they'd return, however briefly, to check up on the old man's flock among the Pine Nut foothills.

There was also a possibility, a slim one Crane conceded, that Masterson and Judah Walsh were with them.

Finding Stark's camp would not be easy either.

The Pine Nut Mountains stretched forty miles north to south, and that was a heap of territory to cover.

After an hour, riding across hilly, broken country fragrant with the musky scent of piñon and sage, Crane swung east around the base of Mineral Peak, a jagged cone of rock standing more than eight thousand feet above the flat.

Ahead of him rose the mountains, a series of low, purple pinnacles that looked like the backbone of a great animal. At this point the Pine Nuts were dominated by the nine-thousand-foot Mount Como, its gently sloping sides heavy with piñon and juniper. Higher, the vegetation thinned to clumps of sage that covered the naked rock like a threadbare cloak.

The sun was higher in the sky, the drowsy day was hot and insects with sawtooth legs made small sounds in the bunchgrass. A flock of sage hens strutted toward Crane, then fled in panicked flight, a few feathers drifting behind them in the motionless air. The feathers settled to the ground, quiet as snowflakes, and in the wilderness all around him nothing moved, nothing stirred nor made a sound.

Crane felt sweat trickle down his back and his horse stamped irritably at a fly, no more fond of the growing heat than he was. The marshal swung out of the saddle, took off his hat and poured an inch or so of water into it from the canteen. He let the buckskin drink, then took a mouthful himself. The water was warm, alkaline, but it tasted wonderful.

His eyes lifted to his back trail and a thin

plume of dust rising into the air did not surprise him.

Hollister had sent others, probably Joe Garcia and some of the Rafter-T hands, to follow him.

The rancher was also playing long odds.

Crane smiled. If by chance he caught up with Masterson, Garcia and his boys could be depended on to kill the sheriff, gun the only witness — himself — and take Judah Walsh into custody.

Problem solved, to the relief of all concerned . . . except the two dead men.

Lifting his hat to shade himself from the sun, the marshal studied the dust: three riders, maybe four, but no more than that.

They would keep their distance, at least for now, waiting to see where Crane led them. They would have some hope that it would be to Masterson and Walsh.

But the marshal was not following a beckoning star, only his instinct, and that had failed him a time or three in the past.

Garcia and his riders could end up riding around in circles following his tracks, getting hotter, thirstier and madder by the minute.

There was also the possibility that if he got within rifle range, the frustrated gunmen might try to kill him out of sheer cussedness, and Crane knew he had to be alert to that possibility.

He stepped into the leather and continued his way east. A couple of times he stopped and took his field glasses from his saddlebags and scanned the shimmering land ahead of him.

He saw no sign of life, human or otherwise.

The sun had reached its highest point in the sky and was just beginning its slow slide to the horizon when Crane reached the foothills of the Pine Nut Mountains.

He drew rein in the shadow of the towering bulk of Mount Como and studied the land to the north with his glasses. He was searching for any telltale drift of smoke that would suggest the cooking fires of a large encampment.

But in that he was disappointed.

His survey to the south yielded the same result, a vista of folded hills and arroyos stretching into a blue distance where nothing moved.

Crane sat the buckskin for a few moments, undecided, then swung north.

He kept to the bottomland where shadows were gathering, trusting that the dancing heat haze to the west would keep him from being spotted by Garcia if the gunman was coming from that direction.

After an hour the marshal rode up on a deep canyon that scarred the landscape, a narrow pass that cut right through the mountains. Here the hills around him were lower and sandier, heavily covered in juniper, Mormon tea and sage. Stands of white evening primrose were in full bloom along with paintbrush and a few mariposa lilies.

The air was thick with heat, but smelled clean, of sage and wildflowers, heralding the new-aborning summer.

A sense of defeat in him, Crane swung his horse to the south again. Hunting for Stark's encampment in this vast wilderness seemed increasingly like an exercise in futility. The mountain canyons and hanging valleys could swallow hundreds, maybe thousands of people, and if they wished to remain hidden, there would be no finding them.

Maybe a cavalry regiment, given time and adequate supplies, could track down Stark's encampment, but it was an impossible task for one rider.

Crane was a man intolerant of his own failings. He realized now that he'd embarked on a fool's errand, but he should have known that much before he left Rawhide Flat. Now he was alone in a land he did not know well, beset by enemies, with the darkness that would soon close on him.

"Well done, Augustus," he said aloud, bitterly chiding himself. "Oh, very well done indeed."

Crane rode head up and alert. He had seen no sign of Garcia, but that didn't mean the man wasn't close, watching him.

By now the gunman must have figured that the man he was following had no idea of what he was doing, so why not take a potshot at him from ambush?

At the very least Crane's death would solve one of Ben Hollister's problems.

The shadows in the arroyos were deepening and had turned a dark purple color as the sun set. Already the coyotes had gotten to their feet, shaken off their twitching dreams, and were now yipping among the hills. The sky was shading from burned-out blue to pale violet, and to the west, above the bronze ball of the sun, it was tinged with red.

Once, far-off and faint, the marshal thought he heard gunshots. He immediately dismissed the notion. A hunter, maybe. That is, if they even were shots. Sometimes open country could play tricks on a man's ears, and his eyes.

Crane rode into a narrow arroyo thick with yellow poppies and cholla and built a cigarette, giving in to a tobacco hunger he'd battled for the past couple of hours.

What the hell, if Garcia was close enough to smell his smoke, he was close enough to shoot.

The marshal sat the buckskin and considered his options.

He could head back to town, but the notion of riding through the dark in strange country with hostile men on his trail did not appeal to him.

The alternative was to find a place to camp.

A rumbling in his belly reminded Crane of his hunger. He glanced at the sack hanging from his saddle, a vision of hot coffee and a thick sandwich of fried bacon and sourdough bread making its fragrant way into his head. But such a feast would require a fire, a blaze Garcia might see.

Crane shrugged. Let him come. He was not about to let a breed tinhorn like Garcia get between him and his supper.

But as it turned out, the marshal's bravado was unnecessary.

One of the booming Washoe zephyrs that from time to time plagued northwestern Nevada had swept down the mountain slopes to the north and was prowling the high plains.

The day had been still, but the wind suddenly picked up with tremendous force, destructive and mindless.

Wave after wave, battalions, then regiments, then divisions of wind assaulted the ramparts of the arroyo, shrieking in rage. The sage and juniper around the gulch tossed like frenzied dancers, their branches shredding as they added their thin wails to the uproar.

With the wind came sand, each grain stinging like a hornet, and jagged chunks of pine branch, lethal whirling dervishes caught up in demented cartwheels.

The sky that until moments ago had caught and held the light of the dying sun was now black from horizon to horizon, throwing a dusky veil over the day as though done with it, content now to leave it to the wind's tender mercies.

To Crane, it seemed that the world had gone mad and had laid siege to the arroyo, howling with the voice of a ravenous wolf.

The buckskin reared, terror-stricken by the madhouse of the storm, then tried to canter out of the gulch into the open.

Crane battled the big stud, sawing on the bit, and finally swung its head around. He leaped out of the saddle and led the horse deeper into the canyon, stumbling, tripping, cursing in the darkness.

The wind was from the northwest and if he rode into the open it would attack him venomously with all its unhindered power. His only hope was that the arroyo, as it cut deeper into the mountain slope, would offer some kind of shelter.

In that he was fortunate, as though the wind had blown away the cheerless light of an unlucky dark star.

The arroyo walls rose in height as they carved into the mountain, but the wind still slapped and pummeled Crane, hissing like a snake, resentful of his presence.

And the scared buckskin was a handful.

Rearing, trying to turn back, it took all of the marshal's strength to pull it farther into the canyon. Its mane flying, eyes showing white arcs of fright, the big stud fought the bit, steel-shod hooves thudding time after time into the dirt with the sound of muffled drums.

Crane tried to cuss at the horse, but the wind instantly snatched his breath away, leaving him speechless. A hunk of pine branch slammed into the marshal's hat brim, then scored down his face, drawing blood. A moment later a tumbling night insect hit his cheekbone, crunching against his skin like a dry leaf.

Battling his horse, Crane struggled deeper into the arroyo, wondering when it would eventually come to an end. He spared a glance at the sky.

The black clouds were being torn apart by the wind and tossed aside in shreds, like an impatient bridegroom rending the undergarment of his beloved.

A blinking moon appeared and its light touched the canyon with a silver sheen, showing Crane the way.

Ahead of him stood a solid wall of rock, but the arroyo made a dogleg to the left and the marshal followed it. Gradually the walls grew closer, barely allowing room for the buckskin to pass. But after twenty yards the coulee abruptly widened again, opening up into a small clearing treed with stunted juniper that grew among scattered boulders.

The area, about an acre in extent, was sheltered by high rock walls and the deranged wind wailed in impotent rage and took out its anger on the mountain, uprooting trees and dislodging loose tumulus that bounced and clattered down the slopes.

Crane listened into the night and heard a small sound of running water.

A search brought him to a cleft in the rock where a thin stream fell from somewhere higher up the wall. Here the floor of the clearing was limestone rock and over the course of years the water had gouged out a shallow tank that held several gallons.

To the marshal's joy, part of the wall close to the stream was undercut deeply. From sandy floor to the rock roof was only about four feet, but that was room enough for a fire and for him to stretch out in his blankets.

Coarse bunchgrass and wildflowers grew among the boulders, enough for the buckskin, who already had two-dollars worth of oats in him. Now out of the worst of the wind, the horse was much calmer and began to graze.

Dry wood aplenty had fallen into the clearing from the trees on the mountainside and Crane soon had a fire going in the cut. He put on the coffeepot to boil and sliced bacon into the small skillet he'd bought in Rawhide Flat.

Soon the delicious aroma of coffee and the frying bacon filled the clearing. Crane stepped away from the fire and built himself a smoke. It was a strange but pleasant experience to stand in comparative stillness and hear the wind roar over his head like a passing freight train.

A few rags of cloud scudded across the sky and the moon was beaming as though its face had been burnished by the breeze.

Crane turned over his sputtering bacon and when it was done, he set it aside and fried two thick slices of sourdough in the grease. Contentedly, he poured coffee, then braced his back against the wall of the undercut. He brought the smoking sandwich to his mouth — then closed it again with a snap.

A voice, a woman's voice, was calling to him out of the darkness.

CHAPTER 12

Irritated, the marshal carefully laid his sandwich on top of his coffee cup and rose to his feet.

There it was again, a small, thin female voice calling from somewhere in the arroyo.

Had Garcia laid a trap for him and baited it with a woman?

Crane pulled his Colt and warily retraced his steps through the arroyo, walking through opalescent moonlight and the raging wind. He heard the voice again, ahead of him.

"Is anyone there?"

The voice was small and the words fluttered like dove wings in the tempest, but Crane heard them clearly enough.

Moving on cat feet, the marshal kept close to a wall of the arroyo where shadows angled. His thumb was on the hammer of his gun. He was ready, his eyes probing the roaring dark.

What the hell was that? An unmoving gleam of white at the mouth of the canyon!

Crane felt an old superstitious dread rise in him. He'd learned such fear young, from the cowboys he'd trailed with, surely the most superstitious of all men. Their talk of ghosts had chilled him to the bone at many a campfire.

"Who's there?" Crane called out. "And don't make any fancy moves while you're talking. From here I can drill ya square in the brisket."

"Don't shoot me, Mister." There was a pause, then, "I'm hungry." And another, then, "An' I'm awfully scared."

"Walk toward me," the marshal said, his voice harsh.

A girl emerged from the gloom. Not even a girl, Crane saw, more a child, no more than thirteen years old. She wore a sleeveless shift that ended just above her bony knees and her eyes were huge and dark in a pale face. Her small feet were bare.

"What in . . ." The marshal's words couldn't keep up with his thoughts. He waited a moment and tried again. "What in God's name are you doing out there by yourself, child?"

"I'm hungry, Mister. And frightened." She looked around her, blond hair tossing in the wind. "It's a terrible storm."

Crane stepped closer, still holding his Colt. The nipples of the girl's tiny breasts budded against the thin material of her shift and he thought he saw her shiver, but whether from cold or fear or both, he didn't know.

He stretched out a hand and the girl flinched away from him, her face showing sudden fear.

"I won't hurt you," he said. He placed his hand on the girl's upper arm and it was icy to the touch. "You're cold," he said.

"And hungry."

"Well, I guess you better come with me."

The girl hesitated. She was so frail, the wind was bullying her, pushing and shoving, teasing her mercilessly.

"You've got a star on your chest," she said.

"I'm a lawman. Deputy United States Marshal Augustus Crane." For a moment he thought he saw a gleam of recognition in the child's eyes, as though she had heard his name before.

But the moment passed and she said, "My ma, when she was alive, said lawmen were safe when you were in trouble."

"Safer than most, I reckon."

He smiled, amused by the absurdity of talking to a frightened little girl in the middle of a dark, far-reaching wilderness where humans were few and the only thing that moved was the wind.

"I'll go with you," the girl said. "I'm scared."

"I know. You've said that before."

"Well, I am." A little flash of fire.

"And hungry."

"That too. Maybe most of all."

"Bacon an' bread set all right you with you?"

"It's better than I'm used to. I've never tasted bacon."

"What's your name?"

"Sarah." She offered no other.

Crane gave a little bow and extended a hand toward the rear of the arroyo. "Well, Miss Sarah, shall we dine?"

Crane draped one of Masterson's blankets over the girl's shoulders and seated her beside the guttering fire. He handed her his sandwich and coffee, then gloomily sliced more bacon into the pan as he watched her eat his supper. Sarah was famished and the bacon and bread disappeared quickly.

She sipped the coffee and made a face. "I don't like that."

"You don't like coffee? Who doesn't like coffee?"

128

"I don't. I like cold buttermilk."

"Sarah, you must have led a sheltered life." Crane grinned. He saw hurt in the girl's eyes, then said quickly, "Hey, I was only funnin'."

"It's all right. Really it is."

Crane built his sandwich, his stomach growling in happy anticipation. The girl was looking at it hungrily and he stopped the sandwich halfway to his mouth.

"Surely you can't still be hungry," he said.

"I've had nothing to eat since yesterday morning, and then it was only corn mush."

The marshal looked at his sandwich, the smoky bacon still sizzling between the bread, then at the girl's thin face. He sighed and handed it to her. "Eat," he said. Then, with a noticeable lack of enthusiasm, "It will do you good."

Crane watched Sarah eat, then resignedly began to slice bacon into the pan again.

"Want to tell me how you got here?"

Crane poured himself coffee, watching the girl's face. Firelight played on Sarah's pale skin, lending her a rosy glow that made her look even younger.

"Of course, if you don't want to tell me, then that's up to you."

"I ran away."

"From where?"

"A man called Reuben Stark. Him and the others." She pushed blowing hair from her eyes, her hands fluttering like white moths.

"You know where Stark is?"

"Yes, I do."

"Who are the others?"

"The people he will save from the avenging angel."

"The Archangel Michael?"

"Yes, him. He will destroy the Comstock, all the mines and the miners and all the towns and cities. No one will be spared but those who bear the mark."

"What mark?"

The girl lifted her right arm. A crude X had been branded into the underside of the arm where it would not show. "This mark." She made a face. "Oowee, it hurt at the time, but it doesn't now."

"Why did you run away, Sarah? I mean, yesterday and not before?"

The girl rested her chin on her knees. Her voice grew smaller even as her thin body seemed to shrink. "Mr. Stark wanted to take me as wife. He already has three wives in camp but he told me he needed to bed a younger woman and I was perfect. He said, 'Lass, you're a scrawny one, but the nearer the bone, the sweeter the meat.' "

Sarah shuddered. "I don't know what he meant by that, but when he told me tonight" — she pointed downward — "this night, would be our wedding night, I ran away. I didn't want to be the wife of a smelly old man. And he's cruel. Once I saw him whip one of his wives because she put too much salt in his stew. He ripped off all her clothes and whipped her until she bled, right there in front of the whole camp."

Crane let that go, but he felt a chill of revulsion he knew would be cured only when he put a bullet in Reuben Stark. He said, "Where are your parents?"

"They're both dead from the cholera. I was an orphan and a farm family took me in. They made me work and beat me and" — she pulled out the thin material of her shift — "and never bought me any pretty clothes. And they never fed me much, said rich food would make me even more lazy and impudent."

Recalling his sandwiches, Crane was about to say, "You sure made up for it tonight," but the girl didn't need any more hurting, so he said, "The sodbusters who took you in, are they with Stark?"

"Sodbusters?"

"Farmers. Are they with Stark?"

"Yes, since maybe two months ago." She managed a wan smile. "There are a lot of . . . sodbusters . . . in camp."

"Where, Sarah? Where is the camp?"

The girl turned and pointed behind her. "That way, a place Mr. Stark calls Sunrise Pass. It's a canyon that cuts straight through the mountains."

Crane remembered seeing the canyon and now he wished he'd stayed longer and scouted the place. Stark and his sons were probably there since the old man was eagerly anticipating his honeymoon. Only the wind had stopped him searching for Sarah.

Crane suddenly felt uneasy. Suppose there had been no wind? Stark could have smelled his fire and attacked the canyon in force. He looked out at the clearing where the junipers were wildly tossing their heads. The wind that had driven him into the arroyo in the first place could also have saved his life.

Sarah was looking at Crane intently. "You seem worried. . . ." She smiled at him. "What do I call you? Marshal?"

"Augu— Call me Gus."

"Gus. That's a nice name, got a ring to it."

"What do I do with you, Sarah?"

The girl poked a stick further into the fire,

her head bent. "I'm not going back there, Gus. I'd rather wander the wilderness and get killed by wild Indians or eaten by hungry wolves."

"There are no wild Indians, at least not any longer, though I reckon there are a few wolves."

"Then I'll just have to take my chances, won't I?"

Crane built a smoke and lit it with a brand from the fire. "I'll take you back to Rawhide Flat with me. Maybe we can find you a home."

"I want to stay with you, Gus. You're a lawman and safe."

"That's not possible. A marshal travels a lot. When my work here in Rawhide Flat is done, I'll be moving on."

Sarah opened her mouth to say something, but Crane stopped her. "When the wind drops, Stark will be out looking for you, and he won't come alone. We'll ride out at first light."

"I don't have a horse."

"My buckskin can carry us both."

Sarah stared into the darkness. "What's his name?"

"Who?"

"Your buckskin."

Crane shrugged. "He doesn't have a

name. I just call him horse."

"Can I call him Buck?"

"Call him anything you like. He don't care."

"Buck . . . Buck . . . here boy," Sarah whispered into the clearing.

The horse did not appear.

Crane threw the butt of his cigarette into the fire. "We'd better get some sleep. We've got an early start."

He spread the blankets, lay down and turned his back on the girl. She snuggled against him, her head on his shoulders. "You feel like a big, cuddly bear," she whispered.

"You ever sleep with a bear?"

"No."

"Then how do you know I feel like a bear?"

"I just do."

The girl's thin arm went around the marshal's waist and a few moments later he heard her soft breathing as she dropped off to sleep with the ease of the young.

Crane smiled.

All at once it felt nice to be a bear.

CHAPTER 13

The night felt wrong.

Startled awake, Crane opened his eyes to darkness, the fire a circle of dull red embers. He rose, stepped over Sarah's sleeping form and walked into the clearing.

The wind had dropped to a whisper, the trees were still and a foreboding silence twined around him like snakes.

He slid the Henry from the boot and walked into the arroyo. The moon watched him, its bland face revealing nothing, and to the south a star hung in the purple sky like a distant lantern.

Heavy, lacking the fine balance of a Winchester, the Henry felt awkward in his hands. It was a weapon he had never favored, though there were a few men of his acquaintance who swore by the rifle and used it well.

But, alone in the night, sensing the menace of something unseen crouching in the darkness like a predatory animal, he took great comfort in the Henry, for all its faults.

Crane reached the mouth of the arroyo, then slipped into the shadows, his eyes scanning the gloom. For the moment the moon was hidden, but as soon as the cloud slid past, the brush flats were bathed in fragile, crystalline light.

A horseman sat his mount a hundred yards away, his face a pale oval in the silvered gloom.

At that distance, Crane could make out only the shape of a tall man on a tall horse standing like a tower of darkness. Perhaps the rider was dressed all in black or it was just a trick of the light.

"Friend or foe?" Crane yelled.

At once he realized how ludicrous that sounded, like a scared picket during the War Between the States.

He tried to make amends.

"I got me a Henry rifle here and I ain't sitting on my gun hand."

The mysterious rider made no answer.

The old campfire talk of ghosts and phantoms prickled at Crane's insides and he touched a tongue to suddenly dry lips. His fingers opened and closed on the rifle. If it came right down to it, he'd shoot first and make his talk afterward.

Suddenly Sarah was at his side.

"What are you doing here, girl?" he said snappishly. "Go back to sleep."

"Who can sleep with all the shouting going on?" she said. "What's out there?"

Crane nodded into the darkness. "Him."

Sarah took a step forward, her eyes searching. "Who is he?"

"Damned if I know. But if he don't speak up soon I'm going to shoot him right off that big hoss."

As though he'd heard, the rider kneed his mount and rode twenty yards closer before he drew rein.

Sarah's fingers dug into Crane's arm and he felt her tremble. "Get behind me," he said. "If our friend there starts shooting, you'll be an easy target in that white shift."

The girl did as she was told and the marshal watched the rider. As far as he could tell the man's hands were empty, though that didn't mean he couldn't reach for a gun in a hurry.

Watching intently for any sign of fancy moves, Crane moved the butt of the rifle closer to his shoulder and waited.

"What's he doing?" Sarah whispered.

"Nothing. Just a-sitting there, watching us."

A short pause, then, "What's he doing now?"

"Shhh," Crane hissed, irritated.

A slow minute ticked past, then another.

The marshal's patience, always a brittle and uncertain thing, finally shattered into shards of anger. "Right," he said, "I'm done. I'm gonna put a bullet into that damned spook's belly."

He raised the rifle, but Sarah, peering around his waist, whispered urgently, "Wait, Gus. Look!"

The horseman had taken a bulging sack from his saddle horn and was holding it out from his side. As Crane watched, the man opened his fingers and let the sack thud to the ground. He waved, swung his horse around and galloped away, disappearing into the distance and dark.

After the sound of the rider's hoofbeats faded to nothing, Crane stepped out from the arroyo. He was tense and alert, ready for anything, including the return of the horseman.

But the silence and emptiness of the land, illuminated by the streaming moon, mocked his caution.

He walked to the sack, stood and looked down at it. He touched it with the toe of his boot and the sack rolled. Sarah stood next to him. Bathed in ethereal moonlight, pale, delicate and blond, to Crane the girl looked as if she were something more than human, like a wood sprite come to see what was amiss in her world.

"What's in the sack, Gus?" she asked. "Did he leave us supplies?"

The marshal looked at her. "Girl, I don't think you want to see what's in the sack," he said.

"It's a head, isn't it? Somebody's head."

"I reckon it is."

"Then open the sack. Let's see who it is."

"If I do, you'll go all female on me and cry for your mama."

Sarah's voice sounded like smoke and steel. "Try me."

Crane took a knee and rolled the head out of the sack. It was a human head all right: the grinning, eyeless skull of Joe Garcia.

CHAPTER 14

Crane told Sarah about Garcia and how he'd been tracking him.

"Well, now his tracking days are done," he said.

"Who would do such a thing?"

"I don't know." Crane looked across the fire at Sarah. "Somebody who was mighty good with a knife. Garcia's head was cut off clean."

The girl shuddered. "But why bring it here?"

"Whoever he was, he wanted me to know he's done me a favor."

"But why, Gus?"

"Beats me. I don't know the answer to that either."

The marshal had made sandwiches with the last of the bacon and bread. He passed one over to the girl. "Eat, then we saddle up. It will be light soon."

"I wish I had some cold buttermilk."

"Well, I don't have any of that. Drink coffee."

Crane poured coffee into a cup and handed it to Sarah. "All milk does is rot your insides."

For a couple of minutes the marshal sat in deep contemplation, prompting Sarah to ask, "What are you thinking about?"

"How I wish I'd drilled that ranny. At least I'd know who he was."

"But he might have been a friend."

"I don't have any friends."

"Am I not your friend?"

Crane sighed. "Right now all you are is a nuisance — a nuisance who talks too much."

The girl smiled, chewing on her sandwich. "See, I knew I was your friend."

There was female logic at work there someplace, and the marshal didn't attempt to follow its twists and turns. He ate his breakfast, drained his coffee cup and said, "I'll go saddle the horse."

"His name is Buck."

"He's only a horse."

Sarah chewed thoughtfully, her small mouth working. "Someday I'm going to have my own horse."

Rising to his feet, Crane said, "What you gonna call it?"

"I don't know. When I see her she'll tell me her name."

"Did the buckskin tell you his name?"

"He sure did. He said, 'Howdy do, Sarah. My name is Buck.' "

Crane shook his head and as he walked away he muttered to himself, "Great, Augustus, as if you weren't in enough trouble, now you got yourself a talkin' horse."

Crane and Sarah rode out of the arroyo just as the night shadows were fleeing long to the west, trying to escape the rising sun.

But they were safe as yet, for there was only the promise of sun, a band of polished gold above the mountains that was setting alight the lilac and blue night colors of the sky.

The marshal rode with the Henry across his saddle, his restless eyes alert for any movement. Sarah seemed to be asleep, swaying to the motion of the horse, her head on his back, thin arms clasped around his waist.

After he passed Mineral Peak, Crane swung north into rolling country under a brightening sky. Ahead of him cottonwoods lined a narrow creek and a high rock rim and talus slope on the other bank reached almost to the water's edge.

But what attracted the marshal's attention was the haze of smoke hanging above the tree canopy and four picketed horses standing near a thick clump of buckhorn cholla.

Crane drew rein and studied the creek. The only movement came from the horses, a tail swishing at a fly or the stamp of a hoof. He listened into the morning but heard only the drone of flies and the soft chuckle of the creek running over its pebble bottom.

He turned and woke Sarah. "Camp ahead," he said. "But I don't see anybody."

The girl blinked and looked over the camp. "Horses," she said.

"I know. I saw that much."

Crane gave Sarah his arm. "Climb down, girl, I'm going to take a look." After Sarah's feet were on the ground he looked down at her. "If you hear shooting, run away and hide someplace. If you don't see me again, head north for Rawhide Flat." He leaned closer to the girl. "Is that clear?"

Sarah nodded but said nothing.

"Good," Crane said, watching Sarah carefully, "then it's clear."

He kneed the buckskin forward and warily approached the trees. Once again he drew rein. He slid the Henry into the boot and drew his Colt. If there was shooting to be done it would be close-in work and the revolver was handier.

When he was twenty yards from the cottonwoods, Crane yelled, "Hello the camp!"

The horses raised their heads and pricked their ears, but there was no answering voice.

He rode on . . . and into a camp of the dead.

The bodies of three men were sprawled around a smoking campfire, the wood green and as yet hardly charred. A fourth man had made it all the way to the horses before he was dropped by a bullet.

One body lay on its back, missing its head. The man's shirt had been torn off and his black eyes had been neatly placed on his naked chest.

Crane hoped Garcia had been dead before his eyes were gouged out.

The other men had not been mutilated. All three were cowboys and the Rafter-T brand on the horses confirmed that they rode for Ben Hollister. Each had been cut down by a single bullet, probably by a rifleman hidden on the rock rim on the opposite bank of the creek.

Four shots, four kills. It had been first-rate work by a man well practiced in arms.

The only gunman of his acquaintance Crane could bring to mind who could have accomplished the feat was Paul Masterson.

Had Masterson been the mysterious rider back at the arroyo?

Crane considered that unlikely. Masterson was a named gunfighter who would come right at you and never let up until you or he was dead. Skulking around in the dark as a man of mystery was not his style.

Then if Masterson hadn't killed these men, who had? Crane hit a blank wall. He had no idea.

Behind him, Sarah let out a startled yip of horror, her eyes fixed on the obscene thing that had once been Joe Garcia.

"I told you to stay away," Crane said.

"You told me to stay away if I heard shooting. I didn't hear shooting."

Sarah stepped closer to the creek, staring around her. "Gus, who would do something like this?"

The marshal shook his head. "Beats me." He nodded toward the campfire. "The killer threw green wood on the fire. He knew I'd see the smoke and come take a look-see. I guess he wanted me to admire his handiwork."

Crane's voice lowered and became almost hesitant. "Well, whoever he is, he knows his craft. By any standard what he did here was excellent work."

"I wouldn't call killing four men and . . . and doing what he did to one of them . . . excellent work. More like murder."

"They were armed. They had their chance." Crane looked at the girl. "I guess it all depends on your perspective. Whoever he is, he's a first-class fighting man and out here that stands for something."

"Why did he cut that man's head off and take out his eyes? He had no call to do that."

"It's strange all right. But who can say why a man does what he does. I'm not walking in his boots."

Sarah lifted her shocked eyes to Crane's face. "How can you be so cold-blooded about it?"

"Goes with the badge," the marshal said.

On his way to the campfire Crane stepped over what was left of Garcia's body. He picked up the coffeepot from the edge of the coals. "Still hot. Want some?"

Sarah shook her head. She detoured wide around the bodies and stepped beside the fire.

The marshal found a cup with an inch of cold coffee in the bottom. He threw it away, then refilled the cup from the pot. Nodding toward the horses he said, "Go pick out a

mount. You can ride it back to Rawhide
Flat."

An incredulous look crossed Sarah's face.
"But there's a dead man over there."

"Sure is. But the dead can't hurt you.
Only the living can do that."

"After you finish your coffee you can walk
me to the horses. I'm not going by myself."

Crane looked down at the girl from his
great height. "Are you going to be a trial
and a tribulation to me?"

"I sure hope so, Gus."

He smiled. The girl had been orphaned,
then abused, beaten, starved and worked
like a slave, but her spirit had not been
broken. Sarah had sand, and he liked that.
He tossed his coffee on the fire and threw
down the cup. "Let's get you a hoss," he
said.

"I like that one, the black-and-white one."

"It's called a paint, and it's sure enough a
mare."

Sarah stroked the pony's cheek for a long
while before turning to Crane, smiling. "Her
name is Koda. That's Sioux for 'friend.' "

"How do you know that?"

"She told me. She says she was a war pony
who once belonged to a great chief of the
Cheyenne nation."

Crane grinned. "Sarah, this pony was foaled on Ben Hollister's range and broke in his corral. That's his brand she's wearing."

"Koda wouldn't lie to me."

"All right, whatever you say."

"What about the dead men?" Sarah asked.

"We'll take them to Rawhide Flat with us. They're Hollister's riders. He should bury his dead."

"Gus, I wish we didn't have to do that."

"Well, that's the way it's going to be."

"There are four bodies and only three horses. You don't want me to —"

"The big bay over there can carry Garcia and somebody else. Now he's lost his head, Joe don't weigh near as much."

The girl looked strangely at Crane, but only to say, "Gus, sometimes you sound hard . . . way too hard and uncaring."

The marshal opened his mouth to speak, but Sarah held up a small, silencing hand. "I know, it goes with the badge. But it doesn't have to."

CHAPTER 15

The effect of last night's windstorm on Rawhide Flat was evident everywhere.

As he and Sarah rode into town under an unblinking sun, Crane passed a store that was canted over at an impossible angle and leaned against an adjoining building like a drunk against a wall.

The entire roof of Paddy Sullivan's Saloon had been blown clean off, and a squad of workmen was already cannibalizing its intact timbers to build a replacement. The rhythmic racket of their hammers sounded like a kettledrum.

Store signs had been blown away and their orphaned chains swayed forlornly in the breeze. Windows were broken up and down the street and over by the station most of the cattle pens were a tangle of wreckage.

The Texas Belle was untouched. An idler sitting in a rocker on the porch saw the big marshal ride in and immediately sprang to his feet and ducked inside. Ben Hollister, flanked by a couple of his men, appeared a few moments later.

Crane sat his horse at the hitching rail and waited for whatever Hollister had to say.

The rancher's cold eyes swept the dead men, lingering longer on the headless body of Joe Garcia. His gaze moved to Crane. "You?"

"Not me. I don't know who did the killing." He eased himself in the saddle, the leather creaking. "Whoever it was presented me with Garcia's head in a sack."

"You saw him?"

"At a distance. It was dark and he never got close."

Seeing the question in Hollister's eyes, Crane briefly described the events at the arroyo and his discovery of the bodies earlier that morning.

"I'd say you got an enemy you didn't even know you had, Hollister," he concluded.

The rancher stepped off the boardwalk and walked through clouds of fat, buzzing flies and looked into the swollen blue faces of the three dead punchers. The sweet stench of death hung in the air and a thick string of coagulated blood hung from Garcia's severed neck.

Disgust on his face, Hollister turned to

the men on the porch. "Take these men to Simeon Pearl and tell him to get them ready for burying. I'll come later."

The rancher waited until the cowboys and a couple of other volunteers led away the horses and their terrible burdens. Then, as though noticing her for the first time, he said to Crane, "Who's the girl?"

"She's an orphaned stray who wandered into my camp last night. Her name is Sarah and she was fostered by a couple of Reuben Stark's followers but ran away after the old man told her he planned to jump the broom with her."

"Can't say as I blame her," Hollister said. "She's a tad young for him." He looked at Sarah more closely. "Skinny little thing, ain't she?"

"She hasn't been eating too well in recent years," Crane said.

"Settin' one of my horses, though."

"Her name is Koda," Sarah said. "That means friend in Sioux. You can have her back if you promise to be kind to her."

"And your first name's Sarah. What's your last name?" Hollister asked.

"I don't know. I was very young when my folks died. I've been in foster homes since I can't remember when."

"And you ended up with old Reuben's

bunch, huh?"

"Yes. He's an awful man. He's mean and unkind and he beats people."

Hollister shrugged. "I can't argue with that." He looked at Crane. "You catch up with him?"

The marshal shook his head. "No, I never did. But I will." He turned to Sarah. "Climb off that horse and tie it to the hitching rail."

Hollister waved a negligent hand. "Keep the pony and welcome. It was one of John Smith's string and he don't have use for it anymore."

Crane was surprised. "That's white of you, Hollister."

"Hell, it's a twenty-dollar pony." He shrugged. "It's nothing. Besides, the girl gave the hoss a name and I'd never remember it."

The marshal made a mental note to himself that if he ever gunned Hollister he'd remember his gesture toward Sarah and shoot him where it hurt the least.

And that time might be right now.

"Think carefully before you answer this, Hollister. Is Paul Masterson alive or dead?"

"No need to think. He's alive."

"Where is he?"

"Why, he's in the sheriff's office where he should be. Got his tin star pinned to his

152

shirt, content as a coon dog lyin' next to a warm fire."

"What happened?"

"Why don't you ask him your ownself?"

Crane looked along the street to the jail. "I will," he said. He turned his eyes back to the rancher. "Hollister, I told you the truth about what happened to your men. How's that sitting with you right about now?"

"I can tell when a man's lying to me. You were telling it straight."

"Mighty strange turn of events, though, huh?"

"Yeah, mighty strange."

Ben Hollister's face was like stone.

"Well, look what the cat drug in."

"I could say the same thing about you, Paul."

"Surprised?"

"You could say that." Crane looked toward the door to the cells. "Is Walsh back there?"

"Judah Walsh is dead."

"I don't understand. I mean, what happened?"

Masterson smiled, sitting back, his boots on the table. "Before I answer that, shouldn't you introduce me to your young lady friend?"

"This is Sarah. She wandered into my

camp last night." For the second time that afternoon, Crane told what had happened at the arroyo and his run-in with the mysterious horseman.

"For a spell there I thought he might have been you," he said.

Masterson shook his head. "Not me, though I would probably have ended up putting a bullet in Joe Garcia eventually. The man annoyed me." His eyes moved to Sarah's worn shift. "Is that rag all you've got to wear, girl?"

"I don't have any clothes, Sheriff, just this. I used to have a pretty calico dress but I outgrew it and they wouldn't buy me another."

"Your foster parents you mean?"

"They weren't parents in any sense, just a couple of nasty people who wanted a servant girl."

Masterson's eyes lifted to Crane. "Gus, look at her. The girl needs some new women's fixin's."

"I wasn't planning on keeping her."

"What are you going to do with her? Throw her out in the street naked? Give her back to Reuben Stark? What?"

Annoyed, Crane said, "What the hell are women's fixin's?"

"You know, dresses, hats, shoes, bloomers,

corsets and such. The fancy stuff females wear."

"She don't need corsets. She's already skinny as a rail. Anyhow, I don't know where to get all that — that — froufrou."

"Take Sarah across the street to the New York Fashion Emporium. Ask for Minnie Lewis and tell her I sent you. Minnie's an old battle-axe but she'll steer you right."

Crane felt a lump rise in his throat. "Dresses . . . bloomers . . . how much does it all cost?"

"A lot," Masterson said without a tinge of remorse.

"Gus, I can't walk around Rawhide Flat in a shift," Sarah said. Her eyes were wide and pleading. "What would the other girls in town think of me?"

"Yeah, Gus, what would the other girls think of her? Leave her with Minnie and then come back. We need to talk."

Glad to take out his irritation on someone, Crane snapped. "Damn right we do, Sheriff. I want to know how Judah Walsh died and why you lit a shuck on me. And then there's the matter of a cowboy who turned up his toes in the Texas Belle."

"Just as I said, Gus. We need to talk."

Weighed down by responsibility not of his making, the marshal looked at Sarah and was forced to admit to himself that the girl needed clothes.

"Sarah, when I take you over there to the store, don't go loco with yourself. A plain dress and shoes, that's all you need."

The sheriff was grinning. "Seems to me the little lady will need a heap more than that."

Crane's eyes were cold, the color of rainwater. "Masterson, do you enjoy spending another man's money?"

"Always," the sheriff said cheerfully.

Minnie Lewis was in her forties, dressed in rustling black, and she looked like she'd been raised on scripture and prune juice. She regarded Crane with obvious distaste as he stood, out of place and awkward, surrounded by female clothing, some of it of an embarrassingly intimate nature.

But the woman was kind to Sarah and when Crane said, "She needs —," Minnie immediately cut him off and snapped, "I know what she needs."

She consulted the watch hanging from a fob pinned to the front of her dress. "Come back in an hour, and be warned, I do not tolerate tardiness."

The marshal was horrified. "How long does it take to buy a dress?"

"An hour."

Minnie shooed Crane out of the store as though she were chasing an egg-sucking hound from the chicken coop. "One hour, Marshal," she said. "No more, no less."

Crane stumbled out onto the boardwalk and looked over at the sheriff's office.

He was overjoyed that he could now vent his rage on Paul Masterson.

CHAPTER 16

Paul Masterson laid a cup of coffee on the table in front of Crane.

"Careful," he said, "it's hot and you don't want to burn your tongue. Then you wouldn't be able to do all that speechifying you've been planning."

"I can talk just fine," Crane snapped, his irritation walking hand in hand with belligerence. "And the first thing I want to talk about is how come Judah Walsh isn't with us anymore."

Masterson leaned forward on his chair and slowly rotated his cup by the brim, regarding with fixed attention the brown swirl of the coffee. "I heard about Maxie Starr," he said. "I took it hard."

"I have a good idea just how hard you took it and I'm leaving that for later. Right now I want to know about Walsh."

"I killed him."

Crane was startled. "You killed him?"

"Shot him out of the saddle. I —"

The door burst open and Minnie Lewis stormed inside, Sarah in tow. The black rustle of the woman's dress made her sound like a vengeful bat.

She pointed an accusing finger at Crane. "You! You monster!"

Sarah wailed, "I told you he didn't —"

"Silence, girl! Minnie Lewis is speaking for you."

The woman turned all her attention to the marshal. "Did you do this?"

Crane was alarmed. He rose to his feet, his mouth working. "Do what?"

The woman had wrapped Sarah in a sheet of some kind and now she ordered the girl to turn around. When Sarah did, Minnie pulled the blanket down from her back.

"This!"

From shoulders to waist, the girl's slender back was a mass of vicious red welts and a few of them had broken the skin, leaving traces of crusted blood.

Crane felt Masterson's eyes on him, mildly accusing, and he protested, "I didn't do this!"

"Of course he didn't!" Sarah pulled the sheet over her shoulders and she turned to face Minnie Lewis. "I told you that, but you wouldn't listen to me."

"Then who did, child?" the woman asked.

"An old man called Reuben Stark. I told him I wouldn't jump the broom with him and he beat me. I — I ran away and Marshal Crane took me in."

"Are you telling the truth, child?" Minnie asked, glaring first at Sarah and then Crane, her gaze searching and terrible.

"She's telling the truth," Crane said. Now he'd gotten over his shock, his patience with Minnie was wearing thin. "Reuben Stark used his dog whip on her and I aim to put a bullet into his dirty hide the first chance I get."

He'd expected the woman to accuse him of being a violent brute, but to his surprise she sniffed and said, "I should hope so. A man who would do this to a child has no right to walk among decent Christian people. He's better off dead."

She took Sarah by the shoulder. "Come, girl, let's get you some clothes."

The girl looked up at Crane, her eyes bright. "Gus, you should see all the pretty dresses . . . and shoes . . . and hats . . . and . . . and . . ."

She paused, expecting a response.

"I'm sure they are pretty," Crane said. Then, the dreadful image of Sarah's back still fresh in his mind, he said, a lump forming in his throat, "Get what you need."

Minnie consulted her watch again. "Fifty minutes, Marshal. And remember what I told you about tardiness."

As she and the girl turned to leave, Crane said, "Sarah, why didn't you tell me about the whipping last night?"

The girl smiled. "I thought you had quite enough to worry about last night."

"You know, Gus, under that rough exterior you really do have a heart of gold."

"I wouldn't go counting on it if I was you," Crane said. "Why did you kill Judah Walsh?"

"I made a deal with him. I told him if he showed me where the town's money was hid, I'd give him a horse, a hundred dollars and free passage out of the state."

"And did he?"

"Yeah. He figured taking my offer was better than waiting around for the ranchers. Besides, he was scared of you after you opened up his face with a spur. He wanted out of Rawhide Flat real bad."

"And did he take you to the money?"

"He sure did. It was at night and hard to find in the dark, but it was there all right, fifty thousand dollars in paper money and some coin hidden under a flat rock."

"Then why did you kill him?"

"Well, you know, by times I'm a thinking man. So I said to myself, I said, 'Paul this is not right. It just ain't true blue.' "

Crane built a smoke. "Go on."

"So, I'm looking at ol' Judah climbing onto his dun hoss, grinning like you please, and I'm thinking, 'He killed a woman and you're letting him go.' He was wearing his gun, so before he rode away I called him."

"And then what?" Crane lit his cigarette.

"He went for his gun and I shot him."

"You should have left him for the law."

"Gus, last time I looked, I am the law."

"And now you're the only one who knows where the money is hidden."

"Right. First person I told was Ben Hollister. Now he's very concerned about my welfare. I'd say he's become my best friend, never wants to leave my side."

"You say Walsh drawed down on you?"

"That's what I say."

"Then you killed him in self-defense."

"Seems that way."

"When it came right down to it, was Walsh fast with the iron?"

"He's dead. I'm alive. What does that tell you?"

Crane's coffee was cool enough to drink and he looked at Masterson over the rim of his cup. "Ben Hollister didn't murder Maxie."

"I know."

"Then why did you try to kill him in the Texas Belle?"

"That was none of my doing."

"You mean somebody else took a pot at him?"

"That's what I mean."

"Why do you take my word so easy that Hollister didn't murder Maxie? He might have thought she knew where you were holed up. Speaking of that, where did you and Walsh hide?"

"I can't tell you that, Gus. Maybe later but not now. Getting back to Hollister, he wouldn't whip a woman. Oh, he might shoot one if it suited his purpose, but he wouldn't cut her up with a whip like that. Besides, he was sweet on Maxie, asked her to marry him a couple of times."

Masterson leaned back in his chair and steepled his fingers. "My guess is that Reuben Stark murdered Maxie with the same whip he used on the girl. I plan to kill him, Gus, him and his sons."

Restlessly, the sheriff rose and poured coffee for both of them. "You think that might have been Stark or one of his boys back at the arroyo?" he asked. "Before he tied in with Hollister, the old man never made it a secret that he's ambitious. He wants to found an empire before it's too late and the quickest way is to acquire range. Hollister's got the Rafter-T and if Stark can't buy, he might be inclined to take it."

"The man at the arroyo was taller than Stark or any of his sons," Crane said. "Maybe he has an inch or two on me."

"A range detective and sure-thing killer by the name of Miles McKenna is tall like that. But he's never been known to leave the Montana Territory. Then there's Bill Canfield down El Paso way. He's a string bean who hires out his gun now and then. But the last I heard he'd married a widder woman and was prospering in the baked-pies business."

"Good business that," Crane said. "Gives a man something to think about. He began to build a cigarette. Without taking his eyes from tobacco and paper, he said, "When are you going to tell the town where the money is hid?"

He expected Masterson to hem and haw, but the sheriff answered without hesitation, "When they decide what's in it for me."

Now Crane looked up. "I don't catch your drift."

"Then I'll toss it out to you again: I want

164

what's coming to me — half of the fifty thousand."

CHAPTER 17

Crane took time to light his cigarette. He felt like a man in a rapidly flooding box canyon, trying to find a way out. Finally he said mildly, "Paul, it's the town's money, not yours."

"This town owes me."

"For what?"

"For taking the sheriff's job when nobody else wanted it. For wearing a tin star on my chest that every crazy drunk and wannabe gun tramp wants to use for target practice. For trying to get by on less money than a puncher makes, for having to say, 'Yes, sir,' 'No sir,' to the bunch of idiots who run this town. And finally because I'm sick and tired of wearing these guns and hearing a rustle in every damned bush and seeing shadows in every alley.

"I want a wife, Gus, children, a ranch of my own where I can sit in a rocker on my porch of the evening and drink coffee and watch the sun go down before the little lady calls me in for supper."

Masterson sank back in his chair. "I'm tired, Gus." He smiled. "Funny, isn't it, that I was a tired outlaw and now I'm a tired lawman. But twenty-five thousand dollars can put back the fire in a man's belly and a spring in his step real quick."

Masterson leaned forward. "All I want is my due. I'm not breaking any laws here."

Blue tobacco smoke wreathed Crane's head. His eyes were level, without heat.

"What you're doing is stealing, Paul. You're holding Rawhide Flat to ransom. I'd say that's breaking the law you've sworn to uphold."

The sheriff sounded like he'd just bitten into a bitter apple. "And what about you, Gus? That star don't seem to sit too heavy on your own chest."

"Maybe not, but I try to uphold the law. Sure, I do it in my own way, but I've not turned my back on this badge and what it stands for."

"You think I'm breaking the law?"

"Yes, I do. The town's money is your hostage and you've gone into the extortion racket."

"You drawing a line here, Gus?"

"It would seem that's the case."

"Take my advice and don't cross it. Get in my way now and I'll kill you, Gus. I don't want to have to do that."

Masterson slammed his fist on the table. "Hell, it doesn't have to be like this. You don't owe this town a damn thing. Listen, your work here is over. The prisoner you came to collect is dead, shot by local law enforcement while trying to escape. Go back to Virginia City and leave Reuben Stark and Rawhide Flat to me."

The sheriff smiled. "I like you, Gus. You bumble around a lot and chase your own tail, but you're a dedicated police officer and I respect you for that. Years from now, maybe we'll meet and I'll buy you a steak dinner, and we'll talk about the old times and laugh about all this."

He stretched out a hand. "For now, let's agree that you go your way and I go mine."

Crane ignored Masterson's proffered hand. He rose to his feet.

"Paul, I won't let you hold this town to ransom. Tell the bank where their money is hidden and we'll forget this conversation ever happened."

Masterson shook his head. "I can't do that, Gus."

"Then the line is drawn." Crane's eyes were bleak. For some reason he felt his talk

168

with Masterson had been a humbling experience, like looking into the muzzle of a .45. He said, "And all my talking is done."

The marshal stepped to the door and Masterson addressed his retreating back. "Gus, I'm faster, a lot faster than you. Maybe you should bear that in mind, give it some deep thought, like."

Without turning Crane said, "Thanks for the advice, Paul. Yeah, I'll give it my due consideration."

"Look, Gus!"

Sarah, wearing a blue dress that stopped at the ankles to reveal lacy bloomers and button-up boots, did a pirouette. "Well, what do you think?"

"You look crackerjack, Sarah." Crane grinned. "Like a New Orleans belle."

As the girl gave a little bow of appreciation, Minnie Lewis scowled at the marshal, as though still unconvinced that he was innocent of abusing her.

The woman finally bent her head to a ledger and chewed on the end of a pencil. Finally her eyes lifted to Crane, wary, as though she expected him to bolt from the store at any second.

"Right, Marshal," she said. "Dress, with bustle, ten dollars and eighteen cents; shirt, three dollars and ninety-eight cents; skirt, split, suitable for riding, nine dollars and twenty-five cents; drawers, cotton, frilled, eighty cents; hose, silk, two dollars and forty-seven cents; boots, button, sold at cost, five dollars even."

Minnie Lewis arched an eyebrow and glared at Crane accusingly, as though she was sure he'd dispute the prices or confess that he couldn't pay.

Using a voice of doom, she said, "Marshal Crane, you owe me thirty-one dollars and sixty-eight cents."

Everything was expensive in the Comstock and Crane knew he'd been charged top dollar for every item Sarah had bought.

But he had gone this far and there was no turning back. The marshal sighed and paid up.

Sarah threw her arms around his neck and said, "You're so good to me, Gus."

A frugal man who felt he'd just walked into a female ambush, Crane's smile was strained. "Don't mention it. Now, let's check into the hotel while I still have a few chips left."

"I get this whole room all to myself?"

Sarah looked wonderingly around her, at the iron bedstead, dresser with pitcher and bowl and two cane-backed chairs.

"Uh-huh, it's all yours," Crane said. "My room is right next to yours." Seeing the girl's delight in her surroundings, he added, smiling, "It's not near as nice as this one."

"I've never had a room to myself before," Sarah said, as she sat on the bed and bounced up and down. "I always slept in a barn or in a storeroom, anyplace I could find."

"You'll be comfortable here," Crane said. "It's not a barn and it's nice and quiet."

Then, to himself, "Augustus, what a really stupid thing to say."

Suddenly he wished he was more practiced at talking pretties to womenfolk.

CHAPTER 18

A small sound in the darkness.

The scuff of a boot.

A muffled voice, cursing.

Crane was instantly awake. He rose, padding long-legged in his underwear. He found his hat, then his gun. He opened his creaking room door.

There were shadows on the stairs. A gun flared and a bullet chipped wood inches from his face.

"Gus!" It was Sarah's voice, followed by the crack of the hard blow that slapped her into silence.

A shadow detached itself from the rest, climbed a single step, stopped and fired. The air beside Crane's head split and without conscious effort the marshal thumbed off a shot, then another, both sounding as one.

The man on the stairs crashed into the wall. Then his gun thudded onto the carpeted stairs. He elbowed away from the wall and remained stock-still, bleeding out right where he stood.

Crane took time to register the gunman's wound as an arterial hit that had taken him out of the fight. Then he was running. He pushed the dying man aside and took to the stairs. But as he passed, the body fell on him, then slid lower, a heavy weight that hit the marshal on the back of his knees.

Thrown forward, Crane tried to right himself, failed, and plunged onto his face, the gunman's body on top of him. As he fell, the marshal's wrist hit the edge of a step and his gun thudded away from him.

Swearing, Crane kicked free of the body and struggled to his feet.

The gas lamps in the hotel foyer had not been extinguished by the kidnappers and the marshal hunted around, found his Colt and lunged for the door.

Behind him voices were raised in alarm.

A door slammed. A woman screamed.

He was through the door and outside.

Under a moon that floated in the sky like a white flower, four riders were galloping north along the street, kicking up a screen of dust.

Crane lifted his gun, but did not fire. Sarah was with them. He dared not risk hitting the girl.

Suddenly Paul Masterson was beside him, his gun drawn. Like Crane he was wearing only his underwear and hat.

"What happened?" he asked.

"They took Sarah."

"Stark?"

"Probably. There's one of them inside."

"Let's get after them, Gus."

"We'd never find them in the dark. I'll track them at first light."

Crane turned and stepped back into the hotel and Masterson followed.

Several hotel guests and the manager, a small, bald, perpetually dyspeptic man, saw Crane and said, "He's dead, Marshal."

Crane pushed the crowd aside. The dead man lay on his back, his eyes wide-open, still stunned by the fact of his dying.

"I think I only winged him with my first shot," Crane said with a professional gunfighter's detachment. "But he rode my second bullet into hell. Recognize him?"

Masterson nodded. "Yeah, that's Eli Stark, the youngest of Reuben's boys, and his favorite." Blue gaslight flickered on the steely angles of the sheriff's face. "Now the old man will give you no rest."

Crane smiled. "Good, then he'll come to me."

His eyes moved to the hotel manager. "I guess you'd better get rid of that."

The little man gulped, then nodded. He rushed out the door to wake the undertaker as though all the devils of hell were on his heels.

The marshal looked around him at the circle of faces. Half a dozen men and a couple of women were looking at him in horrified fascination, as the ordinary citizens of ancient Rome must have once stared at a successful gladiator.

Gun violence was rare in the Old West; named gunfighters rarer. Shooting scrapes were mostly confined to saloons and dance halls where armed men gathered and festering enmities, real or imagined, fueled by raw whiskey, made them fighting drunk.

Violence seldom affected the lives of respectable citizens like those around Crane who were probably seeing a gunshot man for the first time and the terrible effect of the .45 caliber bullet on the human body.

To them, the man who had pulled the trigger was something less than human, a dangerous, killing animal to be shunned and avoided at all cost.

Crane smelled the stench of their fear and saw the dread in their eyes, and the dark angel enfolded him in its wings and embraced him.

His Colt hanging by his side, he said with flat emotion, "Go back to bed, all of you."

The hotel guests stared at him, uncomprehending, statues with eyes that did not see.

Depression drifting through him like black smoke, Crane glanced around, then pushed through the crowd. A tall man wearing only long johns and a battered hat, he climbed the stairs slowly, feeling lonelier than he'd ever felt in his life.

In his mind he saw Sarah.

Laughing.

Face aglow, excited by her new clothes.

Giggling like a child at the perceived luxury of her hotel room.

But now she'd be terrified, riding through darkness with an old man who smelled of lust and hate.

Crane stepped into his room and threw himself on the bed.

Would the light of morning never come?

Crane saddled his horse while the night had yet to surrender to the dawn.

The air was still cooled by starlight and an errant wind prowled through the stable, sniffing in every stall and corner.

Once in the saddle, the marshal stopped outside the barn doors and, like a chess player, thought out his next moves.

Stark had headed north, but Crane was sure the old man would have looped around town and headed for his hideout in Sunrise Canyon. His followers were there and he'd be protected.

Waiting for the dark to shade into light, Crane built a smoke. He was wishful for coffee but had none — the pot and a sack of Arbuckle were in his saddlebags. Once he was sure of Stark's intentions he would stop and light a fire.

He smoked one cigarette, then another.

The violet night turned gray with age and the sky took on a rosy hue to the east. Somewhere a rooster welcomed the dawn and the little calico cat padded out of the stable, stretched, its claws extended, then sat looking up at him with iridescent eyes.

Crane kneed the buckskin into motion and rode north, past the railroad station. Almost immediately he picked up the tracks of Stark's horses. The old man and his sons had stayed close to the rails for about a mile, then headed east, as the marshal had suspected they would.

After another mile, Stark had swung south, giving Rawhide Flat a wide berth.

Although Crane lost it a few times on rocky ground, Stark's trail was easy to follow, heading straight as an arrow to the south.

There was no question of playing catch-up. The old man was probably in the canyon by now. As to what was happening to Sarah, Crane refused to think about it. That would only sprinkle salt on an open wound.

The coffee craving nagging at him, the marshal drew rein when Mineral Peak came in sight, unveiled by the brightening morning. He looked around him at the wakening land, then headed toward a clump of cottonwoods and willows that suggested a creek.

The creek was narrow, no more than a stream, and the trees were stunted and few. But there was water and wood enough, and that was all Crane needed.

He loosened the cinch on the buckskin and let the horse graze before building a hatful of fire.

When the coffee boiled the marshal poured himself a cup and then fetched up to the trunk of a cottonwood. His back against the trunk, he lit a cigarette and tried to let the peace and beauty of the day lift the melancholy that dwelled inside him like a malignant spirit.

Crane's depression was profound, the sort that makes a man look at a beautiful face and see only a grinning skull. He was aware that his melancholy was a form of self-pity that ate at his soul and destroyed his ability to construct a future.

Now he tried desperately to shake it off, recalling that for him, depression was only a short step from a killing rage that in the past had caused him to destroy men who should still be alive.

What was the kid's name in Abilene that summer?

He couldn't remember.

But he could and should have walked away from it.

Everybody in the saloon knew Augustus Crane had nothing to prove and he could have stepped away with his honor and reputation intact. The kid, with his tied-down guns and his sneer, would've been left to stand there looking flat-footed and foolish.

But Crane didn't.

Fired up with whiskey, the blackness riding him, he'd answered the kid's bone-headed challenge with one of his own.

The kid drew and died.

That was three years ago, or was it four? No matter, Crane hadn't ever drunk whiskey in a saloon since, nor would he ever again.

The coffee was hot and bitter, the tobacco

harsh on his tongue. He lifted his head and glanced up at the cottonwood. He thought the leaves looked like Irish lace adorning the blue silk dress of the sky.

A blue dress . . .

What was happening to Sarah?

Thinking about the girl dragged Crane out of his despondency. Concern for another drives a man into action, not depression, and the marshal felt a breeze as the dark angel's wings left him. And folded.

Rising to his feet, Crane poured himself another cup of coffee, then stood, looking into the hazy distance of the day.

In a land where all was still, any movement caught the eye. It looked like a black dot moving across the plain, disappearing, then showing again as it headed north between the low hills.

Crane laid his cup at his feet and retrieved his field glasses from his saddlebags. He focused and the far-off country rushed up to meet him.

A buggy carrying two nuns was traveling slowly, drawn at a walking pace by a single horse. Crane could not make out the faces of the sisters, but he knew where they were going.

They were headed for Sunrise Pass . . . . and Reuben Stark.

CHAPTER 19

Crane lowered the glasses, his face troubled.

Reuben Stark believed, or so he told his followers, that the Archangel Michael would wreak a terrible vengeance on the sinful Comstock.

Nuns were also in the business of ending the careers of the ungodly. Were the two joining forces to rid Nevada of evil when the trumpet of doom sounded?

It was a possibility, an unpalatable one certainly, but there was an eeric, diabolical logic to it.

Cranc threw the last of the coffee on the fire, then stepped into the saddle.

There was one way to find out: talk to the nuns.

Skirting the lower reaches of El Dorado Canyon, Crane swung north, keeping Mineral Peak to his right. The rolling country ahead of him was empty and he saw no sign of the nuns.

The morning was hot, the sun well up in the sky, and a sheen of sweat slicked the marshal's face. Creaking saddle leather and the steady fall of the buckskin's hooves were the only sound, and the silence embraced Crane like a friend.

It was still early in the summer and the grass was green, rainbows of wildflowers growing in profusion everywhere, reminding those who had the eyes to look that spring was writing a fresh new chapter in the book of Genesis.

But beautiful though it is, nature is indifferent and makes no distinction between good and evil. Some instinct told Crane to move out from the open and ride nearer to the Pine Nut foothills.

Closer to the arroyos and sheltering gullies, he felt more at ease, but he rode with the Henry across his saddle, his eyes restlessly scanning the land ahead.

The singing was borne to him on the wind.

Because of the crystalline clarity of the morning, the words and tune of the hymn were plain to hear, long before he saw the singers.

Mine eyes have seen the glory of the
    coming of the Lord;

He is trampling out the vintage where the
    grapes of wrath are stored;
He hath loosed the fateful lightning of his
    terrible swift sword;
His truth is marching on.
Glory! Glory! Hallelujah! Glory! Glory!
    Hallelujah!
Glory! Glory! Hallelujah! His truth is
    marching on.

Stunned, the marshal drew rein.

It seemed that hundreds of voices were raised loudly in song, men, women and children, and in the distance a great dust cloud rose into the air, coming at Crane like the billowing sails of a mighty war fleet.

He reached behind him for the glasses and searched the beckoning distance.

Wagons, three or four abreast, were emerging from the drifting dust, a dozen horsemen riding point.

As Crane looked, more and more wagons appeared, many of them prairie schooners with canvas tops, a sight that hadn't been seen in the West since the great migrations of thirty years before.

The singing was louder now and to the marshal it seemed that an entire people was on the move, grinding across the land like locusts, determined and unstoppable.

Awed by the sight and made uneasy by their sheer numbers, Crane swung his horse into a narrow arroyo. He stepped out of the saddle, then slapped the buckskin on the rump, sending the animal trotting deeper into the gulch.

The walls of the arroyo were fairly steep, but clumps of brush and bunchgrass made climbing easy and Crane scaled to the top, then lay flat on his belly. His clothing was neutral in color and his body would fade into the grass around him.

He raised the glasses to his eyes.

The wagons were much closer, the singing very loud. He scanned the point riders. Reuben Stark rode in front, flanked by his sons and a dozen other riders.

There was no sign of Sarah.

Crane made an instant decision. He had come here for Stark and to free the girl and that's what he would do. He was one man against many, but he had it to do.

He began to ease back from the ridge but stopped when something cold and hard shoved into the back of his head.

"Stay right where you're at, Marshal," a man's voice ordered. "Or I'll scatter your brains."

"I knew you'd be up to some damned

tomfoolery, Gus. I wonder that you've lived this long."

Without turning Crane asked, "You planning to gun me, Paul?"

"Nah, I'm saving your life. If I'd let you ride out there and brace Stark, you'd already be lying dead on the grass. He's got a dozen men with him, for God's sake."

"You followed me from Rawhide Flat?"

"An easy thing to do, Gus. You build fires, send up smoke, ride out in the open, back straight, looking ahead like a cavalry colonel with a regiment behind him. A few years ago the Piute would have lifted your hair quicker'n scat."

"If you don't intend to kill me, why are you doing this?"

"Saving you from yourself, Gus. Despite everything, I like you, even if you're none too bright." Masterson made a shushing noise. "Now, be quiet. We got company and a lot of it."

Stark and his riders were passing the arroyo. All of the men carried rifles, butt down on their thighs, except for the old man who held a Bible to his chest, his head thrown back as he bellowed the hallelujah chorus of the hymn.

Slowly, the wagons rumbled past, most of them drawn by straining ox teams.

Shrouded in gray dust, the prairie schooners looked like sailing ships in a fog, seeking a foreign shore.

It took an hour before the last wagon creaked by; then came the stragglers. First horse-drawn rigs of every kind, then worn, sunbonneted women walked beside their menfolk, who trundled two-wheeled carts loaded with odds and ends of furniture and sometimes children. Older youngsters walked with their mothers, their faces gray with dust and fatigue.

Finally the last of Stark's people vanished into the distance and their upraised voices gradually faded like far-off birdsong.

Crane heard a soft thud as Masterson holstered his gun. His voice held a note of awe.

"My God, Gus, how many of them?"

The marshal rose to his feet. "Hundreds. Maybe a thousand."

"Where do you think they're headed?"

"I don't know. Rawhide Flat? Could be Stark plans to take over the town."

"Take over what? A few saloons and stores and an empty bank? Not much profit in that."

Crane shook his head. "I guess we'll find out soon enough."

"Aren't we going to follow them?"

"No. I saw a couple of nuns headed this

way. I didn't see them with the wagon train stragglers, so they've got to still be at Sunrise Pass. I've got some questions to ask those sisters."

"Like what?"

"Like are they tied up with Stark in some way? And if they are, why? I'm sure the nuns also know where he's headed."

"Mind if I tag along, keep you out of mischief?"

"I have the strangest feeling you want to keep me in sight and under your gun."

Masterson smiled. "Wrong, Gus, at least for now. I haven't quit the law yet, and I want to see Reuben Stark and his boys dead as much as you do. Call what I'm doing co-operation between branches of law enforcement or call it professional courtesy. Call it what you like, but I want Stark any way I can get him."

Something had to be said and now Crane said it. "You saved my life, you know. If you hadn't stopped me, I'd have gone off half-cocked and got my fool head blown off."

"Seems like. You're long on sand, Gus, but short on savvy."

"You were mistaken about one thing, though."

"What's that?"

"If there had been Piute around I wouldn't

187

have made a fire and I wouldn't have rode out in the open."

Grinning widely, Masterson said, "You're noisy, Gus, even when you try to be quiet. The Piute would have followed the racket and got you for sure."

"Damn it, Masterson, but you're an irritating man!" Crane snapped.

The sheriff's grin grew wider. "Listen to yourself, Gus! You're still making noise."

"Let's talk to the nuns." Crane scowled. "And I promise, I'll be as quiet as a snowflake on a feather."

CHAPTER 20

Coyotes have a deep-seated fear of humans and will not venture close to a healthy man or woman.

But they are carrion eaters when no other food is available, and they have a fine nose for the dead, animal or human.

A hunting pair stood on a flat, rocky outcropping jutting out from a mountain slope. The animals were intent on something below them in a sandy arroyo made deeper and wider by winter rains and spring snowmelt.

Wary, but driven by hunger, the coyotes leaped from the rock onto the low wall of the gulch, then dropped lower, vanishing from sight.

"See that?" Masterson asked.

Crane nodded. "Something dead or dying in there, all right."

"Could be a burro."

"Could be. Or a deer."

The marshal slid the Henry from the boot under his knee. "Let's take a look-see."

"Up there," Masterson said.

Crane followed the sheriff's lifted eyes. Buzzards were circling lazily in the polished blue sky, patiently biding their time, knowing that in nature everything comes to those who wait.

"Must be a deer," he said.

Crane rode up to the mouth of the arroyo and stepped out of the saddle. Masterson did likewise, his gaze still on the buzzards gliding effortlessly on the high air currents.

Stepping carefully, the marshal walked deeper into the arroyo, Masterson beside him, a Remington in each hand. The sheriff's handsome face had settled into hard planes, his eyes intent, unblinking.

Both men had the gunfighter's instinct for danger, but this was very different. They sensed evil, an awareness of an entity that clutched at the throat and made the air thick and hard to breathe and the sunlight that streamed around them less bright.

Crane knew, as did Masterson, that an arroyo can't be evil in itself. Therefore something or someone had brought the evil there. And still it lingered, cloying, like an unmoving mist the color of death.

The coyotes had scented the two approaching men. The dog scrambled up the slope, followed by the smaller, nimbler female. Both animals vanished into the sage and piñon covering the lower mountain slope.

A moment later Crane almost stumbled over the body of one of the nuns.

The woman's veil had been ripped off and her throat had been cut, so deeply she'd almost been decapitated. Despite her terrible death, the expression on her face was serene, as though in acceptance of the fate her God had ordained for her.

Masterson called out from deeper in the canyon. "The other one is here. I guess she tried to make a run for it."

The second nun was younger and prettier, Hispanic, with black eyes and hair. Her throat had also been cut, but she had died hard, fighting for her life and there was blood and skin under her fingernails.

She had given her killer a Mark of Cain that would take weeks to heal.

Masterson stepped beside Crane, his face stiff. "Stark?"

The marshal nodded. "Him, or he ordered it done."

"But why? I mean . . . nuns."

"I don't know."

Crane felt a sense of loss. He had not

rescued Sarah and if it hadn't been for Masterson, a man he might have to kill, he would have thrown his life away needlessly. He was doing this all wrong. Suddenly he'd lost his way and didn't know which way to turn.

"What about the sisters?" Masterson asked, adding yet another problem.

"Coyotes, vultures, we can't leave them here. We'll take them back to Rawhide Flat."

"It's a ride," the sheriff said, his face expressionless.

A small anger flared in Crane. "Do you have a better idea?"

"Can't say as I have."

"Then, damn it, do as I tell you."

For a few moments Masterson stood in silence. He seemed to make up his mind about something. Then he said, "Sure, Gus, anything you say. I'll bring the horses."

The day was shading into night as Crane and Masterson rode into Rawhide Flat.

A steady rain fell, giving lie to the bright promise of the day, and clouds curled like lead, heavy and threatening.

Along the street the saloons were already ablaze, spilling rectangles of light on the boardwalks that looked like wet paint.

Hunched in the saddle, a rider in a yellow

slicker passed the two lawmen. He looked, then looked again, startled at the burdens their horses carried.

Crane led the way to the mission. He knocked on the door, then realized it was the empty schoolhouse. He stepped back to his horse and led it around the side.

A door was lit, adorned on the inside by a rectangle of stained glass that hung from a brass chain. The picture was of the Virgin, her pale blue face contorted in grief, her crucified Son across her lap.

The marshal rapped on the door and the stained glass bounced back and forth. Rain fell around him, hissing.

The dark form of a nun appeared behind the door; then it swung open.

"Why, Marshal Crane, what are you doing here?" Sister Marie Celeste asked.

Standing tall, grim and terrible in the downpour, Crane said, "I have some bad news, Sister."

Masterson stepped beside him. He looked like a man who wanted to be anywhere else but where he was.

"Two of your sisters are dead," he said. "Murdered." He shook his head. "I'm so sorry."

The sheriff and nun exchanged a look that Crane could not interpret.

"Where are they?" Marie Celeste asked. Her voice was steady, as though she was trying to hold on to some kind of anchor. But her eyes were a dark tangle of conflicting emotions.

"On the horses," Masterson said. "We brought them back."

"Please, Sheriff, and you, Marshal, carry them inside."

The nun stood at the open door while the lawmen carried the dead sisters into the mission.

"This way," Marie Celeste said. She walked ahead of them, opened a door to her right and stood aside to let them pass. A young nun appeared in the hallway and cast a horrified look at the bodies, her hand flying to her mouth.

"Go, bring the others," the older woman said.

For a moment the nun stood paralyzed, her eyes filling.

"Now!" Marie Celeste snapped.

The nun turned and fled, her sobs falling around her like raindrops.

"This is the infirmary," Marie Celeste told Crane. "As you can see, it's not currently in use. Later we will take the sisters to the chapel."

The room was small. It held four cots and

a glass-fronted medicine cabinet filled with brown and green bottles. A carved wooden statue of the Archangel Michael stood in one corner.

After Crane and Masterson laid the bodies on cots, the nun saw their wounds for the first time. She gave a little cry of alarm and dropped a trembling hand to the rosary hanging from her belt. Black beads clicked through white fingers and the sister's lips moved.

"We discovered the bodies in an arroyo out near Sunrise Pass," Crane said, quietly nudging the nun from prayer to present. "Why were they there, Sister?"

"I sent them," Marie Celeste answered. Her tormented face lifted heavenward. "God forgive me, I sent them."

"Why?" This from Masterson.

Sudden zeal, like black fire, manifested itself in the nun's eyes. "To turn aside Reuben Stark from his madness. He has convinced his followers that he will lead them to a Promised Land here in Nevada and that God will clear the way by unleashing the wrath of the Archangel Michael."

Marie Celeste closed her eyes and quoted from the Bible. " 'Behold, I am sending an angel to guard you along the way and to bring you to the place I have prepared, saith the Lord.'

"The Comstock and all its iniquity will be destroyed by Michael's fiery sword and after the wicked are gone, Stark's chosen people will enjoy a hundred years of peace and prosperity.

"That is what he has told them. I wanted to open his people's ears to the truth, that the Lord has never made such a promise to Reuben Stark. The man seeks only his own gain. That is why he has murdered my nuns and given the blessing of martyrdom."

A dozen sisters had filed into the infirmary and had surrounded the bodies. Now they tearfully looked to Marie Celeste for guidance.

"You must go now, gentlemen," she said. "Thank you for what you have done."

"One thing, Sister," Crane said, "do you know where Stark's Promised Land is? He has . . . something valuable of mine and I want it back."

Marie Celeste shook her head. "No, I don't know, Marshal. But a thousand people with their wagons and livestock can't vanish into thin air. I'm sure you will find it and that . . . item you value so much."

CHAPTER 21

Rain ticked on the roof of the sheriff's office and distant thunder rumbled.

Masterson stood at the stove, pouring coffee into two cups. He set the cups on the table, then got the whiskey bottle from the writing desk. He poured a hefty shot into each.

"I think we need this after today," he said.

Crane nodded in agreement. He got to his feet and looked out the window.

"Town's quiet."

"Uh-huh. That tends to happen when Ben Hollister isn't around."

"I thought he wanted to keep an eye on you?"

"Oh, he still does. I'm sure he's got a few of his boys posted out there somewhere."

Crane took his seat again. He looked at Masterson. "Give the town the money, Paul. I don't want a gun showdown between you and me."

The sheriff smiled. "Did I ever tell you I have a sister?"

"No, I don't think you have. But is it really necessary?"

"I think it is. My sister, she has a daughter. Angie is her name. Well, anyway, when Angie was a little girl her mother would scold her about something or other she'd done wrong, and know what the kid would tell her?"

Crane shook his head.

"She'd say, 'I don't want to talk about it.' "

"And you don't want to talk about the money?"

"Not tonight, Gus."

"All right, I'll take a pass on it for now. What do you want to talk about?"

Masterson sipped his coffee and indicated that Crane should do the same.

"Good, huh?"

"Real good," Crane said. "Puts fire in a man's belly."

"Why did Stark decide to move those pilgrims out of the pass?" the sheriff asked.

"I'd guess he has a couple of reasons. For one thing, he can't get his hands on the town's fifty thousand," he said, then added pointedly, "since you're the only one who knows where it's at."

Masterson smiled and let that go as Crane

continued. "And for another, if he waited much longer, he'd have to feed and house a thousand people and their animals all winter. That takes money Stark doesn't have, so why not lead them to the Promised Land now? Wherever it is."

"It's getting too late in the year for them pumpkin-rollers to put in a crop."

"Maybe Stark is counting on that," Crane said. "Once he has what he wants, he'll let the people starve. Cattle country won't grow crops and he knows that. They'll either have to die or move on. The question is, what does he want?"

"I told you before. Range, cattle. Maxie told me his ambition is to found a dynasty."

"But whose range?"

Masterson smiled. "Everybody's. He wants it all."

A silence stretched between the men, broken only by the rattle of rain against the windows and the sigh of the surging wind.

"How many fighting men you reckon Stark could muster?" Masterson asked finally.

"He's got maybe a thousand people with him. Take away women, children and old men and he still could field two-fifty, three hundred riflemen."

"Even banded together the ranchers

couldn't come up with half that number."

"Stark won't need to send out his fighting men. A thousand people with wagons can cover the range like locusts and take over every ranch. Even Hollister won't let his riders shoot down hundreds of women and children. He knows he'd have the Army down on him and where its sympathies would lie. A lot of them bluecoats are farm boys themselves."

"Kill Stark and we stop it, huh?"

"That's how it shapes up. He's their leader and if he goes, the rest will move on."

"Then that's what we'll do. Kill Stark."

"We have to get to him first. If he's surrounded by three hundred armed men that might not be so easy."

Wearing slickers as they rode through a downpour, Crane and Masterson left Rawhide Flat just before sunup.

The rain had persisted throughout the night and into the morning and the sky was black from horizon to horizon. A keening wind blew from the north and rippled the long grass and the mountains were lost behind low-lying clouds.

The lawmen rode due south for an hour before they cut the trail of the wagon train, a deep scar across the high plains that angled farther to the west toward Hot Springs Mountain.

That was also the direction of Ben Hollister's Rafter-T.

"Unless Stark plans on invading Carson City," Masterson said, "the Rafter-T is where he's headed."

A few minutes later they found the place where the train had bedded down for the night. It looked like Stark had circled the wagons as a precaution. The old man was obviously prepared for war and trusted no one.

Under a thrashing rain and pummeled by wind, the lawmen followed the wagon tracks.

An hour later they discovered the dead men at a cabin just off the trail.

An attempt had been made to fire the place, but the rain had stopped the spread of the flames. Tendrils of smoke rose from a hole in the sod roof, only to be instantly shredded by the wind.

One man lay on his back just outside the cabin door. He looked to be in his fifties, heavily bearded, wearing the rough garb of a silver prospector. He'd been shot several times and his throat had been slashed.

Another man, younger, no more than twenty, was sprawled on the cabin floor. He too had been shot and his throat was cut. A black dog lay near the man. It was also dead. The dirt floor was black with blood.

Crane looked around the cabin. The shelves had been stripped of supplies and two hooks screwed into the wall showed where a rifle had once hung.

"There's a lean-to stable back there, looks like it held a couple of burros," Masterson said.

"Place has been stripped clean," Crane said. "Not even a bean left."

"Stark?"

"Who else? And no more than a couple of hours ago. Maybe a few wagons with women and young 'uns showed up before first light asking for help. The prospectors weren't expecting trouble until the men arrived and started shooting."

"Their throats have been cut. I'd say this was done by the same man who killed the nuns."

"Looks like."

The marshal stepped to the door of the cabin and glanced out at the slanting rain.

"I'm hungry and I need coffee," he said. "We'll eat here where it's sheltered before we take the trail again."

"With that in here?" Masterson asked, nodding toward the dead man and the dog.

"Drag them outside if they bother you. And on your way back bring those beef sandwiches we bought this morning and the coffee."

"Anybody ever tell you that you're a man who loves to give orders?"

"All the time," Crane said. "It goes with the badge."

The fire in the cabin's rusty stove still glowed red. Crane added wood and when Masterson brought the pot he filled it from a stream running nearby.

Later they ate thick sandwiches of stale sourdough bread and black, tough beef that they were glad to wash down with coffee.

"How much did you pay for these?" Crane asked, chewing.

"Fifty cents for the two."

"You were robbed."

"Ma's Kitchen was the only place open."

"Ma must have been a trail cook at one time."

"You do some punchin', Gus?"

"Some. I first went up the trail when I was fourteen. You?"

"Never did. When I was a younker I got a situation in the bookbinding business. I lasted three years, then quit. A while after that I hooked up with a man by the name of Blue Face Pollock and went into the banking trade."

"Were you a teller?"

Masterson shook his head. "Nah, a robber."

"Paid better than bookbinding, huh?"

"Yeah, it did, but it wasn't what you'd call a regular wage. Spend like a drunken sailor one week, broke the next."

Masterson was looking through the door, his eyes fixed on something in the distance.

"What happened to Pollock? He still around?"

"He got hung up Fort Benton way a few years back. Shot the captain of a steamboat and the vigilantes strung him up the next day. I guess they set store by that captain."

Masterson nodded toward the door. "Rider coming. A tall man on a tall horse."

CHAPTER 22

Crane stepped to the door and looked into the rain. After a few moments he said, "Hard to tell, but that may be the man I saw at the arroyo."

"The way he rides, straight up and down like that, he's got a look to him," Masterson said. "A former cavalryman, maybe."

The rider drew rein when he was a few yards from the cabin. "Howdy, gents," he said, touching his hat brim.

Crane nodded and took stock of their visitor.

He wore a slicker, but the thinness of his body and narrow, stooped shoulders were evident. His face was cadaver thin, but burned by the sun to a mahogany color, and his pale eyes moved constantly, missing nothing. A flat-brimmed, low-crowned hat sat just above bushy eyebrows and the man's lipless mouth under his mustache was a mean, narrow gash. His right cheek was scarred with three parallel wounds that were red and raw.

Crane leaned against the doorjamb. Masterson had been right. The rider had a look to him — the look of a professional gunman and a killer of nuns.

"Seen your smoke an' smelled your coffee," the man said. His smile was the cold grimace of a skull. "But then, I've been looking for you boys anyhoo."

"What's your business with us?" Crane asked.

"I have a proposition for you, from the Reverend Stark." Rain drummed on the rider's hat and ran in skeletal fingers down the shoulders of his oilskin slicker.

"So it's reverend now, is it?" Masterson said.

The tall man shrugged. "If that's what he wants to be called, then that's what I call him."

"I don't want to hear Stark's proposition," Crane said. "But give him mine. Tell him if him and his sons surrender to me, I'll make sure they have red, white and blue bunting on their gallows and a well-attended hanging."

"Maybe you should hear what he has to say first."

The tall man looked up at the black,

lowering sky. "You lawdogs gonna keep me out in the rain? It don't seem real polite. But I guess that's what folks are like nowadays, just no consideration for nobody."

"Light, set, drink your coffee, then ride," Crane said. He had made up his mind that the rider was going nowhere but jail. But right now, his Colt unhandy under a slicker, was not the time for a gunfight.

The man nodded. "Much obliged." He said, "Name's Lewt Hope, by the way. No need for you two to give me your'n, on account of how I know them already."

Beside him Crane saw Masterson stiffen. When Hope dropped the reins of his horse, thunder rolling above him, the sheriff made no move to let the man pass.

"You the Lewt Hope that operates out of the Windsor Hotel in Denver?"

The man nodded. "I call it home, when I'm there."

"I hear you're real good with the knife. They say you're better than Jim Bowie ever was."

"They say right." Hope's eyes hardened. "Now, will you give me the road?"

Masterson stepped aside. The man towered over him by a good six inches.

Crane tossed out the dregs from his cup and handed it to Hope. "Coffee's on the stove."

As he built a cigarette he watched the man pour coffee, then looked even closer as Hope shrugged out of his slicker and laid it carefully on the table.

The man wore a plain blue Colt, higher than most, the worn rubber handle between his elbow and wrist. It was a working gun and it had seen a good deal of use. A large Green River knife hung on Hope's left side, the wood handle also showing signs of wear.

He sat on the rough bench at the table and lifted his eyes to Crane. "You got two dead men outside."

"Found them that way," the marshal answered.

Hope showed no interest, or emotion of any kind. "You make good coffee," he said.

For some reason Masterson was on the prod. He made little attempt to hide his dislike for Lewt Hope.

"What's Stark's proposition?" he asked.

Hope sipped more coffee and set down the cup carefully. His fingers were long and sensitive, as you might see on a concert pianist.

"The reverend extends the hand of friendship," he said. He looked long at Masterson, then said, "Oh yes, he really does."

"Why the change of heart?" Crane asked.

Hope spread his hands. "No change. You two and the reverend have a common enemy in the person of Ben Hollister. He wishes to join forces with you — if certain . . . ah . . . conditions are met."

"And what would those conditions be?" Masterson asked.

"Wait, Paul," Crane interrupted. "There are a few things I want to know first."

He took a step closer to Hope. The gunman didn't care for the move, and his right hand dropped from view under the table.

"Did you kill Joe Garcia and his men?" the marshal asked.

"The Reverend Stark deemed it necessary. 'Whittling down Mr. Hollister,' he called it."

"So you didn't kill them on my behalf?"

Hope gave his grinning-skull smile. "Don't flatter yourself, Marshal. You're not that important."

"Then why did you bring me his head?"

Hope shrugged. "I was taking it back to the reverend, but then I smelled your fire and your bacon cooking and thought it might be fun to scare you. See, we'd been more or less keeping an eye on you all day. You're not a difficult man to track, Marshal. And that's a pity, I mean for a lawman."

Crane felt Masterson's eyes boring into

him and he was peeved. "If you knew I was in the arroyo, why didn't you come after me?"

"Well, the Reverend Stark wanted his young belly warmer back, but he didn't want to lose good men getting her." Hope smiled again. "You still have a pretty good gun rep, Marshal. Hell, we lost a man to you at the hotel as it was. How many would have died charging up that arroyo in the dark with a hard wind blowing?"

"A lot," Crane said evenly.

"My point entirely."

"Why did you cut out Garcia's eyes?"

"Just an idle fancy. For a time I thought about letting him go after that, but the reverend wanted him dead. Besides, Joe was squealing like a stuck pig, so I put him out of his misery."

"And the nuns?"

For the first time Hope's eyes were guarded. "How did you know about the nuns?"

"We found the bodies. Did you kill them?"

The gunman was digging a hole for himself, but he didn't seem to care. That took sand, or a supreme, arrogant confidence in his gun skills. Probably it was both.

"They tried to turn the people away from the Promised Land, filling their heads with their popish superstition and lies. The reverend ordered me to take care of the problem."

Hope looked at Crane. "Don't look so glum, Marshal. I didn't have as much fun with them as I did with Garcia. The old woman died quick enough, though I made the one who gave me this" — the fingers of his left hand moved to his torn cheek — "last a spell longer."

Crane studied the man and reached a decision — to hell with jail. Lewt Hope was not going to leave the cabin alive.

But he didn't want the gunman on guard. "All right, what's Stark's proposition? Then be on your way."

"Now you're talking sense, Marshal. It's very simple: Within the next two days, you take me to the place where the bank robbery money is hid. The reverend figgers one of you, or both of you, know where Judah Walsh stashed his loot."

"And if we don't?"

Hope dug the hole deeper.

"Then the cute little gal you're sweet on, the one called Sarah, gets skun." He patted the knife at his side. "Reverend Stark says I'm to gut her like a deer and dump her at the sheriff's office."

Paul Masterson's face looked like it had

been hewn from granite. His eyes were colder than ice, glittering.

"Hope, before I gun you, did you kill a man in the Texas Belle saloon?"

He was digging the hole deeper still.

"Yeah, but I was trying for Hollister." He looked at Crane. "And you ain't gonna do no killing, Crane. That's my job. Now, I want your answer. Do you show me where the money is hid or do I start work on that little Sarah whore?"

Crane opened his mouth to speak, but the sheriff stopped him.

"Ever hear of a woman by the name of Maxie Starr?"

"Sure, everybody knew Maxie." His grin was an obscene thing. "Most of us knew her very well."

Masterson's voice sounded like a death knell. "Did you see her die?"

"Hell, she was only a whore."

"I asked you — did you see her die?"

The hole Hope had dug for himself was now a grave.

"Yeah, I was there. The reverend did the whipping, drug it out, but she wouldn't say where you and Walsh was holed up." His eyes lifted to Crane. "Tell him, Marshal, she was only a damned whore and who the hell cares?"

Thunder crashed outside and for an instant a searing white light filled the cabin.

It sounded as though Masterson was talking from inside a cave, his voice hollow, like a muffled drum.

"Hope, get on your feet, you sorry piece of trash," he said.

The gunman showed no fear as he rose from the table. "Then the answer to the Reverend Stark's proposition is no?"

"That's right, but you won't live to tell him so."

Hope's hand moved closer to his gun. "It won't be that way. The day I can't shade a couple of stupid lawdogs is the day I'll hang up my gun."

His hand flashed for his Colt.

He was fast, very fast and smooth on the draw.

But he died with two of Masterson's bullets in his chest before his gun leveled.

For a fleeting moment, Crane caught a glimpse of Hope's face as he went down. There was horror and disbelief in his eyes. Then nothing at all.

The marshal looked at Masterson, at the smoking Remington in his hand. He knew now that back at the sheriff's office Paul had been right.

Nobody could match his speed on the

draw and shoot. Not he. Not anyone he ever knew.

CHAPTER 23

Paul Masterson punched out the two empty shells from the Remington and reloaded. As he holstered the big revolver he turned to Crane.

"He had his chance."

"Looked like."

"Where do we go from here?"

"Want to bury your dead?"

"Hell no, coyotes got to eat."

Thunder thudded and lightning flashed around the cabin. Rain racketed against the windows and fat drops ticked from the top of the open doorway.

"I can't stand by and let Sarah die," Crane said.

"No, you can't."

"Any ideas?"

"Nary a one."

"We could brace Stark."

"No we couldn't. We'd both be dead and who's going to help the girl then?"

"Paul, I saw you use a gun. You're good, real good."

"I know I'm good." He smiled. "Real good. So maybe between us both we could down half a dozen of Stark's men. But we can't win a gunfight against three hundred."

"Then we ride back to town and round up a posse. If there are enough of us, those sodbusters of Stark's may not be so eager to start a fight."

Masterson nodded. "It's a way."

"But you don't think it's a good way."

"Depends how many men we can muster. Stark is headed for Hollister's range. He'll probably throw in with us, and most of the other ranchers."

"At least then we'll have a fighting chance."

"It depends, Gus. If Stark really does move onto the Rafter-T, Hollister will fight for his range and his punchers will ride for the brand. The other ranchers will fight because they know they could be next. But if Stark heads farther north into his Promised Land, maybe the Comstock silver mines, Hollister and the rest will sit out that dance.

"I tell you this, they sure as hell won't fight for an orphan gal they don't even know."

Crane stepped to the door and looked out at the rain and the ashen, sullen sky.

"The Promised Land isn't a silver mine," he said. "For Stark it's range and herds. For his followers, open ground to plow."

"You're probably right, but what if you aren't?"

"There's one way to find out. We trail the wagon train and see where it's headed."

Masterson nodded. "I'll go along with that, but only because I can't come up with something better." He moved beside Crane and stared into the gray land. "Hell, Gus, I never did cotton to riding in the rain and getting a wet ass."

"Goes with the badge," Crane said.

Ahead of the two riders the seven-thousand-foot McTarnahan Hill was a wedge of rain-gleaming black against the sky. Four miles to the northwest, in Eagle Valley, lay the Carson City boomtown and state capital, bustling with eight thousand permanent residents and on any given day tens of thousands of miners.

The tracks of the wagons veered away from the city and headed toward Hackett Canyon and Ben Hollister's range.

This was a land of unexpected abrupt hills covered in piñon, ephradine and juniper

217

that still held on to the clustered blue-green berries of spring. The fragrant pink blossoms of desert peach bloomed everywhere, as did scattered stands of cholla.

Crane began to see white-faced cattle and a few longhorns grazing on the lush grass near the dozens of narrow creeks that laced the country, and the cottonwoods were heavy with smoke-colored foliage.

The marshal did not know if the cattle belonged to Hollister or someone else, but whoever the owner was, he'd lost money. Three slaughtered cows, their bones stripped of meat, lay on a creek bank.

Masterson swung out of the saddle and examined a slab of dripping hide. His eyes rose to Crane, looking at him through the rain. "Bullet holes there and there."

"I see them."

"Low thing. Shooting another man's cows."

"I reckon."

"Stark's people needed meat, I guess."

"Reckon."

Masterson glanced around him, then at the wagon tracks heading north into the rain haze. "Headed for Hollister's range, all right."

"He'll fight."

"For his ranch? Yeah, he'll fight." The

sheriff smiled. "Isn't that part of your job, Gus? I mean, stopping range wars?"

"Paul, God in his heaven couldn't stop this one." His gaze moved beyond Masterson to a ridge about fifty yards away. "And speaking of wars, it wouldn't surprise me if we have one on our hands right now."

Masterson turned and saw what Crane saw.

Five riders sat their horses on the rim, their faces lost in the shadows of their hats and the shifting steel mesh of the rain.

Crane cursed under his breath. It stood to reason that the canny Stark would have men covering his back trail, probably among the best he had, but he'd totally overlooked that possibility.

It was the kind of mistake that could get a man killed.

Carefully, Crane unbuttoned his slicker and moved it away from his gun, his eyes fixed on the unmoving riders. This was shaping up to be big trouble and those boys up there looked to be quietly confident.

"Don't let them catch you afoot, Paul," he said.

Masterson strolled casually to his horse and swung into the saddle. As he did, in a single, fluid motion, he lifted his Winchester from under his knee.

"Now what?" he asked.

"They'll make a move soon."

"We can take five of them." After a moment's hesitation, he added, "But not a dozen."

More riders had joined the men on the rim. They began to talk among themselves and one of them laughed.

Masterson slowly turned his eyes to Crane. "Know what the Irish say, Gus?"

"No, tell me."

"A good retreat is better than a bad stand."

"Then what are we waiting for? Let's get the hell out of here!"

Crane swung his horse around and set spurs into its flank. Masterson followed at a flat-out gallop.

Bullets splintered the air around their heads as the lawmen ran. The country in front of them promised nothing by way of cover and Crane slapped the spurs to the buckskin.

"Head for the cabin!" Masterson yelled. "We'll make our fight behind walls."

A bullet smashed into the pommel of the sheriff's saddle, then ricocheted away, whining viciously.

Turning in the saddle, Crane cut loose

with his revolver. He fired three shots but as far as he could tell did no execution.

The dozen Stark riders either had sand or they were fanatics, but they came on gamely at the gallop, rifles bucking against their shoulders.

"Gus," Masterson called out, "we've got to slow them."

Crane's mount had the bit in its teeth, his neck was stretched and the marshal had his hands full.

"When you see me turn, stop and give covering fire," Masterson hollered.

"I don't know if I can stop this damned hoss."

"Then shoot him if you have to, but give me cover."

A few tense moments fled past. Then Masterson wheeled the sorrel and charged toward the oncoming riders, firing his Winchester.

Crane leaned back in the saddle and grabbed the reins with both hands. Using all his strength he wrenched his horse's head around.

The buckskin turned and its forelegs flew out from under him. His haunches slammed into the ground hard and Crane nearly flew out of the saddle. But the big horse recovered and the marshal drew rein.

The buckskin stood, trembling, as Crane grabbed for his rifle.

Masterson was already among them.

Surprised by this sudden switch, the riders split into two groups. Masterson charged through the gap, firing. A horse went down, spilling its rider onto the ground. Then a second man, hit hard, toppled backward out of the saddle.

Crane fired at a man in a gray slicker. A miss. He fired again and the man went down, thumping onto the wet ground.

In a state of confusion, Stark's men milled around, looking for a clear shot at Masterson.

But the sheriff was through them again, galloping hell-for-leather toward Crane.

Swinging the buckskin, the marshal slapped spurs and he and Masterson were running neck and neck again.

The sheriff was laughing, his head thrown back. "Hot damn, that will make them think!"

Stark's riders were shooting again and a bullet tore through the loose material of Crane's sleeve.

But Stark's men had lost two of their number and a horse and were wary now.

They slowed to a canter, enough to keep the lawmen in sight, and every now and then one of them tried a hopeless, long-distance pot.

Suddenly, through the shifting gray veil of the rain, the cabin loomed into sight.

Both men cantered to the door and quickly stepped out of the saddle.

"They'll shoot the horses," Masterson said urgently.

"We'll take 'em inside with us."

"Anything you say, Gus, but it's going to be mighty crowded in there."

Masterson stepped into the cabin and pulled his horse after him. Crane did the same.

With two horses and two men inside, the small cabin was crowded, especially since their mounts were still excited from the chase and were restive and in no mood to be accommodating. The presence of a dead man and the smell of blood made things worse, and white arcs showed in their rolling eyes.

Closing the door, Masterson smashed out the glass in the cabin's only window.

The shack had been built solidly of sod and would stop bullets. Only the door was a danger. The horses were big targets and a few rounds through the thin timber could kill them.

Crane saw the danger and dragged the

heavy table to the door, then set it up on its edge. The table had been hammered together from thick pine boards and should stop even rifle rounds.

At least he hoped it would.

An open, flat area of brush and bunchgrass stretched a hundred yards from the front of the cabin, then rose gradually to a shallow hill crowned with a thick growth of juniper and piñon.

Stark's men had dismounted and were strung out along the crest of the hill.

For the next several hours they kept a steady fire on the cabin. The door soon shredded into splinters but, at least for now, the table held.

Masterson had fired a dozen shots in reply but claimed no hits. The riflemen on the hill were well hidden among the trees and were difficult to take down.

Inside the cabin the air was becoming rank.

Horse manure littered the floor and the animals were lathered in sweat and restless, kicking out at the two lawmen every chance they got. Masterson's sorrel had given Crane a bruise on the back of his thigh from a flying rear hoof and had tried to bite him more than once.

"At least he had the good taste to piss all

over the late Mr. Hope." The sheriff grinned. "Probably the first bath he's had in years."

Crane smelled his own rank sweat and the cloying air lay on him like a damp, putrid blanket.

A bullet chipped wood from the table and the marshal swore.

"It's getting too ripe in here," he said. His eyes were red rimmed and gritty. "I'm eating horseshit in air I sucked clean an hour ago."

"What do you suggest we do, Gus?" His eyes traveled over the marshal's face, searching for a reply. But when it came, it was less than he'd hoped.

"I don't know."

"We could rush them with guns blazing, I suppose."

"They'd cut us down before we covered ten yards."

"Then quit complaining and eat your horseshit like a good little marshal."

Crane swore again. "Damn, but you're an irritating man, Masterson."

Another hour drifted past.

Stark's men kept up a desultory fire on the cabin. A ricocheting bullet burned across the buckskin's rump like a metal hornet, sending the big stud into a bucking, kicking frenzy. The sorrel caught his companion's mood and began to kick out on his own account. The lawmen battled to calm them, fearing the animals would injure themselves, and their riders.

In the end the horses settled down, but Crane was seething with rage and directed his anger at the men on the hill.

He stepped to the door, leaned across the table and dusted the hilltop until he shot his Henry dry.

The marshal made no hits that he could see, but did succeed in filling the cabin with greasy, gray gunsmoke.

"Feel better now, Gus?" Masterson asked, grinning.

Suddenly Crane wanted to bash the man's face in with his rifle butt.

CHAPTER 24

The rain stopped, the clouds parted, the afternoon sun scorched and the land steamed. It was like an oven inside the cabin and the hot, damp air around the place shimmered.

Sweat trickled down Crane's face and back and black wedges stained his shirt under his armpits. The stinking air was clotted and hard to breathe, like gulping down the foul contents of a rancid stewpot.

There had been no shooting from the hill for the last twenty minutes.

"Could be they've gone, Gus," Masterson said.

"Could be."

"You think they are?"

"I think, maybe they are."

"Why would they leave?"

"Beats me. We don't even know that they have gone."

"You said they had."

"I said maybe they had. I said maybe."

Masterson thought for a few moments, then offered cheerily, "Why don't you step outside, Gus. See if you draw fire."

"Why don't you?"

"They won't shoot at a United States marshal."

"Hell, they've been shooting at me for hours."

Masterson fell silent, then said, "I'd go, but my leg hurts."

"Are you wounded?"

"Nah, banged my knee on the table, I think."

Crane gave the sheriff the full force of his rainwater stare. "I'm going outside because you've got me by the cojones. But I swear, Paul, if they gun me I'm going to make damn sure I put a bullet in you before I go down."

"I'll cover you, Gus. Don't worry, to me you're gold dust and I don't want to lose you."

"Thanks. I'll carry that thought into hell with me."

Crane pushed the table aside and swung the tattered door wide. He studied the rise. Nothing moved and there was no sound.

"See anything?"

Masterson stood in the doorway, his rifle

in his hands.

The marshal shook his head.

Crouching low, he moved toward the rise. Suddenly Masterson was beside him.

"I reckoned I'd better come with you, Gus." He grinned. "You might bumble right into an ambush."

"Leg isn't bothering you none, huh?"

"Nah, cleared up by itself."

"Maybe it's because I said I'd put a bullet into you."

"Yeah, could be. You did make a powerful argument, Gus."

Then Masterson was running. He stopped at the bottom of the rise, tilted back his head and scanned the rim.

"I don't see anything," he said.

The two lawmen scrambled up the slope and reached the crest. Apart from a scattering of empty shells and cigarette butts, it was deserted.

"Now why would they pull out like that?" Masterson asked. "They had us pinned down in the cabin and all they had to do was bide their time."

Crane's eyes were filled with thought.

"They didn't leave on their own account," he said finally. "They were pulled off by Stark."

"How come?"

"Because he's planning for a bigger battle elsewhere and needs every gun he's got."

"Hollister?"

"You bet. He won't give up his range easily."

Masterson looked down the hill to the cabin. The horses, with the wonderful resiliency of animals, were placidly grazing as though nothing untoward had happened to them.

"I say we ride for Rawhide Flat," he said, "and see if there's any news of Hollister and how he's handling this. Unless you want to ride for the Rafter-T and try to talk reason into Stark."

"I'm not riding into the middle of a war, surrounded by a sight of enemies and mighty few friends. Stark isn't going to listen to me, or anybody else."

The sheriff's eyes focused on the rain-washed blue sky, but he spoke to Crane. "Gus, about Sarah. I'm sorry."

"She's young, only a child really. I . . . worry about her."

The inflections of the marshal's voice suggested there were many layers of hidden meaning in that simple statement and Masterson recognized it.

"I'm real sorry, Gus," he said again, knowing how inadequate he sounded.

Crane sucked it up. "Let's get the hell out of here," he said.

The bullet that had plowed across the buckskin's rump had cut deep and angled under the saddle blanket, scarring the animal's hide.

"It's a sorry cowboy who'll ride a sore-backed horse," he told the big stud. "But right now I don't have any choice."

He swung into the saddle, Masterson beside him, and headed north.

Ahead of them, all the way to the horizon, the sky was a faded blue, but to the west it was the color of blood.

The day was shading into evening when Crane and Masterson rode into Rawhide Flat.

Despite the day's drying sun, the street through town was muddy and the wind whispered a bleak promise of more rain. Shadows hung from shadows in the alleys and around the dark-windowed stores. Only the saloons were brightly lit, optimistically offering the siren promise of whiskey and women to those in need of either or both.

Scores of cow ponies stood at hitching rails or were ground-tied in the street and men were talking loud in the Texas Belle, not from drink but from anger.

The two lawmen left their horses at the livery and walked to the saloon.

The place was crowded with cheering men, and a few of them had drawn their guns and were shooting into the ceiling.

Ben Hollister was being offered helping hands as he climbed down from a table. His handsome face was beaming and it looked like he'd just made a speech that had been very well received by the assembled ranchers and punchers.

Hollister saw Crane come in and he elbowed his way through the backslapping crowd and stopped in front of him. His face was flushed, but the marshal couldn't smell drink on him and guessed it came from either anger or triumph.

"You hear what happened?" he asked. "Stark and them pilgrims of his have moved onto my land, like . . . like . . ." He gave up trying to describe what like, turned his head and yelled, "Jed Battles, git over here."

The big rancher faced Crane again and his face lit up as a simile suddenly came to him. "Like damned locusts."

Battles was a wiry, round-shouldered cowboy with a mustache so droopy it covered his mouth. He had a sling on his left arm and a purple bruise on his forehead.

He stood beside Hollister.

"Tell the marshal what happened," Hollister said. He saw Battles hesitate and yelled, "Damn it, man, speak up."

The puncher swallowed, his prominent Adam's apple bobbing.

"They cut the fences and spread out across the range."

"Like damn locusts," Hollister said.

"Worse than locusts," Battles said. "They took over the ranch house and kilt Ed Grange, the cook, when he tried to stop them. Luke Hill got shot over to the corral, Bill Foster got it in the bunkhouse and so did old Harry Reid, who was down with the rheumatisms. Harry got his head split open with a wood axe. I got shot, but managed to get away."

"You see Reuben Stark?"

"Marshal, there were hundreds of them. All I saw was faces riding by. I didn't wait to tarry and study 'em."

"It's Stark all right, him and his sons," Hollister said. "All those people with him think he's some kind of prophet and the Rafter-T is the Promised Land."

"How do you know all this, Hollister?" Crane asked.

"Because we caught one of them."

Cheers and more gunshots greeted this

statement and the rancher waved a hand for silence.

"One of Stark's sodbusters decided to do a little plundering on his own account. He rode up to Tom Hickman's place when only Tom's wife, Bella, and a colored woman were at home. He had his way with Mrs. Hickman, but then he made the last mistake of his life. He told the colored woman to make him something to eat and while he was waiting, a couple of Tom's hands rode in and caught him.

"Tom Hickman ain't here. He's at his ranch trying to comfort his wife, but from what I was told she won't be comforted. Poor woman doesn't seem right in the head anymore."

Hollister yelled, "Bring me that sodbuster."

A couple of grinning cowboys dragged a man, or what was left of him, and held him erect, showing him off to Crane.

Both the man's eyes were black, so swollen they were closed shut. His nose had been smashed into a bloody pulp and most of his teeth had been knocked out. An ominous scarlet stain drenched the crotch of his pants.

Crane couldn't guess if the man was young or old. It was impossible to tell.

"He won't rape any other women," Hollister said, smiling. "He's all done with that."

"I'll take him into custody," Crane said.

"The hell you will, Marshal," Hollister said loudly, to cheers from some, angry protests from others. "We're gonna hang him."

"That's murder, Hollister," Crane warned.

"He's gonna die anyway. Cut off a man's cojones and his pisser and he bleeds to death. Everybody knows that."

From the man's splintered mouth escaped a whisper that was almost a sigh, like a delicate breeze. "Kill me. . . . Please, Marshal . . . kill me. . . ."

"See, he wants to be hung," Hollister said.

A man knows when it's time to take a stand. Crane knew this wasn't it.

Bowie knife surgery cuts and haggles at the body dreadfully, and Hollister was right, the man could not last much longer.

Besides, here was a rapist, caught in the act, who was begging for death.

Sometimes it was best to forget the law and let rough-and-ready frontier justice take its unforgiving course.

Hollister read Crane's decision in his eyes. In a strangely quiet and subdued voice the rancher said, "Take him out boys. Hang him."

A dozen punchers dragged the man outside. He made no sound. Crane hoped they'd break his neck and not strangle him to death. He'd once seen a man die long and hard that way, and the memory lingered.

Like a novelist who has completed one chapter and moved on to the next, Ben Hollister called out, "Osmond, Dyer, Swenson and the rest of you ranchers, round up your men. We're moving out."

As half a dozen ranchers moved to the door and stepped outside, Crane said, "How many riders do you have, Hollister?"

"Near threescore and another eighteen volunteers signed up for twenty dollars a day."

"You don't have enough."

"It's enough. Every one of my boys is handy with the iron."

"Stark may have three hundred fighting men."

The big rancher laughed. "Sodbusters don't know how to fight."

"Seems to me a bunch of sodbusters in Confederate gray did all right at Chickamauga and Fredericksburg."

Hollister shook his head. "This isn't the War Between the States. It's a battle for my spread and every other rancher's. We don't aim to fight by the rules of war, Crane. If we have to, we'll burn those nesters out and kill them all, seed, breed and generation of them."

"Hollister, you're a squatter yourself. You don't own a square inch of the land you claim. All that mountain pasture of yours is open range. The law isn't on your side on this."

"You're the law, Marshal, you and Masterson there. Are you two on my side?"

Crane clutched at a straw, realizing he was about to drown anyway. "I guess you can say we are, so let us handle this."

"We'll arrest Reuben Stark. Once he's gone, his followers will melt away."

Hollister's blue eyes lay cold on Crane's face. Under his mustache his mouth was a straight, hard line.

"Marshal, in the spring of 'seventy-two I drove five hundred longhorns up from Texas and settled that mountain pasture you say I don't own. I fit Indians and outlaws to hold it and buried friends. I don't give a damn what the law claims. The land is mine and I won't let anybody take it away from me."

A tall, lank man with sad eyes appeared at the saloon door. "Boys are ready to ride, Ben."

Hollister nodded. He looked at Masterson. "Be here when I get back. You and me are going to have words."

The sheriff smiled. "You know my terms. I'll be here."

"So be it." The rancher's eyes moved to Crane. "Will you stand aside and give me the road?"

"Listen, Hollister —"

But the man brushed past the marshal to the door, leaving three words drifting in the air behind him.

"Go to hell."

CHAPTER 25

Crane and Masterson stood at the edge of the boardwalk outside the saloon and watched Hollister's army move out of Rawhide Flat under a starless black sky that threatened rain.

The rancher had a low opinion of Stark's fighting men, but he was cautious enough of ambush that he'd hired a Piute to ride point.

The young Indian was painted for war, the streak of red and white across his nose and cheekbones marking him as a former cavalry scout.

Hollister looked hard at Crane as he rode past, but did not speak.

Behind, in a column of fours, rode every puncher the ranchers could muster, wild young teenagers for the most part who laughed and joked as though they were headed for a Sunday school picnic.

But the faces of the more seasoned men

were somber. A few were married and were aware that, even fired by a sodbuster, a rifle bullet is a widow maker that doesn't discriminate.

Bringing up the rear were the volunteers, frontier drifters of all kinds, from taciturn, professional gunmen to ashen drunks who were determined to stay sober just long enough to collect their twenty dollars a day.

"I guess Hollister plans on a dawn attack," Masterson said.

"Seems like."

"The Piute will be a help."

Crane didn't answer.

"You're thinking about Sarah."

"Some."

"Maybe we should have gone with them."

The marshal shook his head. "It wouldn't have helped none. Not many of those boys are coming back. All we'd accomplish is to die with them. How would our deaths help Sarah?"

"Hell, try looking on the bright side for a change, Gus. That's a tough bunch with Hollister, real door busters."

"But Stark has fanatics filled with the false fire of a false prophet. The only way you can stop people like that is to kill them. That's why, so long as Reuben Stark is alive,

they'll fight to the death and won't surrender."

Crane smiled slightly. "Come sunup, I
reckon Hollister will discover he's got a
cougar by the tail."

"So, what do we do? Wait around to pick
up the pieces?"

"No, Paul, I'm going to trail after them. I
have to do what I can to save Sarah."

"You really cotton to that little gal, don't
you?"

"Yes, I do. After all this is over, I plan on
taking her with me. I've never known what
it's like to have a kid of my own, and she
comes mighty close to filling the bill."

"Then I'll ride with you."

"Sarah is my responsibility, Paul, and only
mine. You got no call to get involved."

Masterson looked like a man about to put
his head in a noose. "Gus, do you have a
conscience?"

"Every man has." Crane smiled. "Yeah,
I've got a conscience. But I manage to sleep
o' night. Well, most nights."

"Mighty strange thing, mine just snuck up
and buffaloed me. Gus, it's like I'm on trial
before a hanging judge, but there's no witness so dreadful, no accuser so horrible as
my own conscience."

Puzzlement showed in every hard line of

Crane's face. "You're talking in circles. I'm trying, but I can't dab a loop on your drift."

"Then I'll lay it out real simple. I'll trade my twenty-five thousand dollars for Sarah's life. If I didn't, it would be the ultimate betrayal of certain principles that at one time, if I recollect clearly, I held dear."

A light had come into Masterson's eyes, like a man lost in the woods who has suddenly found his way. "Stark wants the whole fifty thousand, but I reckon he'll settle for my half of the money. Gus, now we have a bargaining chip for the girl."

"Paul, it's not your money. Did you forget about that?"

"If it saves Sarah's life, do you really care?"

Crane felt that question like a blow to the gut.

He wore a star on his chest and had sworn a solemn oath to uphold the law.

But there could be only one answer to Masterson's question. Reluctantly, the words dragging out of him, he said, "No, I don't care."

"Let's get the horses and ride," Masterson said. He grinned. "I can't leave you to crash around in the dark by yourself. The Piute would figure you're one of Stark's sodbusters and lift your hair for sure."

"No, we wait. How much bargaining are

we going to do in the middle of a shooting scrape? We bide our time and see what tomorrow brings. Who knows, maybe Hollister will bring back Reuben Stark with a rope around his neck."

"It could happen, I guess. Well, we'll play it your way and wait."

Crane's face took on a crafty expression. "When we try to make our bargain with Stark, do we take the money with us?"

"No, Gus. We make the bargain, then meet somewhere to trade for Sarah."

"Where is the money hid, Paul?"

The sheriff shook his head and smiled. "Don't ask me that again, Gus. I said I have a tender conscience, but I don't think adding a marshal's scalp is going to trouble it one bit."

"I declare," Crane said, "you're a mighty irritating man."

Crane stood, sleepless, looking out his hotel window.

He had visited Sarah's room, saw the carefully hung clothes he'd bought her and remembered the girl's innocent joy over her fixings, the hotel and about her life and the living of it.

The visit had been a mistake and it had done him no good. All he'd done was open festering wounds that now bled despair.

Beyond the hotel, Rawhide Flat lay dark and unseen, as though the town was glad to disappear into the deeper darkness of the night. Their patrons gone, the saloons were closed. The street was quiet and unmoving as a tomb.

A gusting wind played with a sheet of newspaper, tossing it into the air, then letting it swoop to earth again. The paper rose a last time, curved around a red and white pole outside the barbershop and fluttered like a stricken dove. Bored, the wind left it alone and moved on.

The sky was black, but in constant motion. Almost invisible, clouds with misty edges of gray toiled in from the north, and white light tremored in their swollen bellies.

A sudden spatter of rain hit Crane's window and for a moment beaded on the dusty panes before trickling downward.

The marshal's attention was caught by a shadowy movement in the street.

Cloaked and hooded, a slight figure hurried toward the sheriff's office, the delighted wind tugging at her.

A gust pushed back the hood and for a fleeting moment before she replaced it, Crane saw the veil and white coif of a nun.

Moving his position for a better view, the

marshal watched as the sister tapped on the door of the office. Masterson answered, smiled, and the little nun quickly stepped inside.

Prepared for a wait, Crane built a smoke, his eyes on Masterson's door.

But he didn't have to wait long.

After a few minutes the door opened and the nun stepped back outside. She looked around and hurried back the way she had come, soon disappearing from sight as he was fenced in by the gloom.

The marshal lit another cigarette, his face thoughtful. Why would a nun make a midnight visit to Paul Masterson? Was she trying to convert the former outlaw and hired gun from his wicked ways?

Hardly likely.

Was it something to do with Reuben Stark? Or the avenging Archangel Michael, about to destroy the Comstock with his sword of fire?

Both were possible, even if they didn't make any sense.

Crane smiled to himself.

But then, what did make sense in Rawhide Flat?

CHAPTER 26

The Piute, Ben Hollister and seven of his men rode into Rawhide Flat at the brightest part of the day.

The rain of the night a memory, the sun burned like a gold coin in the buffed lemon sky and a stifling heat lay heavy on the town, forcing stray mutts into the thin shade of alleys and sending panting lizards scampering under rocks.

Along the street the timber buildings creaked and groaned and purged pungent pine resin like sweat. Local merchants opened store doors wide, tried vainly to catch a breeze and invited inside swarms of fat, black flies nurtured in the rich manure of the cattle pens by the railroad tracks.

Irritable and querulous, businessmen in broadcloth and clerks in plug hats cursed the sweltering heat and the gritty dust that worked its way inside their celluloid collars and under their woolen long johns.

Women layered in bloomers, petticoats, corsets, camisoles and cotton dresses felt flushed and sticky, dark stains in the middle of their backs and underarms. They told one another that the summer dog days had just begun and that temperatures would only go higher. They wondered aloud if cool weather would ever come again or if it had been killed aborning, burned to a crisp by the jealous sun.

But that day none of these, men, women or animals, was more miserable than Ben Hollister.

Crane and Masterson had just eaten in Ma's Kitchen restaurant and were standing on the boardwalk when the rancher's horse, by long acquaintance, stopped at the Texas Belle.

Like his seven men, Hollister was wrapped from his hips to the crown of his head in barbed wire. Wound and rewound, the spikes had cut cruelly into his face, masking his features in blood. He tried to open his mouth to speak to the townspeople crowding around him, but his lips were imprisoned by the wire and could not move.

The Piute, not being a white man and thus a natural enemy, had been treated differently.

He'd been scourged, then crucified.

The Indian, naked, was nailed to the crosspiece of a T formed by two fence posts and later had been roped to his saddle.

Mercifully, he was dead. But hatred and defiance had not yet faded from his open, fixed eyes.

Crane and Masterson joined the willing hands helping Hollister and his men from their horses. A merchant dashed into his dry goods store and returned with an armful of wire cutters.

Three of Hollister's riders were wounded, and they cried out pitifully as the wire was cut from their bodies and the wicked spikes ripped out of their flesh.

"Massacree," Hollister gasped once his bleeding mouth was freed from the wire. He was lying on his back, a woman Crane didn't know supporting his head. "Everybody dead . . ."

"What happened?" This from Masterson.

"They laid for us in Sullivan Canyon. We were bushwhacked real good, pretty as you please. The Piute tried to hold the boys back, said it was a trap, but their blood was up, and since when do punchers listen to anybody, especially an Injun?"

Hollister's eyes were haunted, his face a grotesque, scarlet carnival mask.

"Stark and his sons led us into the canyon

248

and into an ambush. I don't know how many men were hidden on the slopes, hundreds maybe. We were cut to ribbons in the first volley." He waved a hand. "All but these."

"Why did Stark spare you?" Crane asked.

Hollister lifted his gaze to the marshal.

Crane saw fear, resignation . . . no, far worse than that, the shattered, distant stare of a broken man.

"He hates you, Crane, for killing his son. Hates you . . . hates you like poison."

The woman holding Hollister's head made cooing sounds, told him to lie quiet until the doctor got there.

The rancher wasn't listening.

"He — he says you and Masterson have to bring him the town's money by noon tomorrow. He says if you don't, he'll cut the hide of the girl — Sarah — like he did Maxie Starr."

Hollister looked wildly around him. "Where's the mayor?" he yelled. "Where's the damned mayor?"

"I'm here, Ben."

A small, balding man wearing a merchant's white apron took a knee beside the rancher.

Hollister grabbed him by the front of his shirt.

"Ed, he wants it doubled."

The mayor shook his head. "Ben, I don't understand."

"He wants a hundred thousand. He says for the folks in Rawhide Flat to take their money out from under their mattresses and add it to bank loot."

A horrified murmur ran through the crowd, and a man in broadcloth yelled, "The hell we will."

"Then he'll burn the town and kill every male, man and boy, like Quantrill did in Lawrence, Kansas."

"The town doesn't have that much money, Ben," the mayor said. "The loss of the fifty thousand from the bank has crippled us all financially."

"Then you'd better start trying to scrape it up, Ed. If you don't, Reuben Stark will come to kill. Depend on it."

The doctor, a man named Preston, had a lame left leg and the experienced physician's worried look. He immediately started to work on the most badly wounded of the cowboys.

"Hollister, I thought all Stark wanted was range," Crane said.

"Changed his mind, or maybe he always planned it this way. I reckon, after all this killing, he knows the law will catch up with him sooner or later and he wants out. A man can go far and fast with a hundred thousand dollars."

"Found a dynasty someplace else where he's not known," Crane said, almost to himself.

At first glance Mayor Ed Reddy looked what he was, a middle-aged man with huge muttonchop sideburns who was quietly prospering in the drapery business.

But his looks were deceptive.

Reddy had risen to the rank of brigadier general during the War Between the States and had fought with great bravery on the Confederate side at Shiloh, Lafourche Crossing, Chattanooga and Five Forks.

After the war he'd worn a lawman's star in Texas before taking up the tradesman's calling.

Now he looked at Crane with critical eyes. "Marshal, you represent the federal law in the Comstock. Why don't you arrest or shoot Stark and his cohorts?"

"Seems to me that Hollister lost sixty men trying to do just that," Crane said.

The mayor would not be turned aside. "Then what do you suggest, Marshal?"

"I plan on trying to bargain with Stark, see if I can make him see reason."

"And if you don't?"

"Then I'll be dead and you and the other citizens of Rawhide Flat better start searching under those mattresses."

The doctor elbowed Crane aside, made a cursory examination of Hollister, then snapped at the crowd, "All of these men are badly hurt and we need to get them out of the sun. We'll use the saloon as a temporary hospital."

He looked over his shoulder at the marshal. "The Indian is dead."

As hands reached out to lift him, Hollister freed himself from the woman's comforting hands and raised himself on one elbow, looking at Crane. "Remember what I told you. By fair means or foul, Reuben Stark aims to see you dead and he won't rest until he does."

The rancher's eyes took on a distant, lost look again. "He hates you — worse than me, worse than anything."

CHAPTER 27

"Gus, I know I keep asking you where we go from here," Masterson said. "But where do we go from here?"

"Like I told the mayor, we speak to Stark."

"Hollister never asked me about the money."

"Hollister is done. He's beat. I can see it in his eyes." Crane looked at the sheriff. "But I'm asking about the money."

"I can get it, the whole fifty thousand."

"Stark wants a hundred."

"I'd say that's up to the people of Rawhide Flat and ranchers like Ben Hollister."

"Paul, there are no ranchers left, only their widows."

"Then we dicker with the money we have."

"Leave it be. If we ride into Stark's territory with the fifty thousand, he'll just kill us both and take it. We'll tell him we stashed the money along our back trail, then set a time and place to meet."

"So we say, 'Come with only a couple of men,' and when he does, we draw down and gun him?"

"That's the general idea."

"Think it will work?"

"No."

Masterson looked shocked. "Then why the hell did you suggest it?"

"Because it's the only hand we have. All we can do is play our cards and hope they come up aces."

"It's thin, Gus, mighty thin."

"You asked where we go from here. Well, that's where we go."

Crane made an odd gesture, tilting his head to look at the flexing fingers of his right hand. "Know this, when the moon comes out tomorrow night and looks for Reuben Stark, it won't find him. No matter what happens, no matter how many bullets I take, I'll stay on my feet long enough to kill him."

"You're one hard gent, Gus."

The marshal smiled. "Ain't I, though?"

Crane bought a large burlap sack and filled it with every kind of debris he could find in the alleys, from peach cans to scraps of paper.

When the sack bulged enough, he hefted it and said to Masterson, "If Stark has scouts out, they'll expect to see a money bag."

"Suppose the scouts just bushwhack us, shoot us dead and take it?"

"I don't think that will happen. I reckon Stark won't forego the pleasure of killing me himself."

The lawmen were walking past the Texas Belle toward the livery stable but stopped when the doctor hailed them from the boardwalk.

"Sheriff Masterson, Mr. Hollister wants to talk with you. And you too, Marshal."

There was an odd light in Preston's eyes and for a moment it looked like words were hovering on his lips. But he thought better of it, closed his mouth and trapped them inside.

The big rancher was on his back across two tables that had been pushed together. He'd been stripped to the waist and his body and face glistened with some kind of salve. Now that the blood had been washed away, he looked better, but his skin was pocked with angry red welts, like a man who had just done battle with a nest of hornets.

Hollister raised his head as Crane and Masterson entered. Now he reached out and grabbed a handful of the sheriff's shirt, wounded eyes searching the lawman's face as though trying to find responses to words he had not yet said.

"Get the money and give it to Stark," he pleaded. "Every last penny of it. Save my ranch, Sheriff, and save this town."

Masterson nodded but made no answer.

His eyes moving to Crane, Hollister spoke with a keening whimper. "Save me, Marshal, save me."

"You're safe, Hollister, safe now," Crane said.

"Safe." The rancher savored the word like fine bourbon, then smiled. "Hey, Marshal, tell the boys to bring those yearlings in from the west forty, will ya? And tell 'em to ride the damn fences out there now and again. Get Powder River Tom Dowling to do it. He's a steady hand."

Hollister sat up and screamed wildly, "No! No! No!"

"Easy, now, easy," Crane whispered, pushing the man back onto the table.

Hollister's eyes looked like they were staring through a sheet of frosted ice.

"Tom's dead," the rancher yelled. "I saw it happen. The whole top of his head was blown away." He shook his head and stared at Crane. "He couldn't live after that. And

256

Jed Battles . . . dead. Luke Donnelly . . . dead. His brother Mark . . ." Hollister was telling himself something he could not believe. Wonderingly, he muttered, "All of them . . . are dead."

Dr. Preston pushed beside Crane, a small defeat in his eyes. "Better leave him now."

The man was a cow town doctor who could treat broken limbs, gunshot wounds, scurvy, running sores, the croup, the more common social diseases and all the other ailments punchers fall prey to.

But sickness of the mind was beyond Preston's medical skills, an uncharted sea where he dared not venture. He could only stand helpless on the shore and watch Ben Hollister founder.

Crane stepped away, then walked outside, a sickness in him.

Hollister was not his friend but a likely enemy. Yet he felt no joy, no triumph.

Every man has his breaking point and the rancher had reached his.

His will, his spirit, had not been broken, as is the way with slaves. But his mind had been shattered and the horrors he'd seen in Sullivan Canyon would remain with him forever. The gray ghosts of the dead men would be there when he woke, sit with him at table and crowd around his bed at night.

His only way to escape those accusing shades was to retreat into madness as Hollister had now done. He would forever ride a twisted trail that led nowhere until death, in its cold mercy, freed him.

"We'd best get going, Gus." Masterson stepped beside Crane, his eyes questing over the big marshal's face.

"Yeah, I guess we'd better."

Both men left unsaid what was on their minds. Guns, horses, badmen they could handle. But, as it was with Dr. Preston, mental illness was a dreaded unknown and they were content to let it lie.

Crane and Masterson rode north under a searing sun. Despite the encouragement of the rain, the grass around them was already losing its green, turning to gold to match the sunlight. In the distance languid buzzards quartered the sky and once a small herd of antelope crossed their path before vanishing into the shimmering heat haze.

Neither man had felt like talking and for the past hour the only sound had been the creak of saddle leather and the occasional jangle of a bit as the horses shook off flies.

Now, looking around him, Masterson broke the silence. "If Stark's men are watching us, I sure don't see them."

"And that's why we should be worried," Crane said.

Masterson looked up at the circling buzzards. "Want to take a look in Sullivan Canyon?"

"I've seen dead men before."

Unbidden, he had a vision of another canyon in another place and time.

An under-strength patrol of the U.S. 11th Infantry had been caught and wiped out by a mixed band of Comanche-Kiowa near Fort Concho. The dead had been stripped of their uniforms and boots and their naked bodies left to rot in the sun, thick with flies, maggots already curling.

He recalled the swollen bellies, blue tongues protruding from cracked mouths, the eyes that stared at everything but saw nothing.

Sullivan Canyon would be like that, only worse, and it was not a sight any man should see twice in a lifetime.

"Up ahead, where the cottonwoods are growing, we'll stash the sack there," Crane said. "And that's where we'll tell Stark to meet us."

Constantly checking their back trail and the rock-faced hills around them, Masterson looked uneasy.

"Gus, you could hide a regiment among

the trees up there on the hills. They could be watching us."

The marshal's eyes scanned the juniper and piñon cresting the hilltops. This was high rim country and serried ranks of aspen grew in the upper elevations.

"We'll have to take our chances," Crane said. "Hiding the money sack is the only way to lure Stark away from the rest of them."

"Thin," Masterson grumbled. "By God, it's thin."

The man was talking to himself and Crane let it go. He didn't need anyone to tell him how thin it was. He knew.

Cottonwoods stretched along both banks of a narrow mountain creek that ran, surprisingly cold, over a pebbled bottom. Tufted grass grew among the trees along with scattered wildflowers and a few stands of prickly pear. Bees droned sleepily among the blossoms and the heat lay heavy on the cottonwoods, the sun casting dappled shadows on the grass at their feet.

"Over there," Crane said, nodding in the direction of a jumble of sandstone boulders.

He and Masterson stepped out of the leather and Crane stuffed the sack in a space between two rocks. He answered the question on Masterson's face.

"If they're watching us, they'll find it. If they're not, it's as safe there as anywhere else."

"If you say so, Gus."

The marshal nodded. "I say so."

He stepped to the buckskin and loosed the cinch. "The horses are still tuckered from yesterday. We'll water them and let them graze for a while."

The lawmen led their horses to the creek and let them drink. After a while the tired animals started to munch the rich grass among the trees.

Crane settled his back against a cottonwood and began to build a smoke. Masterson took a place beside him and tilted his hat over his eyes as the bees sang a lullaby and the chuckling creek provided a drowsy counterpoint.

The lawmen didn't know it then, but they had just made a big mistake.

CHAPTER 28

When a general knows his enemy, he reinforces his line where he expects an attack.

But what of an enemy he neither knows nor expects? If he's blindsided by a flank attack from this unknown threat and his line is totally unprepared, his only options are to fight and die, or retreat.

Crane and Masterson were now in that position, but they had only one option — and it wasn't retreat.

There were four of them, drifters who had been loafing around Rawhide Flat since the bank was robbed. Warned by some animal instinct, or out of a genuine desire not to endanger their sorry hides, they had elected not to ride with Ben Hollister and had thus escaped the Sullivan Canyon massacre.

The grinning man who seemed to be their leader was tall and skinny, with a ragged mustache that perfectly matched his tattered, filthy shirt, black pants and mule-eared boots.

The other three were close copies of the first, just as dirty, but bearded.

But the guns they carried were clean, oiled and ready for bullet business.

"Howdy gents," the skinny man said. "No need for palaver here. We'll just take the money and then be on our way an' no harm done."

Crane and Masterson rose slowly to their feet.

"There is no money," Masterson said.

"Ah, but isn't that a bald-faced lie?" the skinny man said. "Have we not followed you from town? Did we not see, with our own two eyes, the marshal, there, stash the fifty thousand dollars in the rocks?"

"You boys ride on," Crane said. "You've got no need to die here. We told you, there is no money."

"Die is it?" The skinny man grinned. "My friend, you two are the ones who are going to die. And, I'll tell you no lie, it's truly sorry I am about that."

He turned his head. "Jacob, get the money."

Whatever the skinny man's name was, however long he'd lived, whether he had a loving wife and children or a Bible-reading old ma, no longer mattered to him or anyone else.

He died with Deputy United States Marshal Augustus Crane's bullet in his brainpan.

The man called Jacob drew rein and frantically tried to bring up his rifle.

Crane shot him dead.

Masterson was firing.

Another of the riders went down, grunting in surprise as a bullet thudded into his chest and a second nailed him before he hit the ground.

The fourth outlaw, a big man with streaks of gray in his beard, cursed, swung his horse around and set spurs to its ribs.

Crane fired twice and emptied the man's saddle. A drift of gun smoke crept between the cottonwoods like a mist and the ringing echoes of the gunshots seemed to linger in the motionless air.

Masterson looked at Crane.

"When it comes right down to it, you're not a talking man, are you, Gus?"

The marshal shrugged as he reloaded his Colt. "I'd nothing left to say. They were notified."

Masterson checked the downed men.

"This one's still alive," he called out.

Crane stood and looked at the man. He was the one Masterson had shot.

"Your time is short," the marshal said. "Best you make your peace with your maker."

"My name . . . is . . . my pa named me for a star . . . Epsilon. It — it means 'the swallower.' " He grinned. "I just done swallowed a heap o' lead, huh?"

"Some," Crane allowed.

The dying man's eyes filmed. "I wish . . . I wish I'd never left Texas," he said.

Then he was gone.

"He was game enough," Masterson said with faint praise.

Crane nodded. "Yeah, he died game. But if he was planning to rob somebody, he should have put in a lot more practice with the Colt's gun." He waved a hand. "All of them should."

"Now I come to study on it, I sure thought they would have got their work in better than they did," Masterson said. "The skinny one that done all the talking should have rode up and plugged you right off, Gus. Dropped you where you stood. I would've if I'd been him."

"Well, he talked too much, just like you. And just like you again, Masterson, he was a mighty irritating man."

The lawmen dabbed loops on the four bodies and dragged them behind their horses up a nearby hill, hiding them among the roots of the trees.

The marshal checked on the sack again. Then he and the sheriff swung north.

It's no easy thing to kill a man, and Crane did not take the deaths of the four hapless robbers lightly.

But they had taken their chances and it hadn't worked out for them. They had spit into the wind and in so doing had tried to defy the workings of cause and effect: if you try to do harm to a man, he's going to do harm to you.

From long experience, Masterson read the signs. "Those four dead men troubling you, Gus?"

"Some. I wish it hadn't happened."

"It happened."

"They could have been better."

"You ever think that if they'd been better we could both be dead?"

Crane considered that. "I'll study on that some," he said finally.

"Don't study on it too much, Gus. We're getting mighty close to Ben Hollister's range."

Night shadows were already gathering in the dips and hollows of the craggy land. The sky was tinged with gold and lilac and already a single star hung like a lantern to the north. Eastward, a ribbon of dark purple loomed over the peaks of the Pine Nut Mountains, its leading edge fraying slightly as it sought to spread west. After drowsing away the hot afternoon, the wind was shaking itself awake, stirring the branches of piñon and juniper up on the blue rock rims.

When the lawmen reached the southern edge of the Rafter-T range, they discovered that a wide section of fence had been cut and fence posts leveled to allow the passage of the wagons.

Straight as a lance aimed at Ben Hollister's heart, the tracks cut across prime pasture in the direction of the ranch house.

The moon had begun its slow climb into the darkening sky and the newly awakened wind snuffled at Crane and Masterson like a playful pup.

The sheriff glanced over his shoulder, then turned to Crane. "Riders behind us. Dang, I knew I'd been smelling skunks for the last ten minutes."

"How many?"

"Too many."

"Are they keeping their distance?"

"Seems like."

"Then ignore them and keep on riding."

"Gus, I always had it planned that if I ever got plugged, I'd rather it was in the front than the back. Looks better at the funeral, like."

"They won't shoot. At least not until we talk to Stark."

"Should I go tell them boys that, so we're all on the same page?"

"Paul, you're a talking man for sure, but I never did peg you for a worrying man."

Masterson gave the marshal a sidelong glance. "We're following a wagon road right into hell and there's a bunch of hard cases on our back trail. Don't you think I have the right to be worried?"

Crane smiled. "Like my old pa used to say, never joke with sheriffs, range cooks and mules as they have no sense of humor. Of course you have a right to be worried. And so do I."

"Are you worried?"

"Uh-huh. As a steer in a packing plant."

"Thanks. That sure delivers a heap of confidence to a man."

Like many Western men, Crane was an enthusiastic reader of Sir Walter Scott, when any of his novels could be found.

To him, the scattered campfires blazing in the night around the Rafter-T ranch house looked like the encampment of a vast, medieval army, a barbaric display of scarlet, purple and, where the shadows fell thickest and moonlight lingered, fish scale gray.

Drawing rein, the marshal indicated that Masterson should do the same.

He turned in the saddle.

"You boys! Ride on by. We're giving you the road."

There were eight of them, sodbusters astride good horses, but sitting like sacks of corn in their saddles. But these were the men who had wiped out Hollister's punchers and the marshal did not take them lightly.

The riders came on, warily. All carried either rifles or shotguns, their faces pale blurs in the waxing moonlight.

This close to the camp, they seemed content to pass on by, but Crane caused a few to stop as he said, "Tell Stark we'll meet him outside the camp. We don't plan on riding in there."

"You scared, lawman?" a tall, bearded man sneered. He looked like a hayseed, but under the brim of his hat his eyes burned like coals.

"Just careful," Crane said. "You heard what I said. Now tell him."

"The Prophet ain't gonna like it."

A sudden flare of anger in Crane. "I don't give a —" He thought better of what he was about to say, and settled for, "Just tell him."

The tall man shrugged. "Your funeral."

He rode past and for a moment the marshal's heart stopped beating in his chest.

The man had the burlap sack tied to his saddle horn.

CHAPTER 29

Crane and Masterson drew rein about a hundred yards from the Starks' camp.

Already armed men were drifting out from the wagons in ones and twos to form a loose skirmish line.

All this was done in silence. There was no talk.

A full moon climbed higher into the sky and the rising wind set the campfires to dancing. Tall flames undulated wildly and scattered ruby red sparks into the darkness.

Crane turned his head and whispered, "The sodbusters have found the sack."

Masterson gave an exasperated sigh, then said, "Gus, now you tell me? We should be hightailing it out of here right now."

"No, it's the only chance I've got to free Sarah and I have to take it. Maybe I can convince those folks back there that Stark is playing them for fools."

"And if you can't?"

"Then we cut and run and fight another day."

Masterson shook his head. "This isn't going to work. We're playing it all wrong."

"How else can we play it?"

"Like I said, get the hell out of here before it's too late."

"We'll make our try and see what happens," Crane said.

He kneed his horse forward at a walk and stopped again when he was twenty yards from the pickets standing outside the wagons, now grown to sixty or seventy alert riflemen.

Crane stood in the stirrups. "You men," he yelled, "Reuben Stark has lied to you. This is mountain rangeland, an inch of dirt lying on top of ten miles of bedrock. It can't be plowed or farmed. All you'll grow here is rocks, misery and starvation. Surely, you owe more than that to your wives and children."

Seventy silent statues stared back at Crane. There was no sound but the dry crackle of fires and the mystified murmur of the wind.

"Ask Stark about the hundred thousand dollars he's demanding from the town of Rawhide Flat!" the marshal said. "It's not for you. He wants the money for himself.

He plans to run out on you. All of you, man, woman and child, will be left here to face the law and then prison, and, for some of you, the hangman's noose."

Crane's eyes scanned the ranks of stoical riflemen. If there was any reaction to his speech he didn't detect it.

Defeated, he sank into the saddle.

Masterson was beside him. "Good going, Gus. That got them on your side."

"They don't believe me."

"Or they don't want to believe you. They set store by Reuben Stark. They don't want to hear from you or anybody else that he's a false prophet."

The darkness separated, pulled apart like a dusky curtain, and Reuben Stark took center stage, his sons close behind him. He was followed by a large, silent crowd of women and children, their faces like stone.

When he was yards from Crane, the old man stopped and held up the burlap sack for all to see.

"I asked these men for money to help my people, the much beloved sons and daughters of the Archangel Michael."

A chorus of cries of "Hallelujah!" and "Amen!" arose.

Stark's voice became a hoarse shout. "This was their reply!"

He tipped out the contents of the bag Crane had filled with trash, bottles and cans clanging and clattering to the ground.

"Garbage!" Stark screamed. His white beard streamed in the wind. "Yea, verily, in the minds and eyes of the sinners and deceivers we are as garbage in the wind."

A roar of rage went through the crowd and the women began to scream and pelt the lawmen with rocks and the bottles and cans from the sack.

Crane ducked his head and fought the nervous buckskin.

Masterson revealed his hot temper and was lifting his rifle, unwilling to take much more of this treatment.

"Stop!" Stark yelled. Immediately the shower of rocks stopped.

The man turned his head. "Bring forth the whore."

Stark's sons were grinning and Jeptha's eyes were wild, the eyes of a man enjoying the spectacle and eager to kill.

The night had grown darker and an ominous blackness had crept into the camp like a cloaked thief.

Crane smelled rain on the wind, but faint and far-off. To the east the sky thrummed with heat lightning, a blush of red trembling in the clouds like a virgin bride.

A couple of buxom women dragged Sarah to Stark's side. She was wearing the new nightgown Crane had bought for her. It had been an expensive afterthought addition to Minnie Lewis' bill that had further strained his meager purse. But now the garment was stained and there was blood on the shoulder from a deep cut at the corner of Sarah's mouth.

The girl saw the marshal and hope briefly gleamed in her eyes, quickly replaced by an expression of absolute despair. "Gus, leave here," she said. "You can't save me. Nobody can."

Stark grabbed Sarah by the back of her neck and shook her into silence. The girl didn't look scared, just beaten, defeated.

"Crane!" Stark roared. He drew a bowie knife from his belt and shoved the keen edge against Sarah's throat. "I told you if the money was not forthcoming the whore would be skun. And I meant it."

He looked around and tossed the knife to Jeptha. "Here, boy, carve the hide off'n her."

"Sure, Pa," the man said. He touched his tongue to his top lip, then advanced on the girl. His face was shining with reflected firelight, shifting shades of scarlet and blue, his eyes filled with a lustful hunger.

"Stark! Tell us what you want," Crane yelled.

The old man waved his son away. "Hold your hand for now, Jeptha."

Stark looked at the marshal. "What I've always wanted. It's about the money, the money, the money."

"I'll show you where it is," Masterson said. "Now, let the girl go."

"Not that simple, Sheriff," Stark said. "You tried to trick me once and there won't be a second time. You'll take me to the money, but Crane and the girl stay here until I come back. Just to prove your bona fides, like."

"You won't come back, Stark," Crane said, loud enough for all to hear. "You'll take the money and run."

"That's a damned lie and I throw it back in your teeth." A big, gruff-looking man with a beard down to his navel stepped away from the others. "Prophet, to set the mind of the people at ease, I will accompany you. Remember, a faithful man will be richly blessed, but one eager to get rich will not go unpunished."

"Yes, I am eager to get rich, Lucas, but only because I am a mighty river that flows to my people and does not wish to see them live in want."

Stark turned to his followers and made a dramatic gesture, his hands thrown high in the air. He roared, "The money is yours! As the avenging angel of the Lord is my witness!"

Above the approving shouts of the crowd, a woman's scream, high-pitched and edged with hysteria, tore apart the stretched fabric of the night.

"Look at the sky!" she shrieked. "It's a sign!"

Crane glanced upward and his blood froze.

Alone in a cloudless sky, the moon was disappearing.

CHAPTER 30

Because of the drama unfolding around camp, no one had been paying any attention to the sky. Now the eclipse was almost complete and only a sliver of moon remained.

"Yes, it's a sign!" Stark yelled. "It is proven! Verily, the angel has anointed me!"

The crowd was on its knees, staring at the night sky, hands joined in prayer. And the riflemen in front of the wagons, including the belligerent man named Lucas, had loudly joined in the devotions.

As the moon was lost to sight and the darkness grew more profound, the only light came from the glowing domes of red around the campfires. Beyond the flames, the night was as black as spilled ink.

Stark's people kneeled in the gloom, their whispered prayers rising like the drone of a million insects.

Lightning flashed to the east and Stark

jumped around in a frenzy, the tails of his frock coat flapping around his skinny legs.

"I saw him!" he screamed. "The Archangel Michael has entered the clouds!"

Heads moved, looking toward the mountains where the distant clouds blazed with white and vermillion fire.

"Yes! I see him!" a woman screamed. "The angel of the Lord has come to smite the sinful land!"

"I see him too!"

"And me!"

"And me!"

"Michael is come with a sword of flame!"

People began to sing hymns of praise, as they were caught up in the awful majesty of the moment.

Ignored by all but Jeptha Stark, who held on to her arm, the knife still in his hand, Sarah stood with her head bowed, as though oblivious to the turmoil around her.

Masterson turned to Crane, slid his rifle into the boot and drew his revolver. A slight, bemused smile touched his lips.

"You ready, Gus?"

The marshal drew his own Colt. "Call it."

"Now!"

Masterson set spurs to his horse and the big sorrel leaped forward. He closed with

Sarah very quickly, taking Jeptha by surprise.

The man recovered, took a backward step and hurled his knife at Masterson.

Ninety-nine times out of a hundred, Jeptha Stark could not have made that wild throw effective. But fate, luck, whatever you want to call it, sometimes meddles in the affairs of men, and the knife flew true.

Straight as an iron falcon on its prey, the blade buried itself high up in Masterson's chest, close to the shoulder. For a moment the sheriff reeled in the saddle; then his gun hammered in the darkness.

Jeptha went down on one knee, coughing blood, and Masterson shot him again.

He didn't wait to see the effect of his second shot. At the gallop, he scooped Sarah into his arms, threw her into the saddle in front of him, and swung away from the wagons.

As Masterson began his charge, Stark's riflemen had quickly scrambled to their feet, grabbing for their guns.

Crane saw the danger and cut loose with his .45, fanning the gun to lay down a field of fire with no thought of accuracy.

He made no hits, but his spraying bullets were enough to send the men scattering for cover behind the wagons.

The marshal swung his rearing horse away, reaching for his rifle. Out of the corner of his eye he saw Masterson stiffen as a bullet smashed into him.

Then the sheriff was running for his life, Sarah clinging to him.

Crane drew rein and levered his old Henry, but in the gloom saw no targets. Rifles flared from behind the wagons and a close shot split the air an inch from his nose.

There was nothing to be gained and much to lose, notably his life, by making a fight. He galloped after Masterson, bullets chasing after him like enraged wasps.

Crane caught up with Masterson and the sheriff turned in the saddle. "Take the girl."

Without slacking their pace, their mounts running flat-out, Crane grabbed Sarah and held her in front of him. She immediately threw her arms around him and laid her head against his chest. The girl felt thin and frail and she was trembling uncontrollably.

"Easy, easy," the marshal whispered, at a loss for comforting words, "you're safe now."

Sarah didn't answer, but clung so tight to him he could feel the rapid beat of her heart.

Now the marshal turned his attention to

Masterson. He was bent in the saddle and it took a few moments for Crane to see the knife sticking out of his upper chest.

"Paul, can you make it back to Rawhide Flat?" he asked urgently.

Masterson's face was a frozen white mask in the newborn moonlight.

"I'll make it," he said. His voice was weak and his mouth was stretched in a tight line, a man fighting back pain. He managed a weak smile. "I've got a bullet in my back someplace, but I don't know where. Seems like the bowie's demanding my full attention."

"We have to stop," Crane said. "Get that damned blade out of you."

"They'll be right behind us, Gus."

"It's tough to trail men in the dark. I'll hunt us a place to hole up."

Masterson made no answer, as though the effort of speaking was suddenly too much for him.

Crane was a far-seeing man and his gaze probed the shadowed, high plains country ahead.

Beside him, Masterson reined his horse to a walk, swaying in the saddle.

Suddenly the need for shelter became urgent.

Fate had already intervened in Crane's affairs that night and now it did so again.

To his right, a deer burst out from a thicket of brush and stunted juniper and bounded away. The marshal grabbed the bridle of Masterson's horse and retraced the buck's steps.

The trees grew around the mouth of a sandy, dry wash that cut into what seemed to be an ancient lava flow. Both walls were about eight foot high, very steep, and were crowned with scattered clumps of bunch-grass and prickly pear.

Listening into the night, Crane heard no sound of pursuit behind them. He rode deeper into the wash, pulling Masterson's sorrel behind him.

The wash narrowed slightly, then ended at a sheer wall of rock that showed signs of being smoothed by a heavy fall of water in times of torrential rain or snow melts off the high mountain ridges.

A trickle of water, barely enough to wet the surface of the rock, still ran through a patch of green moss that flourished in a shallow gutter at the top of the wall.

The wash was not an ideal place, but for what Crane had to do, it would serve well enough.

He tried to free himself from Sarah, but the girl clung to him, her head against his chest, fingers digging deep into his shoulders.

"Sarah," he said, "you've got to let go. Paul needs our help."

The girl raised her face to his. "Gus, you won't leave me ever again?"

"No, I won't, and that's a promise."

Reluctantly, Sarah moved away from him and Crane set her gently on the ground. He swung out of the saddle and stood at Masterson's left knee, looking up at his shadowed face.

"How do you feel?"

"Worse than I look."

"Then you feel real bad. I'll help you down."

"I can do it."

The sheriff tried to step out of the leather but collapsed into Crane's arms.

"I guess I'm weaker than I thought."

"Easy . . . I'm going to lay you down on your back."

Once Masterson was settled, Crane took a knee beside him and looked at the knife. "The bowie's got to come out of there. Then I'll take a look-see at the wound in your back."

The sheriff tried to smile. "I reckon I'm shot through and through, Gus."

"We'll see."

"Where's Stark?"

"I don't know. I guess, out in the dark somewhere."

"That damned eclipse was a piece of bad luck."

"Oh, I don't know. It helped us get Sarah back."

Now Masterson's smile was genuine, with sunlight in it. "You're always the optimist, Gus."

"I don't believe that, and neither do you." He studied the knife again. The broad blade was buried in Masterson's chest almost to the hilt. "Now I'm taking that bowie out of you."

Sarah kneeled beside the sheriff and cradled his head in her lap. She took off his hat and stroked his thinning hair.

"I know this is gonna hurt," Masterson said.

"Seems likely it will. But a man can stand more than he thinks he can."

"Thanks for the words of wisdom, Gus. I reckon —"

Masterson gasped and arched his back against the pain as Crane pulled the knife free. Immediately the wound began to bleed.

Crane studied the man's face, then lifted his eyes to Sarah. "I think he's passed out."

"No, I didn't pass out," the sheriff

snapped. "And be damned to ye, Gus Crane."

Smiling, Crane said, "Anybody ever tell you that you're a rotten patient?"

He looked at Sarah. "We'll turn him over. I want to take a look at his back."

By nature, Paul Masterson was not a cursing man, but he gave vent loudly and passionately enough to singe all the grass within ten yards when Crane and the girl pulled his upper body upright.

"Unbutton his shirt, Sarah," Crane said.

"Damn it, Gus," Masterson growled, "did nobody ever tell you, 'Don't interfere with something that ain't bothering you none'?"

"All the time." The marshal grinned. "But I've always gone right ahead and interfered anyway."

He pushed up Masterson's shirt . . . and what he saw horrified him.

CHAPTER 31

A heavy caliber bullet, possibly a big .50, had entered Masterson's lower back close — dangerously close — to the spine. The wound looked raw and angry, but there was little blood.

There was no exit wound.

Crane let the man's shirt drop.

"How's it look, Gus?"

Gently, the marshal laid Masterson's head on Sarah's lap again. It was then that the sheriff read the answer to his question in Crane's face.

"That bad, huh?"

"Yeah, it's bad, Paul."

Masterson tried to move. "I can't feel my legs. They're not numb. . . . They're just . . . not there."

"I think maybe the bullet nicked your spine."

"Done broke it, you mean."

"I don't know. I'm not a doctor."

"Dang, I would never have guessed."

Crane rose to his feet. He stepped to the rock wall and stripped a handful of moss from the runnel, then kneeled beside Masterson again.

"This will stop the bleeding from the knife wound," he said.

He placed a moss poultice on the cut and bound it up with his bandanna. There was nothing he could do for the bullet wound.

"I'm going to put you on your horse, Paul," he said. "We've got to get back to Rawhide Flat and take you to Doc Preston."

Suddenly Masterson seemed tired. He made no objection and the eyes Sarah turned to Crane were filled with sympathy and something else that looked like resignation, a small surrender to the inevitability of destiny.

The marshal felt uneasy. The girl claimed horses spoke to her, and now maybe she was hearing another voice, the thin whisper of death skulking close by.

"Let's get him on his horse," Crane said to her. Even to his own ears, his voice sounded hollow.

Freed from the shadow of the jealous earth, the moon was restored to its former glory.

The steep faces of the high rock rims glowed like tarnished silver, but on the flat, the hollows were mysterious places, shrouded in deep blue shadow. Moonlight tangled itself among the branches of juniper and piñon and hung there immobile, like dewy spiderwebs. To the east, the sky still throbbed with heat lightning, as though the Archangel Michael was indeed getting ready to pass judgment on the land.

Masterson drifted in and out of consciousness and talked to dead men. Sarah rode behind the cantle, supporting him in the saddle, her arms around his waist.

Crane's head moved constantly, searching their back trail and the way ahead.

Nothing moved, not even the wind. The country before and behind him was still, vanishing into distance and darkness, populated only by Paul Masterson's dusty ghosts.

Where was Reuben Stark?

It was likely that Paul had killed Jeptha. Was the old man taking time to grieve for him? Or was he saving himself for something else? Perhaps the invasion of Rawhide Flat?

That last possibility seemed more likely to Crane.

Stark would hold the town to ransom and if it didn't pay up, he would attack and loot everything of value he could find. And what could not be moved, he would burn.

Ambition is bondage, and the man who hoped to found a dynasty must know that the last grains of sand were rapidly running through the hourglass. He had but two sons left, the least of them, and he had to act now.

Crane no longer troubled to search the trail.

Stark would come as surely as night follows day and it would be at a time of his own choosing. Today . . . tomorrow . . . soon.

When Crane rode into Rawhide Flat, the moon had dropped below the horizon and the dark of night was shading to a somber blue. The sky was the color of a sour apple. There was no one on the street and the saloons and stores were locked up tight.

In the harshening light, the town looked gray and gaunt, like a tired whore who had just stripped off her makeup and wouldn't paint her face again until nightfall.

Only the mission of the Sisters of the Cross and Passion was lit, shining like a beacon of hope in a dark world.

The marshal rode directly to Doc Preston's office, a squat frame building with the surgery in front, the dwelling at the back.

Masterson was conscious, but his eyes were unfocused and he could not walk.

Sarah went on ahead and pounded on the doctor's door as Crane lifted the sheriff from the saddle and carried him.

"Bring him inside," Preston said, holding the door wide. He wore a long, red and white striped nightshirt that fell to his ankles and a pointed cap with a tassel hung over his shoulder.

Crane had never seen such a sight before.

"Through here into the surgery," Preston said, opening a frosted-glass door to his left. "Lay him on the operating table, Marshal. Gently now."

Crane did as he was told, then said, "He took a knife to the shoulder and he's got a bullet in his back. He says he can't feel his legs. I put moss on the knife wound to stop the bleeding, but I couldn't do anything about the bullet."

"Very wise of you, Marshal." The doctor had already rolled Masterson onto his side, examining the bullet wound.

"The bullet's still in him. Maybe you could probe —"

"That child needs sleep," Preston said. "Look at the dark circles under her eyes. Perhaps you could take her to the hotel."

"She's got a room there, Doc. But about that gunshot wound? I'd say it was made by a Sharps 'Big 50.' Now that's what we call a buffalo gun around these parts and —"

"Please, Marshal." Preston's eyes hardened. "Take the girl to the hotel before she falls asleep on her feet."

"I am very tired, Gus," Sarah said, more in league with the doctor than Crane realized.

"Come back in an hour, Marshal," Preston said. "I'll have completed my diagnosis by then."

"Will he be all right?" Crane asked.

"Marshal, at the moment I have no idea. Come back in an hour."

"Don't you want to know how it happened?"

The physician was already involved with Masterson. "Come back in an hour," he said. "Right now I'm interested in what happened, not in how it happened."

Crane felt Sarah grab his arm. She was trembling again and when he looked at her eyes, they were brimming with tears.

CHAPTER 32

The sight of her hotel room cheered Sarah considerably. She ordered Crane to step out into the hallway and when she called him back inside, the girl had changed out of her nightdress and was sitting up in bed, the sheet pulled up to her neck.

The marshal poured water into the basin from the jug on the dresser and used a clean patch of Sarah's soiled clothing to dab away the blood from the corner of her mouth.

"You're good to me, Gus," she said. "And for such a big huggy-bear of a man you've got very gentle hands."

Crane made no answer and Sarah said, "What's going to happen to me?"

Now he made eye contact with the girl. "I've been studying on that. I reckon when this is over I'll take you with me to Virginia City, or Carson City, wherever the United States marshal is hanging his hat."

"He's your boss?"

"Yeah. He ramrods the whole outfit."

"Gus, what will I do in the city where the marshal is hanging his hat?"

Crane smiled. "Go to school, I reckon. Learn how to read and cipher."

"I've already learned that."

"There's still a lot of stuff you don't know."

"Will you marry me in Virginia City, Gus?"

The marshal laughed. "No, you're far too young for that and for me."

"Then will you adopt me?"

Crane rose to his feet, the basin with its pink-stained water in his hands. "Sarah, you ask too many questions."

He placed the basin on the dresser. "I'll empty that later," he said.

"Reuben Stark wants to marry me in the worst way."

"I know. Did he . . . harm you?"

The girl shook her head. "No, but he told me he plans to keep me as a breeder. He wants many sons and he said I'm young enough to have a dozen litters before I'm worn out."

Sarah's words hit Crane like a punch in the gut. He tried not to let it show but failed because suddenly the girl looked frightened. "Will he come for me, Gus?"

"He might try. If he does, I'll kill him."

"He hates you. He told me that."

"I guess you could say the feeling is mutual."

Crane stepped to the girl's bedside. "Now, you close your eyes and get some sleep. I've got to ask that uppity doctor about Masterson. The man just won't listen to advice."

Sarah's eyes misted. "Paul will die," she said. "But not in his bed — he won't let that happen."

"How do you know this?"

"I see it in my mind. It's very clear, like a picture in a book."

"I won't let him die, Sarah. He's an irritating man and I'm looking forward to the pleasure of gunning him myself."

"That's not true, Gus. You like him a lot."

"Is that another picture in your book?"

"No, I can see it in your eyes. You're worried about him."

"You go to sleep."

"Gus, you'll stay close?"

A small joy in him at Sarah's trust, Crane said, "You bet I'll stay close."

As Crane walked along the boardwalk toward the doctor's office a scarlet sky rode point for the oncoming day.

Now the storekeepers were astir and one

of them, his glasses as far down his nose as possible, watched him draw near, his eyes full of speculation.

The marshal stopped and spoke to the man. "Tell the mayor to arrange a town meeting for eight o'clock. And I want every able-bodied man who can shoot a rifle to be there."

"That's early, ain't it?"

"It might be too late."

"I'll tell Mayor Reddy, but he won't like it."

"Tell him that Ben Hollister was right and that Reuben Stark is coming. Mayor Reddy either comes up with fifty thousand dollars or loses his town. The chances are he'll see it burn anyway."

This time the storekeeper made no objections. He hurried away, his face troubled.

Doc Preston must have seen Crane coming, because the door to his office opened immediately when the marshal arrived.

"Get inside," the physician said abruptly.

He led Crane past the surgery and into a small parlor at the end of a hallway.

"Take a seat," he said, ushering the marshal onto an overstuffed tapestry sofa. "Can I get you coffee?"

"I could use some."

Preston rang the small brass bell that sat on a table next to his chair. A pleasant-looking, middle-aged woman appeared at the door.

"Martha, coffee for two please."

"Yes, Doctor."

After the woman left, Crane showed Preston the makings. "Mind if I smoke?"

"Please do. I'm told by colleagues in Texas, where cowboys and Mexican vaqueros are much given to the habit, that tobacco is very good for congestion of the lungs and ailments of the throat."

Crane took time to build a smoke, putting off the time he had to ask the question. He lit the cigarette, inhaled deeply, then asked it. "How is he, Doc?"

Crane's heart beat once, twice, three times. Then Preston said, "He's dying, Marshal."

The middle-aged woman bustled inside and handed Crane and the physician a cup and saucer. She filled the cups from a flowered coffeepot, which she then set beside Preston.

"Will there be anything else, Doctor?"

"No, nothing, Martha. Thank you."

The woman walked out and Crane said, "Paul Masterson is a tough man, Doctor. He's mighty hard to kill."

"He is indeed. If he weren't, he'd be dead already. In time, he could recover from the knife wound, but a bullet is still inside him and it's deep. I don't have the skill to go digging for it, and even if I did, the surgery would surely kill him."

The coffee steaming forgotten in his cup, the marshal drew deep on his cigarette and said, "Doc, there has to be a way."

"There is no way." Preston looked tired, as though all the life had been drained from him. "The bullet smashed the sheriff's spinal column, then ranged upward. His legs are paralyzed, both lungs are damaged and I believe he has suffered a heart injury."

The doctor sipped his coffee with all the apparent enjoyment of a condemned man eating his last meal. "Marshal Crane, your friend has only hours to live."

Crane absorbed the blow, but, like that of a punch-drunk pugilist, his head reeled. Without being fully aware of what he was doing, he stubbed out his cigarette in his saucer, drank coffee, then began to build another smoke.

Finally, his hands still, he said, "Sarah saw it. She saw it all."

"Saw what, Marshal?"

"She saw Paul's death, like a picture in her mind. But she said he wouldn't die in his own bed, that he wouldn't let that happen."

"He won't die in his own bed, Marshal. He'll die in my surgery. I don't want him moved."

"Can I see him?"

Preston rose. "Of course."

Crane shoved his half-built cigarette into his pocket and he too got to his feet.

The physician led the way down the hallway, opened the surgery door and stepped aside. "I'll leave you alone with him. All I can do for him now is to ease his pain if it gets bad."

His heart thumping in his chest, Crane stepped into the surgery.

CHAPTER 33

Masterson was lying on a steel cot, covered by a spotless white sheet and a gray blanket.

He was completely still and for a moment Crane thought he was asleep or dead.

"Come in, Gus. I'd recognize the thump of those big feet anywhere."

The marshal stepped to Masterson's bedside. Like everyone who visits the sick, he frantically ransacked his mind for something uplifting to say.

"Relax, Gus. I know I'm dying," the sheriff said, solving Crane's dilemma. "I asked the doc to give it to me straight and he surely did."

"I'm sorry, Paul." It sounded inadequate, but it was all the marshal had.

"Is the town getting ready for Stark?"

"I've had the mayor call a meeting for eight in the Texas Belle."

"That's late, Gus. It's already daylight. Stark could attack at any time."

Masterson's face was ashen, and blue shadows were gathering under his eyes and in the hollows of his cheeks. His voice was a pained, wafer-thin whisper.

"Get scouts out, Gus," he said. "The town will need a warning."

"I'll do that."

"How many fighting men can we muster?"

"I don't know." Crane shrugged. "Maybe a couple dozen, or less than that. I really have no idea."

"Well, we're starting with two good men. You and me."

"Paul, you're not going anywhere. Doc Preston wants you to rest."

"Yeah, he wants me to rest in peace. Gus, I'm not going to die in bed, looking down at the holes in my socks and wondering how in hell I ended up like this. I want to go out in a moment of hell-firing glory with Reuben Stark in my sights."

Crane had no decorated words that would change Masterson's mind.

Tense, his mouth dry, he knew that in the sheriff's place he would have said the same thing.

Now he uttered an admission of defeat in a voice that flattened every word. "What do you want me to do, Paul?"

"Help me into my boots, bring my gun

301

belt from the chair over there by the window and we'll head for the Texas Belle."

"How you plan on getting there?"

"You're gonna carry me, Gus. Now, help me sit up and get me my hat. My head feels nekkid."

Crane manhandled the sheriff to a sitting position and Masterson looked at him with fevered eyes. "Before we start out, Gus, I got something to tell you."

"About the money?"

"Yeah, about the money. It's at the mission. I told the nuns that some mighty bad men might be searching for it and they should keep it until I asked for it back."

Masterson's lips were white as life took its own sweet time to drain from him. He managed a smile.

"It wasn't too difficult to convince the sisters. I told them they could keep a thousand dollars to expand the school and put a new roof on the building. Even nuns aren't above a little larceny when it's used for God's work."

"All that searching . . . but nobody thought to look in the mission."

"I know. Why do you think I left it there?"

Now Crane understood why a nun had visited Masterson late at night. She was probably reassuring him that the money was still safe.

"Would you have kept half of it, like you said?" he asked.

"Hell yeah, maybe all of it less the thousand."

The sheriff was holding on to his life by a sheer effort of will. Crane wondered how long it would take before he gave up and descended into darkness.

"Gus, I'm an outlaw who happens to be temporarily wearing a lawman's star. I can no more change my ways than you could turn in your badge and start selling women's corsets."

Crane made no answer and Masterson said, "If any of us are still alive after this is over, get the money from the nuns and give it back to the bank. Don't forget the thousand for the roof."

The marshal nodded. Then he said, "I don't think you would have kept the money."

"Now you'll never know, will you?"

"I guess I won't."

"Then let's get out of here. This place is enough to clabber a man's blood."

Augustus Crane was a big man and it took little effort to lift Masterson and carry him to the door.

Dr. Preston was waiting for them.

He made no comment but opened the door wide and let Crane pass with his burden.

"Doc, I —," the marshal began, pausing in the doorway.

"It's all right," Preston said. "I understand."

A disciple of science though he was, the physician was a Westerner and he accepted all that implied, the unwritten code that required a man to ask no more and give no less than courage, honesty, loyalty, generosity and fairness, courage uppermost.

He understood Masterson's decision, respected it, and would not demean the man's grit by standing in his way.

"Good luck," he said. "Good luck to both of you."

Procrastination is a thief of time and just another way of concealing cowardice.

Crane's opinion of the citizens of Rawhide Flat was low, and procrastination was what he expected . . . talk, delay, whispers of surrender, flight.

In that, he was wrong.

It was not yet eight, but a large number of men were already piling into the Texas Belle. Behind Crane the mission school bell was ringing and children were walking inside, but there were no half-grown boys among them.

Masterson tense and alert in his arms, the marshal's boot heels thudded along the weathered boards of the walk as he headed toward the saloon.

But stunned, he stopped in his tracks as a magnificent vision in gray stepped out of the Texas Belle.

Mayor Ed Reddy wore the uniform of a Confederate brigadier general, the French blue of the infantry at his collars and cuffs, gold braid on his sleeves. A plumed hat sat rakishly on his head and a sword was buckled around his waist.

The uniform had transformed the little, unprepossessing man into a figure of considerable authority and poise.

"No time for a meeting, Marshal," he snapped. His eyes dropped to Masterson, but he made no comment. "I've already given my orders and the boys know what to do. I have pickets out to the north, all of them good, steady men."

As if to underscore his point, a gangling teenager stepped beside Reddy and touched his forehead. "Gen'l, my pa's compliments, an' he says do you want us to start on the barricades now?"

"Yes, son, right away. Tell him to take ten men and get to work. I want works on both sides of the sheriff's office. Tell him to close off the entire street. Use barrels, hay bales, wagons, whatever he can find that will stop a bullet."

"How 'bout bob wire, Gen'l?"

"Can't hurt, son, and it might help if you can find any."

Reddy turned back to Crane. When he realized the extent of Masterson's wounds, some of the ramrod stiffness went out of his back. "What happened?"

"Reuben Stark's men," Crane said, feeling no further explanation was needed.

"Bring him inside," Reddy said.

"No," the sheriff said. "Get a chair out here. I want to be where the fight is."

Reddy stepped to the door of the saloon. "One of you men bring a chair out here."

A Southern voice from inside said, "It's a-comin', General."

The chair was set on the walk and Crane gently eased Masterson into it. He straightened and said to Reddy, "How many do we have?"

The mayor waited until the men spilling out of the saloon ran past him. Then he said, "Including you, Sheriff Masterson and me, forty-three men and boys. That includes storekeepers, bank clerks, butchers, bakers and candlestick makers. We also got a couple of Ben Hollister's wounded cowboys, some dance hall loungers and three gamblers. The light-fingered gentry ain't up yet, but they're all good with a gun and they'll be here when we need 'em."

"Ed, will your men stand?" This came from Masterson.

"They'll stand. About half of them boys fought in the War Between the States, on both sides." Reddy nodded his reassurance. "They'll stand and steady the rest."

The little mayor drew himself up to his full five foot six and directed his remarks to both lawmen. "Not a penny for tribute, Marshal. We've talked and all have agreed to make our fight on this ground."

Crane made no answer.

He didn't know how many men Stark had lost in Sullivan Canyon, but if there were any grieving widows at the old man's camp, he didn't remember seeing any.

Stark must still have well over 250 riflemen.

The odds were not in Rawhide Flat's favor.

CHAPTER 34

The morning passed and grew into a hot, oppressive afternoon that smelled of dust and man-sweat.

Ed Reddy, his face flushed above the collar of his splendid uniform, had finally deployed his men to his satisfaction. Three pickets were out, twenty men and boys manned the barricade at the end of the street and another ten horsemen had been sent on a wide flanking movement to the east and north.

It was the general's intention that after the fight began, those riders would hit the enemy from the rear and sow confusion and death among their ranks.

Except for the gamblers, the remaining men were at the barricades as a reserve should the attack come from a different direction, as Crane suspected it would.

He doubted that a man as savvy as Stark would recklessly charge down the street into rifle fire. His men would probably hit the town from the four points of the compass and try to overwhelm the defenders by sheer weight of numbers.

Rawhide Flat was a city without walls, but right now it needed ramparts, bulwarks, towers and a mighty big citadel. And maybe a better brigadier general in charge.

Crane stood beside Masterson outside the Texas Belle. The gamblers, pale, taciturn men with cold, calculating eyes, were inside, determined not to expose their sensitive skins to the sunlight until the fight started.

Masterson was weakening. He had refused the doctor's offer of laudanum but was easing his pain with a bottle of whiskey.

"Gus, where is Stark? My clock is running down fast."

"I don't know. The pickets just reported that they've seen no sign of him."

"We can't beat him here in town."

Crane smiled. "I know, but I don't think we can beat him anywhere, so making a stand on this ground is as good as any."

"You scared to die, Gus?"

"Yeah."

"You thinking about it?"

"Some."

"I'm thinking about it. I don't know what happens . . . afterward."

"I don't either. Nobody does. Maybe you go back to being what you were before you were born."

"What was that?"

"I don't know."

"You're a real helpful man, Gus."

"I surely try."

"Gus?"

"Yeah?"

"Don't bury me here in Rawhide Flat." Masterson's eyes scanned the sky as though he were seeing it for the first time. "Take me into the mountains, huh? I want to sleep under the pines and hear the wind."

"Well, that's a dang chore an' no mistake."

"Will you do it? Take me to the mountains?"

Crane looked down at the dying man, a bleak kind of sadness tugging at him.

"I guess you figure on being an irritating man right to the end."

"Will you do as I ask?"

The marshal nodded. "Yes, Paul. If I'm still alive I'll take you to the high rim country."

"You'll still be alive, Gus. You're too all-fired mean and ornery to die." He smiled weakly. "You made a promise, Gus, and I'll hold you to it. If you renege, I'll come back and haunt you."

Crane said nothing.

The oppressive day was pushing down in on him and he squinted against the hard, bladed sunlight that lanced into his eyes.

Rawhide Flat was silent, drowsing in the heat; yet the town seemed strangely off-kilter, tense, as though at any second it would wake up, screaming, from a nightmare.

Ben Hollister's closing of the railroad was now only a memory and a train clanked into the station, followed by a screech of brakes and a loud snake-hiss as the locomotive jetted steam from between its wheels.

The crew and passengers, if there were any, should be warned that they'd just entered a battlefield. Crane could neither muster the energy nor the will. Maybe by-and-by.

But it seemed others would do it for him.

Five men Crane didn't know had left the barricades and were walking quickly toward the station, dropping their rifles in the dust.

Reddy ran after them. "You men, get back to your posts!" he yelled.

One of them called out over his shoulder, "You go to hell, General. We ain't waiting to be massacred like what happened to Ben Hollister's punchers."

His face blazing with fury, Reddy drew a

cap and ball Navy Colt and fired into the air.

The five men broke into a run.

Reddy watched them go. The revolver dropped to his side, his shoulders slumped in defeat and his head bowed. In his Confederate gray, he looked like he probably had when he stood outside Wilmer McLean's house at Appomattox and watched Robert E. Lee come down the steps after his surrender.

Crane moved to the edge of the boardwalk. "They wouldn't have stood anyway, General," he said. "Good riddance to them."

Reddy turned to the marshal. "Now we don't have near enough men, do we?"

"We didn't have near enough to begin with."

The mayor looked up at the sun-bleached sky as though seeking a solution to his problems there. Apparently he didn't find one because he trudged dejectedly back to the barricade.

Brigadier General Reddy had suffered one crushing defeat before and it seemed likely that he was anticipating another.

It did not bode well.

Crane returned to Masterson's side and looked down at him. "The rats are deserting the sinking ship," he said.

The sheriff nodded. "The no-accounts are always the first to quit."

The man had been marked for death and it was branded on his face. His skin was tight to the bone, eyes burning with blue fire, and the shadows in his cheeks had grown darker.

Masterson was struggling to breathe, chest rising and falling in pained shudders as his open mouth grasped at the thick air.

A man with the bark on him, he was dying hard, struggling every step of the way. But this was one battle he was fated to lose.

"How you feeling?" Crane asked.

Masterson's eyes lifted to the marshal, but he obviously did not think his question was worth an answer. Now he asked one of his own that he knew could have no constructive reply either.

"Where the hell is Stark?"

"Out there, someplace. Who knows?"

"Go find him, Gus. You've got no call to stay here and nurse me."

Crane smiled. "And if I find him, then what?"

"Stir up the hornet's nest, throw him off balance. Up until now he's pretty much had things all his own way. It's time we took the fight to him."

"It's a thought, I guess."

Masterson took a swig of whiskey, then wiped off his mustache with the back of his hand. "Gus, Sarah's life and this town's existence are on the line. You don't have the luxury of wallowing in depression, nor the time."

A quick anger flared in Crane, but he immediately let it go. Calmly he said, "I'm open to suggestions, Paul. Or do you want me to go it alone?"

Masterson jerked a thumb over his shoulder. "Roust out them idle gamblers. At one time or another each of them has killed his man. They're good with guns and they've got fast horses."

"Fast horses go with the profession," Crane said. He thought aloud. "I could round up the pickets. That would be seven men, including myself."

"Seven men won't scare Stark, but it might be enough to at least inconvenience him."

By an effort of will Crane freed himself from the seductive embrace of the dark succubus that had been wooing him for hours. He said, "I'll talk to the gamblers." He hesitated, looking at Masterson.

Anticipating what the big man was about to say, the sheriff said, "I'll be all right."

Then, as Crane turned away, he added, "Gus, be careful what you say in there. By times those boys can be touchy."

The marshal nodded and stepped into the saloon.

Three men sprawled at a table, glasses at their elbows, a bottle standing between them. The gamblers were unenthusiastically playing poker, no chips or money on the table. It was a friendly, if unexciting, game between professionals. The real thing was reserved for the suckers and rubes.

"Howdy, boys," Crane said, remembering Masterson's warning.

The men looked up at him but said nothing. One of them, a lean, cadaverous man, reached inside his frock coat and conspicuously adjusted the hang of his shoulder holster.

"I need three volunteers," the marshal said. He was smiling, trying to appear friendly and at ease.

The lean man said, "You're Augustus Crane, ain't you? Made quite a stir in Texas a few years back."

"And other places," Crane replied. "You must be new in town."

The man shrugged. "No, but I sleep a lot." He studied his cards, then lifted his eyes to

315

the marshal again. "What's the job?"

"Go after Reuben Stark. Shake him up some."

A younger man wearing a gray frock coat with a velvet collar frowned and said, "The old man sets himself up as a preacher. I hate preachers." His cold eyes moved to Crane's face. "I hear Stark has two, three hundred men backing him."

The marshal nodded. "Uh-huh, and chances are you'll be seeing all of them real soon."

"You want to slow him down, huh?"

"Yeah, and make him realize that taking Rawhide Flat isn't going to be as easy as he thinks it is."

The cadaverous man threw down his cards. "Hell, anything's better than sitting here in an empty saloon. Even the bartender's out there at the barricade with a six-gun he don't know how to use."

He rose to his feet and stuck out his hand. "Name's Clinton Thorp. The feller in the fancy coat is Jack Palmer and the one over there who doesn't talk much is Silent Sam Chase."

After Crane shook hands with them, the other gamblers rose.

"I guess we'll ride along," Palmer said. "Give us something to do."

Silent Sam lived up to his name and said nothing.

Fifteen minutes later the four men left Rawhide Flat and swung north.

CHAPTER 35

The sun was dropping lower in the sky, but as yet the coming of evening was just a vague promise and the heat remained a scalding liquid that pooled around the four riders and their horses.

Crane had seen no sign of Reddy's pickets, nor of the ten flankers that were supposed to surprise Stark's hordes from the rear.

Maybe all of them had run away and were hiding out in the hills.

A carrion stench rose from Sullivan Canyon as the marshal and the others passed and now they slowed their pace, guessing that Stark must be close.

Only Crane carried a rifle, the old Henry in the boot under his knee. The others carried short-barreled Colts in shoulder rigs, adequate for close work but not for a long-range fight.

The marshal had only the merest fragment, fraction, morsel of a plan, and now, with the effectiveness of his artillery in doubt, he sought to modify it.

He did not succeed. The plan, such as it was, broke apart in his mind and crumbled into dust.

So much for sniper fire.

"Smoke ahead."

Silent Sam had broken his vow of silence.

"Where away?" Thorp asked, his use of the nautical term suggesting a youth spent on board a ship.

"Straight ahead," Sam said. He clamped his mouth shut like a man who'd just decided that his talking was done.

"I see it," Crane said. "It's coming from the Rafter-T."

"Cookhouse, maybe," somebody suggested.

"No, it's from a heap of campfires. Damn it, Stark hasn't moved."

Clinton Thorp sat his dun like a sailor, looking lumpy and uncomfortable in the saddle. "What's he waiting for?" he asked.

"Beats me," Crane answered.

"More men?" Thorp said.

"I doubt it. He knows he's got more than enough already."

The marshal shook his head. "What is Stark up to?" None of the gamblers attempted to answer that question.

But then Jack Palmer, young, sharp-eyed and intelligent, said, "He's waiting for something. An item he thinks he needs."

Crane was willing to clutch at straws, at any suggestion. "What might that item be?"

"I don't know," Palmer said. "But I'm willing to bet it's being delivered to him and he doesn't have it yet."

"By wagon? Pack mule? A man on a horse?" Crane asked.

Palmer smiled. "Marshal, I don't have a crystal ball. If I did, I'd be at the gaming tables in Denver, not Rawhide Flat."

The marshal watched a hawk fold its wings and dive on something skulking in the long grass. Then a shriek. It was a small death that would have gone unnoticed had he not been there.

"Whatever Stark thinks he needs will come from the north," Crane said after some thought. "Probably out of Carson City or Virginia City."

"Whores?" Silent Sam suggested.

Crane shook his head. "Stark has set himself up as a holy man. Holy men don't import whores."

"There's Gardnerville to the south," Palmer said. "It's a fair-sized town."

"Sodbuster town," Thorp said. "Nothing

there, unless Stark's bringing in food supplies."

Crane thought that unlikely, but he was not willing to take a chance.

"Palmer, you and Sam stay here and keep a watch to the south. Thorp, you come with me. We'll swing wide of the ranch and scout to the north." He looked around at the sallow, hard-faced men. "Unless one of you has a better idea?"

"You called it, Marshal," Palmer said.

"Then let's get it done."

Crane and Thorp headed east for an hour, then swung north, riding parallel to El Dorado Canyon, the limit of Ben Hollister's range. Carson City was now almost due west of them and that meant they had miles of country to cover.

Unless luck was on their side, it might well prove to be an impossible task.

The heat of the day still hung heavy on the broken land, but the afternoon light was fading and shadows were slanting longer under the high ridges. Unused to riding, Thorp looked tired and irritable. "This is impossible, Crane," he said. "Hell, it's like trying to sweep sunshine off Ma's front porch."

The marshal readily agreed. "It's a heap

of ground to cover for two men."

"Heap of ground to cover for a cavalry regiment. Up here the Piute rode rings around the Army for years because it couldn't find them in these hills."

"We have to try," Crane said. "Whatever Stark is waiting for must be all-fired important. If we get to it first maybe we can upset his plans."

"You really believe that?"

"Not entirely. But I'm holding on to it because it's all I got."

"Then what's your call?"

Aware of Thorp's pained expression as he shifted in the saddle, the marshal said, "I'll scout to the west and you stay here and keep watch. If a rider or a wagon or whatever shows up, hold it here. I'll be back."

"Suits me," Thorp said. He swung out of the saddle, then rubbed his rump. He looked like a very uncomfortable man.

Crane reached behind him and took his field glasses from his saddlebags. "These will help."

Thorp nodded and took the glasses. "Ride careful," he said. Then, with a smile that reminded Crane of Paul Masterson's wide grin, he said, "A tall man on a tall hoss can be seen for miles, and you ain't exactly anybody's idea of Dan'l Boone."

"I'll keep that in mind," the marshal said, annoyed.

When Crane estimated he was about six miles east of Carson City, he rode along the broad, rocky spine of an arroyo that rose steadily upward in a gentle incline.

The slope was covered thickly with juniper, piñon, and, unusual at this elevation, a few cedar. Bunchgrass grew among the trees and clumps of sagebrush.

The wall of the arroyo topped out at about fifty feet above the flat, then leveled off for a hundred yards before beginning a sharp descent.

Crane rode to the end of the level area of the spine and dismounted. From here he could see for several miles in all directions, but the day was hazing a darker blue and when night came it would rob him of his eyesight.

He had two hours, maybe less, to accomplish what he'd come here to do. He looked around, his eyes reaching far, but the empty, still land mocked him with its breathless silence.

Crane led the buckskin into the trees and let the animal graze on the sparse bunchgrass. He squatted on his heels and built a smoke.

To the west, the wild country still brooded and held its counsel.

Night fell, drifting downward from the dusky sky like black soot. The wind picked up and a desert cold chilled Crane to the bone.

But, contrary to its secretive nature, the darkness extended the marshal a helping hand.

Anyone who has traversed a lonely land knows that a light of any kind can be seen for miles, unless it's cleverly hidden by canny men.

But the men who had built the campfire that glittered like a red star in the distance had made no attempt to conceal it. Why should they? The Indians were all dead or in captivity, and though this was outlaw country, getting fat and sassy from the easy pickings of the Comstock, few were night riders.

Crane allowed himself a wry smile. Thorp and Masterson before him had been right — he was no Dan'l Boone.

Some deputy marshals, a different breed, were chosen for their tracking skills and woodsmanship. Others, like him, because they were what they were, were named gunfighters who would brace a man straight up, take their hits and keep on a-comin'.

He grudgingly accepted the distinction, but now it did not help him calculate how far away the campfire was. A mile, two miles, halfway to the end of the earth? He had no idea.

He rose to his feet. There was only one way to find out.

CHAPTER 36

Crane led his horse down the spine of the arroyo to the flat.

The moon was out, but from where he stood he could not see the campfire. He swung into the saddle, trusting the sure-footed buckskin to find its way through the pressing darkness.

When the marshal topped a rise, the campfire came in sight. When he dropped down to a hollow or wash, it disappeared again. But, like the three Wise Men of old, he kept following his glittering star.

The camp was much closer than he expected, so close that he almost rode right into it.

Crane crossed a creek with a high bank, a broken-down section next to a wide dog-wood tree visible in the moonlight. Ducking his head, he rode under the lower branches of the dogwood, and when he raised it again the camp was in sight.

Immediately drawing rein, he sat his saddle and studied the layout.

A man sat at the fire, his back to the marshal. Off to the right, half-hidden among trees, a light freight wagon was parked, its tongue raised. Nearby was a tethered team of four rangy mules.

After a few moments, Crane rode closer, then stopped again. The delicious odors of frying bacon and simmering coffee assailed his nose.

"Hello the camp!"

The man at the fire immediately sprang to his feet. He turned, then faced into the darkness, silhouetted by the fire.

The marshal pegged the man for a pilgrim to expose himself that way, but there was nothing of the rube about his harsh, shouted challenge.

"What the hell do you want?"

"Smelled your coffee," Crane said.

"Then ride on. I have only enough for myself." He hesitated a moment, then added, "I don't plan on feeding every saddle tramp who rides up to my camp."

"Unfriendly sort of cuss, ain't you?" Crane grinned.

"Ride on, or I swear I'll take my whip to you."

"I don't advise that."

Something in the tone of the marshal's voice gave the man pause. But he decided to bluff it out. "I said ride on, and be damned to ye."

Crane kneed his horse closer.

The man by the fire inched his hand closer to the gun in a cross-draw holster buckled to his waist.

"I told you, I don't advise that."

Swinging out of the saddle, Crane advanced on the man. Even in the uncertain light, he saw the mule skinner tense, getting ready to make a play.

Crane's Colt came up smooth and fast.

"Drop the gun belt and kick it over here," he said. Crane heard the sizzle of bacon in the pan and the soft crackle of the fire.

The man looked startled. Then he said, "You're a lawman."

"Deputy United States Marshal Augustus Crane. I can't say I'm pleased to make your acquaintance." His voice hardened. "Now, do as I say and unbuckle the gun belt or I'll drop you right where you stand."

"But lawmen don't do that to innocent folks."

"This one does."

Hastily, the man unbuckled the belt and let it fall around his ankles.

"Now kick it over here."

He did as he was told.

"Take that damned bacon off the fire," Crane snapped, shoving the mule skinner's gun into his waistband. "That's my supper you're burning."

Again the man, obviously frightened, was quick to comply. When he straightened up after shoving the fry pan aside, the marshal said, "I've given you my handle, now what's yours?"

"Nathan," the man gulped, "Nathan Tull."

"Where are you bound, Nathan?"

Tull managed to look scared and sly at the same time. "Carson City."

"You're a liar. You're coming from Carson City, headed for the Rafter-T Ranch and a man by the name of Reuben Stark."

Robbed of his chance to play coy, Nathan settled for surliness. "Then if you know, why the hell did you ask me?"

"Just trying to see if you were honest." Crane shook his head. "You're not."

He smiled. "Now, give me my supper like a hospitable gent, and later we'll stroll over there together and see what's in the wagon."

"I don't know what's inside the wagon and I'm not lying to you, Marshal. A couple of men gave me twenty dollars to drive it to the Rafter-T Ranch, said to deliver the goods to a man named Stark. The back of the wagon was covered by a canvas and I didn't see what's inside."

Crane held out his plate and as Tull filled it with bacon and sourdough flapjacks, he asked, "You didn't look?"

Tull, a shifty-eyed little rodent with a thin, pockmarked face, shrugged. "I didn't figure it was any of my business."

"Wagon could be full of silver," Crane said.

The little man looked like an angler who has just seen the lord of the lake break his line and swim into the reeds. But after a few moments his face cleared.

"Nah, them hard cases in Carson City wouldn't have trusted me with a wagonload of silver."

"Probably not. I wouldn't trust you with anything, Nathan."

The marshal scraped his plate clean, then rose to his feet. "Let's go take a look-see."

Pushing Tull ahead of him, Crane undid the rope ties. "Now, haul the canvas back and let's see what you were asked to deliver."

The contents of the wagon came as a shock to the marshal, and Tull looked genuinely startled.

"Gunpowder in barrels," the little man said. "But what the hell's that thing?"

"It's a Gatling gun," Crane said, "mounted on a light cavalry carriage. I saw one at an army barracks down Texas way a few years back, but it wasn't near as fancy as this. An officer shot it off for some visiting folks from Washington and it made some big bangs that went on for quite a spell."

Beside the Gatling, a wooden box was packed with long rectangles of metal wrapped in wax paper. On the lid, stenciled in black paint, were the words:

50 × 40-ROUND STEEL MAGAZINES —
CALIBER .45

Tull was staring openmouthed at the Gatling. "Who needs a big gun like that?"

"Reuben Stark does."

Tull was perplexed. "What's he plannin' to shoot with that? An elephant?"

Running his hand over the bronze housing that enclosed the gun's ten .45 caliber barrels and breech, he said, "This has got to be a new model." He shook his head. "I was told a man can buy anything in the Comstock if he's got the money to pay for it. Maybe I didn't quite believe it then, but I do now."

"Where did them hard cases in Carson City get a big gun like that?" Tull asked.

"I don't know. Could be they stole it, or bought it in Mexico. The Diaz government always needs money."

"You didn't tell me, Marshal. Who's this Reuben Stark feller gonna shoot?"

"Maybe nobody, maybe just a few. Nathan, my questioning friend, this gun is designed to intimidate and terrify. Reuben Stark is holding a town to ransom, and with this he would've had no need to fight a pitched battle. A little demonstration of what a Gatling can do and the good citizens of Rawhide Flat would've anted up the money he's demanding real fast."

"How much money?"

"A hundred thousand dollars."

Tull whistled between his teeth. "With all that dough at stake, no wonder them boys could pay me twenty dollars just to drive a wagon."

Crane smiled. "But it works out that when Stark bought the gun, all he did was to sow the seeds of his own destruction."

"What does that mean, Marshal?"

"It means, Mr. Tull, that I've got him by the cojones."

CHAPTER 37

"Hitch up your team, Nathan," Crane said. "We're moving out."

The little man looked horrified. "But . . . it's dark."

"Scared of the dark?"

"Driving a wagon full of gunpowder across rough country at night, you bet I am."

Crane nodded. "Yes, I understand your point of view. That's why I'm giving you a choice: drive the wagon or I'll blow your brains out."

"What kind of choice is that?"

"My kind."

Cursing and grumbling under his breath, Tull began to hitch the mule team.

Drinking the last of the coffee directly from the pot, Crane watched him. When the team was in the traces he doused the fire and tossed the coffeepot and pan into the back of the wagon.

He swung into the saddle and rode beside Tull, who was already up on the driver's seat. "Move out," he said.

"Marshal, if we're both blown to kingdom come, don't blame me," the little man said.

"I won't. And later we'll have a real good laugh about it in hell."

Tull let rip with a string of words under his breath that Crane couldn't hear, but that probably questioned the legitimacy of his birth.

They traveled south under a luminous moon that shone a lamp above the way ahead, but shrouded the hidden hazards in shadow. Twice the wagon hit rocks that threatened to topple the rig onto its side, and once Tull got bogged down in a muddy seep caused by one of the numerous underground streams that flowed through limestone beneath the high ridges, only to immediately surrender their water to the thirsty ground.

It took Crane, slowed by the wagon, three hours to reach the spot where he believed he'd left Clinton Thorp.

He stood in the stirrups and called out the gambler's name. A few minutes passed and the marshal tried again.

This time the shadows parted and a man stepped into the moonlight, leading a horse.

"Right here," he said. Only then did he slide his Colt into his shoulder holster.

Thorp was framed in moonlight and Crane saw his head move. "That's what Stark was waiting for, the wagon?"

"Yeah. Gunpowder and a big gun, .45 caliber Gatling on a wheeled carriage."

"Heard about them repeater guns. With that, he could've chopped up Rawhide Flat and everybody in it."

"I'd say that was his idea. Some insurance, you could say. 'Pay up, or I start shooting.' "

"He doesn't know we have it," Thorp said.

"No, he doesn't. The only one who could have told him is Mr. Nathan Tull here. But, as you can see, I brought him along."

"The Gatling will even up the odds considerable."

"It will, if Stark and his men oblige us by charging straight at it."

"How do we do that, Marshal?"

"I've got an idea. It might work, but it's mighty thin."

"You mind telling me?"

Crane did. Then Thorp stood silent for a while. Finally, without a trace of enthusiasm in his voice, he said, "It's your call, Marshal." Then he shook his head, smiled faintly and said, "God help us all."

Crane picked up Jack Palmer and Silent Sam; dawn was breaking as he led his little party back into Rawhide Flat.

A quick glance around told him the barricade at the end of the street was still manned, though there was no sign of Mayor Reddy. Paul Masterson still sat on a chair outside the Texas Belle, and someone had covered him with a blanket.

The gamblers left to put up their horses, and Crane told Tull to park the wagon outside the saloon.

He swung out of the saddle and stepped up onto the boardwalk. Masterson's head was bowed and for a moment the marshal thought he had died.

But as soon as Crane's boots thudded noisily on the boards, the sheriff lifted his head. "I reckoned it had to be you, Gus. You're the only tangle-foot I know who can make that much of a racket just walking."

Masterson looked as though he had aged fifty years overnight.

His face was gaunt, a colorless death study in gray and charcoal, lips bloodless, drawn tight across his teeth. But the eyes still lived, bright blue jewels in the shadowed sockets of a skull.

"How are you —" Crane backed up, tried again. "Glad to see you're still with us, Paul."

Masterson read the clumsy sympathy in the big man's eyes and it made him laugh, a pained, choking sound. "Gus, did anyone ever tell you that your bedside manner leaves much to be desired?"

"Sorry, I —"

"I'm dying. A little more slowly this morning, but dying still. But I'll be with you until I get a bullet into Stark. Then I'll let go."

"Are you in pain?" Now Crane was really trying to reach the man, attempting to share his burden.

"I got my whiskey. It works most of the time."

"You should go into the saloon, Paul. What if it rains?"

"Then I'll be wet, outside as well as in."

Crane opened his mouth to speak again, but Masterson's raised hand stopped him. "Tell me about Stark," he said. "Did you slow him?"

"He hasn't even started out." The marshal waved a hand toward the wagon. "He was waiting for that."

In reply to the question on Masterson's face, Crane told him about the gunpowder

337

and the Gatling gun.

"As far as I can tell, it's one of the newer models," he said. "Ten barrels fed by a forty-round magazine."

"A real door buster," Masterson said. "With that Stark could have —"

"Extorted every last cent out of this town without a battle." Crane grinned. "But we've got it and Stark doesn't know we have it."

"You got a plan, Gus?"

As he had with Thorp, Crane told Masterson what was on his mind.

After he finished speaking, the sheriff thought for a while, then said, "It could work, if Reddy and the others play their parts."

"They'll play their parts. If they want to save their town they have no choice."

A middle-aged man carrying a rifle was stepping along the boardwalk toward Crane, but as he stepped around to go past, the marshal stopped him.

"Where's the mayor?"

"General Reddy is at home taking breakfast and talking strategy with his subordinates," the man said with great formality, obviously impressed by the mayor's uniformed splendor. He would have spoken in the same reverent tone about Robert E. Lee.

Crane suppressed a smile and said, "Please give the general Marshal Crane's compliments and ask him to meet me here at his earliest convenience."

For a moment it looked like the man might salute, but he seemed to think better of it and said, "I'll tell him, Marshal."

Crane watched the man go. Then he said to Masterson, "We have to get Stark to lead his men into the street. Even with the big gun, if he attacks from all directions we're finished."

Speech was a struggle for the sheriff as his strength faded. His voice was barely above a whisper as he said, "I only met Stark a couple of times. To me, he seemed more sly than smart."

"But maybe he's both. That's what's troubling me."

"I guess we'll find out soon enough."

Crane looked up as feet pounded on the walk. Reddy, booted and spurred, was hurrying toward him.

While he was still a ways off, the mayor yelled, "Is he close?"

"He hasn't started out yet," Crane said. "And that's good, because we've got matters to discuss."

The marshal showed Reddy the Gatling gun and explained yet again how he'd come by it. "Now it's our ace in the hole," he said.

Then he told the mayor his plan.

Reddy listened in silence, his face growing paler and more horrified with every passing second, and when Crane was finished he almost strangled on his words.

"But that's — that's dangerous, Marshal," he choked. "It puts me and the other town dignitaries right in the line of fire."

"Yes, it does," Crane said. "That's why, when the shooting starts, you'll have to skedaddle fast."

"I'll cover you, Mayor," Masterson said. "I'll be right here."

Reddy glanced at the dying lawman and took no comfort in what he saw.

"It's suicide," Reddy said. "We'll be gunned down fastern'n scat."

"We have to get Stark and his men in the street, General," Crane said, using his military title to recall him to a sense of duty. "There's no other way."

"How many of us would you want to sit at the table?"

"The more the better — make it look dignified and official, like. I'd say at least you and four others."

Reddy took a step back, as though to put distance between himself and the marshal.

"We'll all be killed," he spluttered. "You're

crazy, insane, mad as a hatter."

"Goes with the badge." Crane smiled, not an ounce of sympathy in him.

CHAPTER 38

One of Reddy's pickets rode in just before noon and reported a huge dust cloud to the north. The man said the others were scouting in that direction and would report back as soon as they confirmed it was Stark's wagons.

Crane and the mayor got the news in the Texas Belle where Dr. Preston was setting up a field hospital, helped by several nuns who were not teaching in school that day.

The marshal knew the risk of allowing classes to continue, but Sister Marie Celeste insisted, and Crane reluctantly conceded they would give the town an air of normalcy.

The last thing he wanted was for Stark to smell a rat and launch an all-out attack.

"Mayor," he said, "you'd best get changed into your best Sunday-go-to-prayer-meeting suit. The uniform will be a red flag to Stark that something's up."

Reddy nodded. "I filled the money bags

from the bank like you said, Marshal. I don't even want to think what Stark will do when he finds they're full of sand."

"If it comes to that, we'll all be dead anyway, Mayor," Crane said.

The marshal walked out onto the boardwalk where Masterson was keeping his painful vigil. His eyes swept the street.

A table and chairs had been set up a few yards in front of the sheriff's office. The table was piled with canvas money bags and, a nice touch, a water jug and glasses. Nearby someone had raised the U.S. flag and red, white and blue bunting, taken from the gallows, was swagged around the table.

All the barricades had been cleared and the sign he'd ordered was being lettered with painstaking, tongue-protruding care by Simeon Pearl, the undertaker.

Four carpenters were working on the front wall of the sheriff's office. One of the men saw Crane and called him over.

"Just shove on her and she'll come down, Marshal," the carpenter said. He had a solemn, long-jawed face that was badly pockmarked. "Of course, the whole damned roof might collapse on you at the same time."

"I'll take that chance." Crane studied the man. "What's your name, pardner?"

"Jake Hooper. My friends call me Hoop."

"Well thanks, Hoop. And say the same to the others."

Hooper nodded, then said, "You think Stark will hooraw this town? Me an' the missus kinda like it here. Well, up until recent."

"I don't know, Hoop. I'll do my best to stop him."

"Folks are talking about the big gun you brung in."

"It might make the difference."

"I'm sure it will."

Jake Hooper nodded, but he didn't look like a man who was setting store by the marshal's reassurances.

The pickets rode into town at the hottest part of the day with the news that Stark and his men were getting close.

"Marshal, it looks like there's a whole town on the move, and it's a bigger town than Rawhide Flat," one of the men said. His eyes were haunted, as though he'd added up the odds for the first time and didn't like the bottom line.

"When will he get here?" Reddy asked. The mayor wore his best broadcloth suit and a silk top hat.

"Two hours at most. The wagons are slowing him."

A crowd had gathered after the pickets returned, eager to hear their report.

Shorn of his sword and gray and gold finery, Reddy looked what he was, a worried little man sporting huge side whiskers that bookended a face that was usually ruddy but was now ashen.

He held up his hands and said, "Listen folks, all them as wants to leave should do it now. There's nobody in this town will hold it against you."

One of the pickets, a young man wearing a plug hat, a dusty suit and a high celluloid collar, leaned forward in his saddle. "Mayor, my Nora is in a delicate condition as most here present know. I don't want her in town when the fighting starts. This will be our first young 'un."

"I understand, Ezra," Reddy said. "Get your wife and ride on out."

As the young man rode away, the mayor asked, "Is there anyone else?"

Men muttered to each other and shuffled their feet, but no one elected to quit.

"Good," Reddy said. "Now, I suggest we send our womenfolk and children to safety. We'll start them out for Carson City immediately."

"That's not how it's going to be, Ed

345

Reddy." This came from a tall, string bean of a woman in a white dress and sunbonnet. "I'm not leaving my Tom alone, and I think I can speak for the other ladies in Rawhide Flat when I say we will not desert our husbands," she said.

The score of women present, including several saloon girls, nodded their bonneted heads.

"We're with you, Edna," one of the younger matrons said. "We're not going."

Reddy looked alarmed. "Ladies, you'll be in harm's way, and think of the children."

"Our children will be by our sides where they belong," the woman called Edna said. "We live as a family, and if need be we'll die as families."

Crane stepped beside Reddy. "Listen, you women," he said, "Reuben Stark is a madman. If he takes this town, he'll let his men kill and plunder, and none of you will be safe. You've all read the history books, and I don't have to tell you what happens to women when a conqueror takes a town."

"You're talking about rape, aren't you, Marshal?" Edna said. She was thin and hatchet-faced and her skin was as brown as an old saddle.

Taken aback by the woman's frankness, Crane struggled to find words, but when he eventually tried to speak, the woman talked over him.

"There's one way to avoid all that, Marshal. Just make sure you defeat Reuben Stark and destroy his followers, even if you die in the attempt."

Two hours later, the drumming started.

It began as the afternoon sun parched the sky to the color of a dried-out lemon. Heat fell oppressively on Rawhide Flat. The air buzzed with flies, and the lizards and panting dogs sought shade. The outhouses behind the saloons ripened, adding their odors to the stench of the cattle pens and acrid counterpoint of dust and sweat.

Crane had relieved Mayor Reddy of his command and had deployed his riflemen along both sides of the street, concealed in the saloons, stores and a few houses. He had called in the flankers and they now added their rifles to the others.

In total, he had around forty men to defend the town. How many of those would stand when the shooting started, he did not know. Most of them, he hoped.

No matter, the big gun would have to make up the numbers.

It sounded to Crane that Stark's disciples were beating on their wagons with sticks, the rhythmic throb of dim drums traversing the dreary distances of the day.

Masterson had been dozing. Now he lifted his head wearily and said to Crane, who was standing at his post beside him, "Gus, what the hell is that?"

The marshal smiled. "Stark's drum corps."

"What's he doing that for?"

"Trying to scare the hell out of Rawhide Flat."

"Looks like he's succeeding," Masterson said. He nodded into the street.

Men were stepping out of their hiding places, asking each other what the noise was about and what it boded for the town.

Crane walked to the edge of the boards. "Men, it's only Stark trying to soften us up and scare us." He smiled, trying to make light of it. "Must be a trick he learned from the Indians."

A short, stocky redhead who had the beaten-down look of a man with a nagging wife and a bunch of kids, said, "Well, if he's trying to scare us, he's doing a real good job, Marshal. Them drums has me spooked."

"Don't fret none about the drums," Crane said. "It's time to start worrying when they stop." He waved a hand. "Now you men get back to your positions."

Reluctantly, the street cleared and the marshal looked at Masterson. "I've got some things to do, Paul. Will you be all right?"

"Before you go, get me another bottle. From the waist down I can't feel a thing, but every inch of me above my gun belt buckle hurts like hell."

Crane got a bottle of whiskey from the saloon, handed it to the sheriff and stepped into the street.

The drumming grew louder, setting the marshal's teeth on edge and twanging his stretched-taut nerves.

He was scared to death and it was a realization that did not sit well with him.

CHAPTER 39

One thing every cowboy learns sooner or later is that if you're riding point on a herd, look back every now and then to make sure it's still there.

Now Crane stood at the door to the sheriff's office and glanced up and down the street, checking on his men.

To his relief, riflemen still stood behind doors and windows, their eyes on the street outside. He had feared the drumming had so unnerved them that a few of the men might skedaddle. But they were still there and vigilant, some with wives close, and the marshal's confidence grew that they would stand on this ground.

But how many men would he lose, even in victory? How many widows and orphans would be left to cry salt tears and bury their hurting dead?

It was not a thought to dwell on, and Crane dismissed it from his mind.

He wished the drumming would stop.

Gingerly, wary of the whole place tumbling down on his head, he stepped into the office. The Gatling gun stood in the middle of the floor, spare magazines stacked beside it.

Earlier, before the carpenters got to work, Crane had helped manhandle the gun inside. Now, squat, ugly and venomous, it was ready to spit out a thousand rounds a minute.

The gun's inventor, Richard Gatling, had thought the weapon's presence on the battlefield would be so devastatingly lethal that it would put an end to wars.

Thousands of dead men had since proved him wrong.

Satisfied that all was in readiness, the marshal was about to step outside, when a tap at the door stopped him.

"Gus, are you in there? It's me."

Sarah's voice.

The girl wore her new dress and hat and looked young, pretty and vulnerable.

"You just wake up?" Crane asked with pretend gruffness.

"The drums woke me. Who's doing that?"

"Stark. He wants us to know he's near."

The girl didn't have to pretend fear. It was clear in her eyes for anyone to read.

"Gus, I want to stay close to you," she said. "Don't leave me for a minute."

"When the shooting starts —"

"Then more than ever."

"Come in," Crane said. "And step careful."

Sarah walked inside. Everything but the stove had been cleared out of the office to make room for . . .

"What's that thing?" Sarah asked.

"It's called a Gatling gun."

"What does it do?"

"It shoots a heap of bullets in a very short time. Stark doesn't know we have it."

Sarah was silent for a few moments as her child's mind tried to grapple with the concept of an automatic gun and the implications of its effect on charging men and horses.

Finally she gave up, resorting to what she knew and could handle. "Gus, I'm starving."

"Then let's get something to eat."

They had steak and potatoes at Ma's Kitchen and were the only customers. It seemed that the relentless racket of the drumming had spoiled appetites all over Rawhide Flat.

After they ate, Crane borrowed a hammer from a hardware store and he and Sarah sought out Simeon Pearl.

The undertaker met them at the door of his house.

Yes, the sign was ready. And it was as fine a piece of artistry as had ever graced the fair town of Rawhide Flat, even if he said so himself.

Crane thanked the man and complimented him on his work; then he carried the sign to the edge of town. He planned to set it up between the mission and the railroad station where it would be seen by riders coming from the north.

He used the hammer to stake the sign deep and steady, then stepped back to admire his and Pearl's handiwork. The marshal had to admit the sign was simple but very professionally done.

WELCOME REV. STARK~
PEACE TALKS THIS WAY>

When loved ones pass on in Rawhide
Flat, let Simeon Pearl, undertaker,
guide them through the Pearly Gates

"It's very pretty," Sarah said. "Nice colors."

"I hope Stark heeds it, is all," Crane said. "I need him and his men in the street."

353

"For the Gatling gun?"

"For the gun to do its work, yes."

Sarah was quiet for a moment. Then a small frown gathered between her eyes.

"Gus, will a lot of men die?"

The rattle of the Starks' drums sounded like rain on a tin roof.

"Some. I hope not many."

Suddenly the girl's eyes seemed distant, as though she was looking into a hidden place that only she could see.

"Men will die, Gus. And a woman."

She shook her head, clearing the vision from her mind.

"What woman?"

"I saw a woman in black. A holy woman. A nun, I think."

Crane felt a chill, recalling that night in the train. It seemed like a lifetime ago.

"The drumming is getting to you, Sarah," he said. "You're seeing things."

He was lying to the girl, and to himself.

"Well, yes, maybe that's it," Sarah said.

When the marshal looked into her eyes he saw that she did not believe him.

"I'd like to see Paul now," she said.

"You look real purty, Miss Sarah," Masterson said.

The girl smiled. "How are you feeling, Paul?"

"Great, from the waist down. Above that, not so good."

"I'd like to take you back to the hotel where I can look after you."

"I'd just die on you real quick. You don't want to see that happen."

"No, I don't. But I think Gus and I should be with you."

Masterson managed a small laugh. "The last thing I want is to see that long, Yankee face of Gus' looking down at me while I lie abed. I'd swear he was the angel of death."

"He refuses to move from where he's at, Sarah," Crane said. "He's a mighty irritating man."

"You know why I'm here, Gus." The eyes the sheriff lifted to Crane were fevered and sharp with urgency. "I hope he comes soon. I don't think I can make it much longer."

Masterson read the question in Sarah's eyes and said, "I want to kill him for what he did to Maxie Starr. You didn't know her, but she was a friend of mine."

Sarah looked at Crane. "Gus, I'd like to stay with Paul for a while. Is that all right?"

"Ask Paul."

"Bless your heart, girl, sure it is," the sheriff said, without waiting to be asked.

"I'd admire to spend time in the company of a beautiful little gal like you. But as soon as Stark's sighted, you go."

Masterson lifted the bottle from beside his chair. "And one other thing — I hope you won't object to my drinking ardent spirits."

The sun sank lower in the sky and soon would relinquish center stage to the cratered moon. The night birds would peck at the first stars and the darkness throw a thick cloak over Rawhide Flat, hiding its shabby, weathered ugliness.

Crane had walked to the edge of town, staring into gloom that stared back at him, and now he retraced his steps, the wind talking to him.

And only the wind.

The drums had stopped.

Filled with a sense of urgency, he started to run. As he passed the Texas Belle he yelled to Sarah, "Get the mayor! Tell him we need lamps! Every lamp he can find."

Without waiting to hear the girl's answer, he ran to the end of the street, then into a saloon. Only a startled bartender was inside, and Crane told him to light the inside lamps and those on the boardwalk.

He did this in every saloon in town, and

when he returned to the Texas Belle, Reddy and a few men had gathered a large collection of oil lamps and outdoor kerosene lanterns.

"Mayor, put a couple of lanterns at the table. Then you and the other men take your places," he said. "Use as many lamps as you need. I want Stark to be able to see you and the money bags."

Crane grabbed a couple of larger lanterns and said to the men with Reddy, "Stand all the lamps you can find on the walks along the street. I need this town to be lit up like a Mississippi steamboat."

After getting a few nods and mutters in reply, Crane walked swiftly toward the sign he'd erected. He hung a lantern from the top of the support post and laid another in front.

Stepping back, he decided that the lamps lit up the sign just fine. Stark couldn't fail to see it.

Now all he needed was some luck, of late a commodity in very short supply in Rawhide Flat.

CHAPTER 40

It looked to Crane as though every available lamp in town had been lit, and a rose and orange glow filled the street. Wicks guttered in the rising wind, trailing smoke that hazed the air and filled the night with the acrid smell of whale oil and kerosene.

Mayor Reddy and four other of the town's notables, including the corpulent, slightly bug-eyed banker, sat at the table. All were dressed in broadcloth and top hats, but looked distinctly uncomfortable.

With a nod to Masterson, Crane got a bottle from the bar of the Texas Belle and hurried back to the table. He handed the whiskey to Reddy.

"For God's sake, pass this around. I don't want anything to scare off Stark, and you men look like you're attending your own wake."

Reddy drank gratefully, then passed the bottle to the man sitting next to him.

"You think he'll come in the dark, Marshal?" Reddy asked.

"He'll come. Stark has a keen sense of the dramatic and he loves to make an entrance."

"I don't like this, Marshal, a gunfight in darkness when you can't see the other man a-coming at you. Seems to me we're trying to run a bluff with an empty poke."

"We got the Gatling gun in our poke, so it isn't near empty. Besides, in the dark you'll have a better chance of getting away clean when the shooting starts."

Reddy shook his head. "A night engagement against a superior enemy is a recipe for disaster. Look what happened to Longstreet and Bragg at Brown's Ferry in 'sixty-three when they launched a night attack. They were routed."

"We're not attacking, Mayor. We're defending."

"Yeah, like that's going to make a difference."

Depressed by Reddy's defeatism, Crane turned away, but someone shouted his name and he raised his eyes to the flat roof of a false-fronted butcher shop.

"Better come see this, Marshal," the man on the roof said. He was one of Hollister's punchers who had survived the canyon massacre, and had a bandaged left shoulder.

"What is it?" Crane yelled.

"Better you come look fer your ownself."

Helped by a water barrel and its drain pipe, Crane scrambled onto the roof.

"Lookee," the puncher said, pointing with his bearded chin.

The man's gesture was unnecessary. The marshal could see for himself.

It looked like a piece of the night sky had fallen to earth and the stars had settled on the high plains. The hard glitter of two hundred pinpoints of light scarred the darkness, coming on relentlessly. Crane was awestruck, like a rookie Roman sentinel on the border of the empire seeing the torches of an invading barbarian army for the first time.

"What do you want me to do, Marshal?"

Crane tore his eyes away from the advance of Stark's hordes.

"Huh?"

"Want me to stay on the roof?"

"No, get down and take up a position in the street. And keep out of sight until the shooting starts."

Crane led the way and when he regained the street, he yelled to Reddy, "They're coming, Mayor. Now stay at the table."

Then a thought struck him.

He needed a band! But was there time?

Quickly, the marshal walked along both boardwalks, calling out to his hidden riflemen for musicians. After a few minutes he'd attracted three volunteers, a banjo player, a trumpeter and the cowboy from the roof who claimed he could squeeze out a tune or two on the concertina, if one could be found.

The trumpet player, a small, plump man with a pleasant face, said there was such an instrument gathering dust in Nathan Goldberg's dry goods store.

Fretting over the delay, Crane told the man to go get it. A few moments later the marshal heard glass shatter and wood splinter.

"No key," the cowboy said.

The plump man returned with the concertina and Crane said, "We need a good, rousing tune to welcome Stark and his men."

"I can play lead on 'Dixie,' " the plump man said. He looked enthusiastic.

"I can play that," the puncher said. He looked scared.

"I can fake it," the banjo player said. He didn't look anything.

"Right," Crane said, hoping he hadn't left it too late, "get your instruments, then come with me."

Several more agonizing minutes dragged by before the musicians returned.

Crane led them to the welcome sign. To the north the flare of bobbing torches was very close, no more than half a mile away.

Stark's people were coming on in complete silence, the ominous hush unnerving the marshal even more.

To the musicians he said, "Play the tune —"

Nervously the trumpeter put his instrument to his lips.

"Not yet," Crane snapped. "Wait till I give the word." He pointed. "See that white rock?"

The men nodded.

"When the first of them get to the rock, turn and lead them into the street. Don't stop playing. You got that?"

"Marshal, what are we going to do when the bullets start flying?" the banjo player asked.

"Just run like hell for cover."

Now the dangers of the job they'd volunteered for dawned on the three men and they exchanged concerned, frightened glances.

"As soon as Stark's men are in the street, run," Crane said. "You'll have plenty of time before the shooting starts."

The men didn't look convinced, and the marshal said hurriedly, "They're almost at the rock. Now, let's strike up with 'Dixie,' boys."

Reluctantly, the musicians launched into the rousing requiem for a lost cause.

The result was a discordant cacophony of sound that hurt the ears, though the melody was there, playing hide-and-seek among the tangled notes.

Crane raised his hands and conducted his men for a few moments, his head swiveling constantly to look over his shoulder.

Stark was very close . . . and getting closer.

"Crackerjack!" the marshal yelled over the "Dixie" din. "Now, remember, don't stop playing until they're turning into the street, boys."

He turned and walked quickly, yelling for everyone to take their positions.

Masterson waved weakly as Crane hurried past. Sarah bent, kissed the sheriff on the forehead and ran after the marshal.

"Go to the hotel, girl," Crane said, not slowing his long-legged pace. "Wait there until I come for you."

"I'm staying with you, Gus," Sarah said. Her chin was at an obstinate angle as she dug in her heels. "If I'm not there, you might do something crazy."

"Sarah, I don't have time to argue."

"Then don't," the girl said.

They'd reached the table, heavy with the fat money bags and lanterns. Reddy was sitting, facing the street, as were the other men. They were still far from relaxed but looked half drunk. It helped a little.

"Soon, Mayor," Crane said. He stopped. "Now, you men start practicing your smiles. Remember, you're a welcoming committee, so look welcoming."

None of the men answered and Reddy looked surly.

Crane shook his head and walked past. None of this boded well. At least the band was still playing, but Dixie was winding down to a grating dirge.

Those boys must be watching Stark's progress and were likely to bolt at any minute.

His heart heavy, Crane reached the sheriff's office. To Sarah he said, "You still here?"

"Gus, I'm not leaving," the girl said. Her eyes were stubborn and determined.

Carefully the marshal opened the door. "Get inside," he snapped.

Sarah smiled. "Thank you for the gracious invitation."

Crane shook his head. What could you do with a female child who was almost a woman and gave you sass?

He admitted to himself that he had no idea.

Before he closed the door, the marshal looked down the quiet, lamp-lit street, the only humans in sight Reddy and his reception committee.

The band had stopped playing and run away.

CHAPTER 41

The rising moon added a steady, bone white light to the shifting orange palls cast by the lamps. At the table, lonely in the middle of the street, the wind tugged and teased at Reddy and his committee.

Looking out the office window, Crane was pleased. So far the town notables had shown some sand. But what would happen when they were confronted by Stark and his men, he didn't know.

Minutes dragged past in chains. The office clock ticked slow seconds into the room like drips falling into a tin bucket. Beside him, Crane heard Sarah's breathing, soft, but shallow and quick. The girl seemed to be every bit as scared as he was.

The marshal wiped his sweaty palms on his pants. He had told his men not to shoot until the Gatling opened the ball, but it would only take one man to cut loose with a nervous shot and his entire plan would collapse like a house of cards. Crane smiled. Once the firing started, the same might be said of the sheriff's office.

"Gus, you need a shave and a bath, and your mustache needs to be trimmed," Sarah said. "I can trim it for you later."

"Thanks, but I trim my own mustache."

"You don't make a very good job of it. It always looks ragged."

Crane stared out the window until his eyes hurt.

Where was Stark?

If he was busy surrounding the town, all was lost.

"And I can cut your hair. You look shaggy."

"Sarah," the marshal said, trying to sound patient, "get away from me. Go back and lie down in one of the cells where you'll be safe."

"What's this thing?"

"It's a magazine for the Gatling. Put it down."

The girl did as she was told, then said, "Could be Reuben Stark has gone away."

"He'll be here."

"Then what's keeping him?"

"I don't know. Maybe he's talking it over with his sons."

"I heard the band, Gus. They weren't very good and I couldn't make out . . ."

Crane wasn't listening. Three mounted men, their rifles propped upright on their thighs, had just entered the street.

Ed Reddy played his part well.

He rose to his feet, doffed his hat and yelled in a friendly, if slightly strained tone, "Welcome boys. Welcome to Rawhide Flat, the pride of the great state of Nevada."

One of the riders walked his horse closer.

"You got the money, Reddy?" he asked.

The mayor held up one of the money bags. "We've got it all here. One hundred thousand dollars for the Reverend Stark to pick up at his convenience."

Crane's heart pounded in his ears and his mouth was dry. If the three men took the sand-filled bags and left, it would be all over — for him, for Sarah and for the town.

The seemingly undecided rider sat his horse, a still figure silhouetted by moonlight, amber lamplight gleaming on his rifle and the Colt at his waist.

Finally the man came to a decision. He turned and threw a few words at the rider closest to him and the man swung his horse and walked back the way he had come.

Crane had never considered himself in good with God and was not a praying man, but he prayed fervently now.

Please . . . let them all come . . . every last man jack of them . . . let them come. . . .

Time passed. Crane had no idea how long. Reddy had taken his seat again and was whispering to the man beside him; their heads were bent.

The wind kicked up veils of dust from the street and across at the Texas Belle, Paul Masterson was motionless in his chair.

Crane looked at the sheriff intently, searching the gloom, trying to see if he was still alive. Masterson's head was slumped on his chest. It seemed like his time had finally run out.

The marshal's focus changed. Horsemen were filling the street and Reddy and the others were all on their feet.

Stark rode in the lead, flanked by his surviving sons. His riders were ten abreast, some of them holding flaring torches above their heads.

Crane smiled grimly. Stark had been just a tad too confident, in his numbers and in himself. He had thought Rawhide Flat cowed and beaten, his point riders had told him so, and now, all unaware, he was riding into hell.

Crane watched the men come. More and more had crowded into the street, forming a thick mass of riders and horses, torches guttering above them.

Stark rode with an old man's stiffness, but his head was held high with the proud, arrogant bearing of the conqueror.

"Closer . . . ," Crane whispered. "Just a little closer . . ."

Stark threw up a hand and halted his men. He and his sons Abe and Ike rode forward until they were a few yards from the table.

"Mayor Reddy," Stark called out in a hollow, booming voice, the utterance of a prophet, "you have the people's money?"

"Yes, Reverend Stark, every penny, though I wish it were not so."

Crane nodded to himself. So far so good. The mayor was a better actor than he was a general.

"All one hundred thousand dollars?"

"All of it."

Stark laid his hands on the saddle horn and leaned forward. "There is one thing more. You will deliver to me, for my swift justice, the murderers Augustus Crane and Paul Masterson."

Reddy shrugged. "I don't know where they are."

"Find them, because I warn you that our God will not be silent." The old man's face was an ashen blur in the gloom. " 'A fire will devour before him and around him a tempest will rage. The Archangel Michael will smite the unbeliever with his terrible, swift sword.' "

The mayor nodded. "I'll find them, Reverend. But I'll need some time."

"My men will spread out and help you. The criminals who hide behind stars of justice will hang this very night."

At least a hundred riders were jammed into the street. It was time.

Crane stepped to the front wall of the office and pushed. The wall creaked but did not budge. Panicked, he tried again. This time the top of the wall separated a couple of inches from the roof joist.

One more push . . .

But it was Paul Masterson who opened the ball.

Crane heard the gunfire, ran to the window and looked out.

Firing from his chair, his Colt grasped at eye level in both hands, the sheriff cut loose with a barrage. A black hole appeared in Ike Stark's head and he tumbled off his horse. Men were firing in Masterson's direction, but he had taken no hits.

All along the street Crane's hidden riflemen were shooting. Abe Stark tried to charge Masterson; the sheriff dropped him. Now he fired at Reuben Stark; the old man jerked and swayed in the saddle. Then Stark swung his horse and disappeared into the crowded riders behind him.

Alarmed, Crane shoved hard on the wall, Sarah beside him, adding her small strength to his.

The wall crashed into the street and Crane saw a sea of faces turn in his direction.

He ran to the Gatling and cranked the handle. Immediately the big gun roared into life, throwing a deadly hail of lead, spent brass cases tinkling to the floor around him.

Quickly Crane changed magazines. And the distinct Gatling sound, like the rumble of an upstairs neighbor dragging a rusty iron bedstead across a rough pine floor, again shattered the scarlet-streaked night.

Screaming riders and horses were being cut down and the street's boardwalks framed a horrific tangle of plunging hooves, glossy hides torn by fire, and the bloody, shredded bodies of men.

Through a gray, greasy cloud of smoke, Crane caught quick glimpses of the mayhem he was causing. He saw Reddy and the others run for their lives.

And he saw Paul Masterson die.

Three of Stark's men who made it to the front of the Texas Belle clubbed their rifles and drove them again and again into

Masterson's skull. Finally the sheriff fell from his chair and lay unmoving on the boards.

Raging, with shrieks keening through his clenched teeth, Crane swept the boardwalk; all three men fell. He swung the Gatling and again fired into the milling riders. He changed magazines, then shot that one dry and reached for another.

It would take almost another four decades before horsemen finally learned the folly of charging rapid-fire guns, so perhaps Stark's men could be excused for acting out of ignorance.

After flanking the dead and dying men and horses, thirty riders spread out and charged the sheriff's office, galloping headlong into a hail of lead from the chattering Gatling.

Only a few managed to turn back.

The rest lay in grotesque heaps of groaning men and bellowing animals, like barbaric trophies of vanquished enemies set up by conquerors.

Enclosed by walls and a roof, the sheriff's office was filled with smoke. Crane was firing blind but still cranked bullets into the street.

He fed magazine after magazine to the ravenous Gatling, and the barrels grew hot, smelling of burning oil.

"Merciful God, stop! They're all dead!"

Mayor Reddy was standing at the very edge of the fallen wall, his mouth still wide-open from the shout that had just fled his lips.

Beyond words, being ripped apart by a killing rage, Crane kept firing.

"Gus! Stop!"

Sarah grabbed his hand on the firing crank in both of hers.

"Please, Gus, no more," she said, her eyes full of tears.

Like a man waking from a terrible nightmare, Crane stilled his hand, blinked and looked at the girl as though she were a perfect stranger to him.

"It's over," Sarah said softly. "It's all over."

Reddy stepped into the misty room, his boots clinking through the thick carpet of spent shells. "I think you'd better come outside now, Marshal," he said. Suddenly he looked old and tired and his eyes were haunted.

Crane blinked again. "Outside?"

Reddy nodded. "Yes, to see what we've wrought, and may God forgive us."

CHAPTER 42

Crane straightened and stepped over the fallen wall that rocked back and forth under his feet. The moon was full and fair in the sky, its genial, mother-of-pearl light illuminating a charnel house.

At least a hundred men lay dead, dying or wounded on the street and twice that many horses. Nuns moved among them and all the women and girls from the wagons stepped noiselessly, like gray ghosts, as they sought husbands, sons and sweethearts.

The riflemen of Rawhide Flat had disarmed the numbed survivors, and now shots sounded as they put injured horses out of their misery.

Crane tried to swallow the hard knot in his throat. "Reddy, how many —"

"Hard to say, Marshal. At least half of them, I reckon. A Gatling gun is a terrible weapon up close."

Forcing himself to speak, his eyes never

leaving the carnage in the street, Crane asked, "How many did we lose?"

"One dead, Sheriff Masterson. The gambler they call Silent Sam was winged in the shoulder and a couple of other men have cuts from broken glass and splinters."

The marshal's laugh was bitter. "A great victory."

"You could call it that," Reddy said.

The mayor looked at Crane, at the way the tall marshal had closed down within himself.

"Marshal, Reuben Stark sold these people a bill of goods. He said he'd take them to the Promised Land, but all he did was lead them into hell. If there's blame to be laid at anyone's feet, the sin was his, not yours, not mine."

"What will they do now?"

"Go back to where they came from. Stark deserted them as soon as the shooting started and the Archangel Michael did not come to their defense in their hour of need." Reddy shook his head. "They'll go home now, bury their dead and wait for another messiah to lead them."

"Seems to me they've had a bellyful of messiahs."

"Could be, Marshal. Could be."

"Is Stark among the dead? I saw Paul

Masterson hit him."

"I don't know. I'll find out, but I think he skedaddled." Reddy hesitated, frowning, a man with something on his mind. "Marshal, about the town's money —"

Crane's eyes were cold. "It was always about the money, wasn't it? When you come right down to it, all those men out there died for the dollar."

"The town needs its money, Marshal," Reddy said defensively.

"It's at the mission. I'll get it. And you can tell Ben Hollister he can go back to his ranch now."

"He's not going anywhere. He's dead."

Crane was surprised. "How did it happen?"

Reddy shrugged. "After the battle of Sullivan Canyon, Ben wasn't right in the head. He took to his bed at the hotel and sometime earlier tonight cut his throat with his shaving razor. A maid found him on the floor, weltering in his blood."

Crane realized Sarah was standing beside him. "Go back to your room and stay there, girl," he said. "You're safe now."

"Where will you go, Gus?" she asked fearfully.

"I'm going to hunt for Reuben Stark, make sure that son of a bitch is dead."

"You've done enough, Gus. Let Mayor Reddy do it."

"Girl's right, Marshal. You've gone through a hell that ain't over yet an' might never be."

Crane stood in silent agreement for a few moments, then said, "Take Sarah to the hotel, Mayor, will you?"

"But Gus, I want to stay with you."

"For this once, Sarah, do as I say. I'll be back soon, I promise."

The girl saw that arguing was hopeless. "Take care of yourself, Gus."

Crane nodded, then crossed the street toward the Texas Belle.

The bonneted women who were searching for their dead did not even glance in the marshal's direction. Their faces looked stunned, like wooden dolls with painted, expressionless eyes as they glided through the pall of gray smoke that drifted like an evil mist.

The women knew only that the Gatling gun, an infernal machine beyond their comprehension, had exacted a terrible price in blood. The modern dogs of war had been let slip and had savaged their men. For now they would think no deeper than that, content to grieve.

A deadness in him, Crane almost wished

that curses, accusations, hate, had been hurled his way. It would have been better than the cold, moonlit silence that pressed down on him.

Paul Masterson lay facedown on the boardwalk, black blood and brains pooled under his head. But when Crane turned him over, his face was serene, somehow impossibly young, the slight smile on his lips one the marshal remembered.

He used a thumb and forefinger to close the sheriff's eyes, but the lids instantly opened again, as though Masterson wished to witness this, the final act that concluded his life.

Crane smiled. "Paul, you're still an irritating man."

He picked up the whiskey bottle that lay beside the body. There were still a couple of inches of bourbon left. He tipped the bottle toward the dead man.

"To you, Paul Masterson. By God, you had sand."

He put the bottle to his lips and drained it.

Crane rose to his feet, just as Dr. Preston stepped out of the saloon. The white apron he wore was drenched in blood and the physician gulped at the cool air like a drowning man. His face was ashen and he had dark shadows under his eyes.

"Doc, have you seen Reuben Stark?" the marshal asked after waiting until the man had regained his composure.

It took a few long moments for Preston's eyes to focus. "Oh, it's you, Marshal Crane." He made an obvious effort to remember what Crane had asked him. Then he said, "I've seen fifty dead men tonight and twice that number of wounded, but I don't recall seeing Stark."

The marshal nodded. "Thanks, Doc."

Preston grabbed Crane by the arm, a thin anger on his face. "Tell me one thing, Marshal. Tell me why."

Roughly, Crane pulled his arm away. "Ask Mayor Reddy. He knows why."

CHAPTER 43

Crane smelled rain in the wind, as though nature were preparing to wash clean the town of Rawhide Flat and conceal the evidence of a senseless slaughter.

As his boots thudded along the boardwalk, a nun glanced at him, hurriedly made the sign of the cross on her chest, then looked away.

The marshal saw and hurt from the gesture, but with the whispers of his conscience echoing within him, he laid no blame on the nun.

The results, the ramifications, the guilt of this night would lie heavily on him for the rest of his life. Perhaps a stronger man could deal with it . . . tomorrow, the next day, the day after . . . but Crane, imprisoned within the wings of a dark angel, knew he never would.

Motionless dim light filmed a few of the mission windows and the rope of the school bell swayed in the wind. The brass bell chimed with a soft *clink . . . clink . . . clink. . . .*

The front door was ajar and Crane stopped outside, sensing danger. Suddenly the air became hard to breathe and his heart quickened.

He drew his Colt, opened the loading gate and thumbed a cartridge into the empty chamber that had been under the hammer.

The open door tempted with an invitation to step inside, like the entrance to the witch's house disguised as the portal to a gingerbread cottage.

Gun in hand, the marshal backed away.

He stepped to the rear of the mission and found yet another open door. A feeling of unease raking him like spurs, he glanced over at the livery stable. The wagon he'd brought in was parked alongside the wall facing him.

The strings of instinct controlling him like a puppet before his mind caught up, Crane crossed the bottle-littered patch of open ground and looked into the wagon bed.

All the barrels of gunpowder were still there. Or were they? He couldn't be sure.

His jaw tightening, Crane studied the mission. Was that where Reuben Stark was hiding out?

The marshal did not have a good feeling

about this entire situation. Maybe he should go back for more men. As soon as that idea came to him he dismissed it. As did he, everyone in town must have had a bellyful of killing and he would not impose on them further.

He was the law and he had it to do.

Crane crossed the open ground again and stepped through the mission's back door. He stopped at the entrance to the hallway, listening into the quiet.

A woman's voice, soft but broken up by alarm, was followed by the crack of a hand meeting flesh, then a man's harsh rebuke.

The voice was Reuben Stark's.

As quietly as he could — a tall, heavy man in Texas boots doesn't move like a wraith — Crane made his way along the hall.

Stark's voice had come from a door on his left, the entrance to the chapel.

His gun up and ready, Crane put his hand on the doorknob, turned and pushed. The door creaked open and he stepped inside.

The chapel was dimly lit by half a dozen oil lamps suspended from a rough, wooden chandelier, and candles in red, blown-glass votives glowed on each side of the altar.

But most of the illumination came from the flaring, smoking torch held aloft by Stark. The crook of his left arm was around

Sister Theresa Campion's neck like a vice and at his feet was an open barrel of gunpowder.

For a reason known only to the sick, tormented mind of the old man, he had stripped the little nun naked, leaving only her veil.

But for an angry red welt on her cheek, Theresa Campion's face was pale but composed, as though she'd accepted that what had happened to her was God's will and she would not question it.

Not so the stiff, frightened face of Sister Marie Celeste and the three young children who huddled next to her on the pew. One of them, a little girl, was whimpering softly, the others, boys, were trying to look brave and failing badly.

Somebody, maybe Masterson, had told Crane that the nuns had taken in orphans. These three must be them.

Stark saw Marshal Crane step inside, and his eyes filled with an unholy light, a tangled weave of hatred and calculation.

"Come in, Marshal," Stark said. His voice sounded like a snake's hiss. "You're just in time to join the party."

Crane weighed his chances. He was only ten paces from Stark, but he had pulled the nun in front of him and taking a shot would be an uncertain thing.

Reading the marshal's eyes, Stark dropped the flaming torch closer to the gunpowder.

"Don't even think about it, Crane, or, by Christ, I'll blow us all to kingdom come."

The marshal hesitated, the gun in his hand wavering.

"Drop it," Stark said. "I mean it. If you don't, I'll kill all of you."

Crane was buffaloed and he knew it. He dropped the Colt.

"Now kick it toward me."

The marshal did as he was ordered. The revolver skated across the wood floor and thudded into a carpeted ledge in front of the communion rail.

"What do you want, Stark?" Crane asked.

There was a smear of blood on the old man's shirt just visible under his coat. It looked like Paul Masterson's bullet had only grazed him.

Stark let go of Theresa Campion. "You stay right beside me where you're at, woman," he said. "I'm taking you with me."

He transferred the torch to his left hand, then drew a long-barreled Colt from under his coat. "I want the money, Crane. Masterson was in tight with these nuns, maybe taking his pick every night. I think they know where the money is hid."

"You've lost your sons because of the money, Stark," the marshal said. "Let it go."

"Damn you, Crane, I've got the hammer" — he elbowed Theresa Campion closer to him — "and the anvil to make more sons. I want the money." His eyes revealed his greed as his voice rose almost to a scream. "The money, the money, the money!"

"Stark, if you set off the gunpowder, you'll die with the rest of us," the marshal yelled above the racket of the man's voice.

"No!" Stark pointed to a plaster statue of the Archangel Michael scowling from an alcove in the wall. "He will protect me from the terrible blast and vanquish all my foes."

"Old man, you're mad and you've started to believe your own lies. There are fifty dead men outside who could testify that you're a damned liar, and now you're even lying to yourself."

"No lies, murderer! I believe, nay I know, the angel of the Lord will save me."

Stark thrust the torch close to the barrel again. "Now, I want my money!"

Marie Celeste was staring intently at Crane and their eyes met.

"Get him the money, Sister." Seeing a look of surprise on the nun's face, the marshal said, "Paul Masterson told me."

For a few moments Marie Celeste sat

where she was as though deep in thought. Her eyes moved to Sister Theresa Campion, naked and silent in the power of a madman. Then she rose to her feet.

"Not you," Stark said. "Tell the kid next to you where the money is hid. Then send him over to me."

The nun's hands clenched into white-knuckled fists and her obsidian eyes glittered. She nodded to Stark, almost graciously, then whispered into the boy's ear.

The youngster listened intently, the emotion on his face changing word to word, from fear, to interest, to amazement.

"Do you understand, Matthew?"

"Yes, Sister."

"Good boy. Then go do as I told you."

Matthew rose and stepped out of the pew. Stark's voice stopped him.

"You bring the money right back, boy, or I'll gut you like a hog. You hear me?"

The child nodded. He looked scared.

"I know what to do with boys," Stark said. "A boy might think he's all safe and warm, tucked up in his bed, but I can find him. And when I does, I cut his liver out and eat it afore his very eyes. You hear what I'm telling you?"

Matthew swallowed hard. "Yes, sir."

"Good. Now, go get the money where the

sister told you it could be found."

After the boy left, Crane said, "Stark, you don't think I'm going to let you leave here alive?"

The old man grimaced. "Big talk, murderer, coming from a man without a gun. But see, afore I leave I mean to kill you all, except this little whore here. I'd a done it already, except I'm savoring the moment, like."

Shaking with anger, Crane took a step forward.

Stark's gun swung on him.

CHAPTER 44

"Stay right where you're at, Crane," Stark said, grinning like a death's-head. "No need to die right now. I'll give you a couple in the belly soon enough."

The marshal figured the odds. Nine, maybe ten paces lay between him and Stark. The old man was a shootist and he'd get off at least four rounds.

Crane's shoulders slumped. With that much lead in him he'd die before he reached the altar.

"Wise decision," Stark said. Then, as though he could read minds, he added, "I'd have dropped you before you covered half the distance."

Long moments stretched between Crane and the old man, and the torch in his left hand sputtered, dropping sparks into the gloom.

Beside him, covering her nakedness as best she could with her arms and hands,

Sister Theresa Campion looked like a demure Renaissance statue in white marble. Her head was bowed, her face hidden within her falling veil.

The boy called Matthew returned, walking backward as he dragged a heavy burlap sack into the chapel.

"Over here, boy," Stark said. "Right here in front of me."

His eyes lifted to Crane. "Soon," he said, a world of menace in that one, quiet word.

Crane raised his head; he smelled smoke. Had the kid set the mission on fire?

Then Matthew made a sudden diving movement. It was the last thing the marshal expected and he made a mess of it.

The boy reached into the sack and with a fluid movement he'd probably learned playing stickball, he threw a gun underhand to Crane.

Taken by surprise, the marshal made no attempt to catch the Colt, which flew over his head and clattered among the benches behind him.

Knowing he was going to take a hit, Crane went after it. He dived into a pew, frantically hunting cover, but Stark's bullet crashed into his left shoulder. A second chipped wood from the top of a bench, driving splinters into his cheek as Crane hit the floor.

Where was the gun?

To his relief, the Colt was lying on top of the bench next to him, but several feet way. He crawled to the gun as Stark shot again, firing blind.

Grabbing the gun, Crane sprang to his feet.

He fired at Stark, just as the old man was dragging Theresa Campion in front of him. The little nun took the bullet and suddenly a bloodred rose blossomed between her small breasts.

The nun fell and Stark, no longer able to support her deadweight, let her drop to the floor.

Beyond rage, looking at Stark through a tunnel of blackness, Crane fired, then fired again.

Hit twice, Stark staggered back a step. He shrieked his own demented fury and tried to plunge his flaming torch into the gunpowder barrel.

Quickly, Crane raised the Colt to eye level and shot again. The bullet crashed into Stark's open mouth and blew out the back of his skull in a grotesque halo of blood, brain and bone.

Stark's eyeballs rolled up in his head. He staggered back and he went down hard. He didn't move.

Like a man walking through a thick fog, Crane stumbled to the altar. He stomped out the torch, then stepped to where Marie Celeste kneeled beside the dead nun.

The smell of smoke was thick in the air. Outside, men were running, shouting at the top of their lungs, and a frantically clanging bell told Crane that the volunteer firemen had rolled out their hand-pump fire engine.

He didn't care.

He looked down at Theresa Campion, her face calm and beautiful in death.

Marie Celeste was sobbing, hands joined in prayer. The children, too frightened to come closer, stood at a distance, fidgeting, unsure of what was expected of them.

Crane ushered them out into the hallway, then told them to fetch a blanket.

After the children were gone, he returned to the chapel and said, "That night on the train, she told me I would kill her, and I did."

Marie Celeste nodded, her head bowed. She did not answer.

Suddenly aware of the Colt in his hand, Crane let it drop to the floor.

Surprised by the noise, the nun turned, the expression on her tear-stained face unreadable. Finally she said, "The fault was not yours, Marshal." She pointed in the direction of Stark's sprawled body. "It was his."

"There's plenty of blame to spread around, Sister," Crane said. "I reckon I'm due my share of it."

"Marshal, you must have faith that Sister Theresa Campion's death was God's will. She saved us all by dying for us. You must believe that you were the instrument of our Savior's will."

"Faith, Sister? I don't even have faith in myself."

A child handed Crane the blanket and he spread it over the dead nun's body.

Outside the uproar was growing, the smoke smell stronger.

He picked up his Colt from the floor and looked at it for a long time before he shoved it back in the holster.

"Take the other one, Marshal. I don't want it here," Marie Celeste said.

Crane picked up the gun. "Paul Masterson?"

"Yes, when he gave us the money he said we might need it. I told him nuns are armed with prayer, not revolvers, but he insisted."

"By rights, a thousand dollars of the money is yours."

The nun shook her head. "It's tainted by

blood, Marshal. I don't want anything to do with it."

Crane picked up the money sack. He searched his mind, but found he had nothing else to say. Somehow "I'm sorry" wasn't even close to adequate.

He turned and began to walk out of the chapel. Behind him, Sister Marie Celeste called out, "Marshal Crane, I will pray for you."

He stopped, his head bowed. "Thank you, Sister. But I don't think that will help none."

Crane walked out of the mission and into an inferno.

Fire was a constant hazard in the tinder-dry wooden towns of the West, and Rawhide Flat, its timber buildings jammed close together, was proving to be no exception.

Oil lamps had been lit all over the volatile and vulnerable town to greet Stark and his men, and now Rawhide Flat was paying the price.

A lamp or lantern may have been tipped over or smashed in the fight, spilling coal oil. Anything could have started the blaze, a carelessly tossed cigar butt or a burning match. No matter, the cause would never be known.

But the result was obvious — Rawhide

Flat was doomed.

Panic rose in Crane. Sarah was at the hotel.

Weak from loss of blood, he pushed his way through the crowd of men and women thronging the street, seeking an escape from the flames.

Buildings on both sides of the street were ablaze. Crane saw sparks and leaping flames from a burning store jump to the roof of the Last Chance Saloon at the end of the street, then to Samuel Reed's rod and gun store next to it. As he watched, both buildings caught fire, the heat intense, and cartridges in the gun store began to go off with a sharp *pop! pop! pop!*

The hotel was close to the saloon and Crane quickened his pace.

Suddenly flames found stacked barrels of gunpowder in Reed's store. With a tremendous roar, the roof of the gun shop lifted clean off. The blast leveled the walls and sent fiery, splintered timbers flying across the street.

More buildings surrendered to the passionate embrace of the flames, the surging wind creating a roaring, crackling firestorm that cartwheeled in a scarlet ball through the town.

The sky, no longer holding the promise of

rain, shaded from purple to cherry red, barred by dozens of slender columns of smoke.

Crane pushed through a jostling, frightened tide of humanity. Their sooty faces were carved from black marble, only their panicked eyes showing white as they fled their burning town, carrying what few possessions they could salvage from their homes.

The Texas Belle was on fire and Dr. Preston, the nuns and a few volunteers were dragging out the wounded. The dead would be left to burn.

Mayor Reddy was in the street, supervising the men operating the pump engine. A thin stream of water jetted from a hose into a blazing store, about as effective as a man pissing into a forest fire.

The money sack tight in his fist, the marshal tried to reach Reddy, but he was swept along by the crowd and he gave it up for now. He continued toward the hotel, trusting that the building had been evacuated before the fire took hold and that Sarah would be waiting for him.

But, apart from a few people running toward the open ground between the town and the railroad station, this part of the street was empty.

Around Crane buildings were collapsing, groaning loud in pain as fire gutted them. The town was a scorching furnace and scarlet sparks danced in the air like a fire-storm in hell.

A man tried to dodge past Crane, but the marshal grabbed his arm and stopped him. The man's face was wild, beyond fear, beyond sanity.

"Where are the hotel guests?" Crane yelled above the roar of the flames.

The man wrenched his arm away. "I don't know!" Then, as he started to run, he said, "Everybody's dead in there."

The first floor of the hotel was a raging torrent of fire, but only a dull red glow showed in the upstairs windows.

Sarah was up there!

Calling the girl's name, Crane ran into the hotel . . . and gleefully the ferocious flames welcomed him.

CHAPTER 45

"Sarah!"

The fire cracked and bellowed, mocking Crane's puny shout.

Flames licked at him like the hungry tongues of the gigantic hellhounds who roam the realms of the ancient Celtic dead. Fire blackened his shirt and sought out the raw bullet wound in his shoulder, probing, branding, tormenting.

The stairway was a rippling inferno of scarlet, yellow and orange that barred his way. Heedless of his own safety, Crane plunged into the morass, his lungs burning from the dry, hot air he was forced to breathe.

He took the stairs two at a time and reached the hallway, where serpents of black smoke curled.

"Sarah!"

"Gus! In here!"

She was still in her room.

The girl had closed the door as protection from the fire and Crane kicked it open.

Sarah stood in the middle of the floor, her new clothes bundled under her arm.

"I couldn't get out," she yelled as she ran into his arms. "The stairs —"

"I know."

Large sections of plaster were falling from the ceiling, and smoke and fingers of flame were reaching for them. There was a tremendous crash as the stairs collapsed, and immediately the floor tilted at a crazy angle. Now the fire was also reaching upward, threatening to engulf the room.

Crane stepped to the window. He pushed with one hand, but it wouldn't budge. He realized he was still grasping the money sack in a death grip and he angrily threw it aside.

He tried the window again, this time pushing with both hands. The frame moved an inch, then another, and finally screeched open.

Now the fire was an evil entity in the room, grabbing for them as the roof, angled floor and walls burned.

"Climb out the window, Sarah. Then give me your hands," Crane yelled.

The girl did as she was told and clambered outside.

The marshal took her hands in his and, as

her feet swung free, he leaned outside as far as he could, taking her weight.

As she dangled above the street, Sarah looked up at him. "Gus, my new clothes! I dropped them."

Crane bit back the rebuke on his lips and said, "I'll get them."

He let go of the girl's hands. Sarah had time to emit a single, short shriek before she hit the ground. She rolled, stayed still for a moment, then slowly got to her feet and looked up at the burning hotel.

"Hurry, Gus! Hurry!"

Crane looked around the burning room, found the girl's bundle of clothes and threw them out the window. He tried to reach the money sack, but it was already on fire, bundled paper money burning with a strange, lilac flame.

Feeling no sense of loss, the marshal strode to the window, climbed through and dropped to the ground.

Sarah ran to him, a slight silhouette against a wall of fire.

"Thank you for saving my clothes, Gus," she said. She put her arms around Crane and hugged him close.

The marshal smiled and stroked the girl's hair. "Let's get out of here."

"Where are we going?"

"Home."

"Where is home?"

"I have no idea."

"It doesn't matter, Gus. Home is any-where you are."

Together they walked along the street, framed in fire.

Sarah looked out at the beautiful landscape of the high plains flashing past the railcar window. She turned her attention to Crane.

"Do you think Paul will like the spot where we buried him, under the trees on the ridge?" she asked.

"He should," Crane answered. "But being such an irritating man, I wouldn't be sur-prised if he comes back to haunt me for one reason or another."

Sarah was silent for a few moments. Then she said, "Gus, what will the people in Rawhide Flat do now that their money is gone?"

"There is no Rawhide Flat, not any longer." He glanced out the window, then back to the girl. "They're Westerners, Sarah, and they don't give up easily. They'll pick up and start over and maybe even rebuild the town. I don't know."

"What will we do, Gus?"

"Us? Well, you're going to school in

Virginia City. And as for me, I always thought I might prosper in the restaurant business. Pies, maybe. I'd like to sell pies, meat pies, fruit pies, all kinds of pies."

"Pies are good."

"You bet they are."

"You really don't want to be a deputy marshal anymore?"

"Yeah, I'm sure about that. As long as I live I'll never again draw a gun on a human being."

Sarah was silent, thinking. Then she said, "Gus, when I get older, will you marry me?"

The marshal laughed. "No, I don't reckon so. You'll meet a nice young feller who's making his way in the world, and fall in love and that will be that."

"I don't think so. I see us getting married, like a picture in a book."

"It won't happen."

Sarah, a girl just growing into womanhood, flounced in her seat. "We'll just see about that, Augustus Crane," she said.

ABOUT THE AUTHOR

Ralph Compton stood six foot eight without his boots. He worked as a musician, a radio announcer, a songwriter, and a newspaper columnist. His first novel, *The Goodnight Trail,* was a finalist for the Western Writers of America Medicine Pipe Bearer Award for Best Debut Novel. He was also the author of the *Sundown Riders* series and the *Border Empire* series.

The employees of Thorndike Press hope you have enjoyed this Large Print book. All our Thorndike, Wheeler, and Kennebec Large Print titles are designed for easy reading, and all our books are made to last. Other Thorndike Press Large Print books are available at your library, through selected bookstores, or directly from us.

For information about titles, please call:
  (800) 223-1244

or visit our Web site at:
  http://gale.cengage.com/thorndike

To share your comments, please write:
  Publisher
  Thorndike Press
  295 Kennedy Memorial Drive
  Waterville, ME 04901